GW00686345

## Praise for *Confu*

*"Smart, captivating and hilarious."* – Kirkus Reviews

*"Don't read this book when you are hungry."* – Scandalicious Book Reviews

*"Art of cooking."* – Book Riot

## Praise for *Brown Sugar & Spice*

*"Bailey's prose is warm and engaging."* – Kirkus Reviews

*"Brown Sugar & Spice crafts a series of colorful backdrops."*
– The Midwest Book Review

*"Amusing and also realistic."* – Reader's Favorite

## Praise for *Black Truffle & Spice*

*"Psychologically exciting"* – The Book Commentary

*"Story will simply delight culinary fans"* – The Midwest Book Review

*"I loved the characters, plot, and (Mathis Bailey's) food descriptions"* –
Samantha Verant author of *The Secret French Recipes of Sophie Valroux*

*"I absolutely adore this book!"* -- Archaeolibrarian

*"Smart, steamy, fun."* – The Prairies Book Review

Copyright © 2021 Mathis Bailey

ISBN: 978-0-9959193-5-8 eBook
ISBN: 978-0-9959193-4-1 Paperback

All rights reserved, including the right to reproduce this book or portions thereof in any form whatsoever. Apart from any fair dealing for the purpose of research, private study, criticism or review, no part of this publication may be reproduced, stored in or introduced into a retrieval system, or transmitted in any form or by any means (electronic, mechanical, photocopying, recording or otherwise), without the prior written permission of the copyright owner.

# BLACK TRUFFLE & SPICE

a novel

By Mathis Bailey

Bon appétit

2002

To Stephen

Mathis Bailey

Thank you so much for support

# TITLES BY MATHIS BAILEY

*Confused Spice*

*Brown Sugar & Spice*

*Black Truffle & Spice*

# PROLOGUE

**F**rench roast. **French** toast. French vanilla. French kiss.
Everything delicious was always French, Anushka thought. Like
Darshan Singh. He was half Indian and French.

He stood in the bistro wearing black. His aura screamed expensive chocolate truffles, and when he spoke there was a midnight edge.
He just flew in from Paris, tearing apart another restaurant with his
sharp food reviews. Now, chefs and staff were on pins and needles.
The crew jumped like hell every time he asked an imposing question. He paced back and forth judging everyone's every move, arms
locked, sleeves rolled.

Every time he was near Anushka, she would tense up. An anxiety
attack was imminent. He was a mystery to her. She had read some
of his online reviews and knew he was a harsh critic. Sweat trickled
down the middle of her back. It didn't help she was the new kid on
the block. Still learning the ropes in this culinary jungle.

Darshan sauntered around the kitchen. Eyes sparkling like black
diamonds cut from an ancient world. He didn't say much, just noting
everything with those eyes. He stood next to Anushka and released

an intoxicating smell. Maybe it was sandalwood. No, she believed it was pink peppercorns and burnt leather. Whatever it was she could roll around in it naked.

Darshan watched her over stuff a crêpe with tandoori chicken, green peppers, and onions; their edges charred to a crisp. Gooey Camembert cheese was added last, with a thick dollop of spicy crème fraiche to finish it off. The dish was an Indian *dosa* spinoff, this was what the Indo-French fusion bistro was all about.

He helped her chop a bouquet of parsley for garnish, the muscles in his arms flexing this way and that way, showcasing his dedication to the gym. For a moment she fantasized being stretched out on the workbench under his touch. She wondered what his hands felt like. Maybe full of energy to turn something raw into something sensual and amazing. She suddenly felt jealous of the bundle of parsley that he possessed.

The parsley released a floral grassiness. They sprinkled some on a few crêpes. Anushka stuffed another crêpe. He watched, eyes intense. Smoldering. Stirring every muscle fiber within her body. The noise in the kitchen occasionally stole his attention; she hated it. *Fuck!* She wanted to be his main focus. Screw everything else. Every time he spoke, it felt like she was on vacation at a tropical beach. Every brush up against him felt like a missile going off in an open potato field.

He watched her as if she was some exotic bird from another world. She felt his eyes pressing. She dropped a whisk on the floor. *Oh crap!* The loud noise in the kitchen stifled the rattling. She picked it up and dropped it in the sink. She stole a quick glance at him, and he hadn't noticed her silly mistake.

The kitchen was so clean, there wasn't one bug in sight. Anushka felt proud. All thanks to her late-night scrubbing. If the place weren't clean properly, she would get blamed, just because she was new. She was the only one without a battle scar to show she was a real cook.

She was everyone's scapegoat. Who burned the baguettes? Anushka! Who over-cooked the chocolate soufflés? Anushka!

She'd only been working there for a month, and she already knew the dirt on everyone, including the customers who ate there regularly. She turned around again, and he was still there. Watching, with those eyes. His dark lashes looking like they spoke several languages.

Waiters moved around like beautiful music, wearing long black aprons while balancing things like ballerinas, unlike Anushka, who was bumbling around. She almost knocked over a tray of madeleines twice. *Fuck, Anushka! Get yourself together*. A chef called out Darshan's name. He wanted Darshan to taste his *bouillabaisse*. Anushka wanted him to taste something else, but that was a different story.

She wondered if Darshan knew about their matrimonial arrangement. Did he like her? Was this the reason why he was here, to spy on her, to see what he was getting himself into? Why did she let her mother talk her into this? Questions simmered inside her.

"Hey, Anushka! Quit daydreaming and get the food out," shouted one of the cooks.

She would have cussed him out. Told him to go fuck himself. Put up a middle finger for good measure. But since Darshan was there, she was on her best behavior. She couldn't mess up her chances being Mrs. Singh. Hell, no! She wasn't going to jeopardize her chances with the man of her dreams.

# CHAPTER 1

**B**utter marked Pierre's black apron as he flirted with two hot men.

Their skin the shade of honey maple and sweet cinnamon. Pierre's eyes were bubbling with delight. He suddenly wanted to do a blind taste test to see which flavor he liked the most. He assumed they were successful executives or some other high profession…well, at least one of them looked that way. The other looked like he was good with his hands.

The men were curious about the Spice Café's grand opening. Pierre could have sworn he recognized one of them from a gay dating app. He hoped one of them played on his team.

Two ladies in heels strutted by. Their pretty dresses flowed in the summer's breeze. They stared at the three men up and down, as if they were expensive art. Pierre noticed the men didn't look in their direction and thought there was hope. He was holding a sampling tray of sweet potato tarts. The cute guy with a manbun took one and bit slowly into the filling. Pierre knees turned into butter as he watched him devour it in two bites.

Pierre's business partner, Zola, watched from a distance. She wished she had such boldness to talk to handsome men so easily. Pierre made it look like a piece of cake. She figured the two men were charmed by Pierre's Detroit accent. She hated her southern voice. She thought it was too country. The way she stretched her syllables was a constant reminder she wasn't from Toronto.

She sauntered through the cafe, mentally checking things off her to do-list. Some boxes of coffee cups, knives, and forks still needed to be unpacked. She couldn't believe her dream was finally coming true. They were the only Black owned business on the block, stuck in the middle of a fashion boutique and an antique shop. The area was high-end Bloor West. Some people thought they were opening a cannabis cafe. Why on earth would they think that? They were dishing out delicious Southern food. The first in downtown Toronto matter of fact.

She looked over at Pierre and thought they were exchanging phone numbers or secret recipes. She tried to guess their ethnicity: Indian. Latino. North African. Persian. She gives up. That's what happens when you live in a cosmopolitan city, so many flavors.

Suddenly she was in the mood for some Moroccan tea. Before she made her way to the kitchen to make herself a cup, one of the guys looked her way. She froze. His eyes dark as black ice. His lashes whispering all kinds of naughty suggestions. His hair was cut close. His eyebrows were fine like silk. His whole face looked as if it was forged in fire in the high mountains.

He was dressed in black. His sleeves were folded to his elbows, arms exposing wisps of black hair. He wore a gold Rolex: the face on it was black, and his tall height was delicious.

Zola quickly looked away. She suddenly wanted to fade into the brick walls. His dark eyes stirred something hot and dark deep within her. *Those lashes! Damn!* His glance was like a warm feather caressing an arm. His tall frame looked like an amusement park waiting to be explored.

A part of her wanted him to stay a stranger because she was fresh out of relationships. She was done with men. The only romance she needed was with her brand-new cafe. A man entering her life now would ruin everything, just like the last one. She needed to focus solely on herself. She was finally living her dream. This was no time to play games. There was no room for mistakes. Everyone back home was rooting for her. Her mother was already telling her church buddies her daughter owned a café, in Toronto! It made Zola's stomach turn upside down even more. The pressure was on.

She didn't understand why the guy was making her so nervous. He wasn't her type but there was something about him. It would be silly of her not to take a chance.

She looks down at her black shoes, it was dusted with powder sugar. She gives them a quick clean with the back of her legs and smoothed out the wrinkles on her apron.

When she finally gathered the courage to introduce herself, the men had vanished. Gone. The sound of the door shutting loudly like a full period. She let out a deep breath. She wondered if she would ever see him again.

Mathis Bailey

# CHAPTER 2

**C**hefs moved frantically at the bistro.

A security guard working front desk texted a master chef, *She's here*. Cooks smoking outside on the rooftop stomped out their cigarettes and leaped down a flight of stairs. Customers' orders were shouted out in every direction in the kitchen. Anushka was chopping an onion when the mood around her shifted.

"*She's coming!*" someone yelled out. A half-eaten sandwich was chucked in the garbage. Waiters tucked in their white shirts and moved swiftly to refill customers' drinks. Hostesses changed out of their comfortable ballerina flats into fashionable stilettos.

Someone threw a bundle of white asparagus over Anushka's head, instead of green. Then a bundle of rainbow carrots flew over her head, instead of orange. The sounds of cooking bounced around the kitchen like a Super Bowl. She looked around, trying to figure out what the hell was going on. She had never met Mrs. Singh, and she was in for a treat.

A cook took the onion that Anushka was chopping and replaced it with shallots. She whispered, "*Don't ever let her see you use onions...*

*Ever!"* Then turned away and wiped off her red lipstick using a frying pan as a mirror.

The driver opens Mrs. Singh's car door. She stepped out of the silver Mercedes wearing a striking black sari. Gold Indian prints snaking up the sleeves and slash. She strutted through the immense revolving glass doors. Shiny gold heels pounding black marble in the lobby. Veins pumping with caffeine. Hair snatched back into a French twist. Spanish earrings swung from her ears like an ancient goddess, while Chanel shades decorated her face.

Meanwhile, cooks scrambled on top of each other, eyes crazed with fear or some illegal substances. Flambés were flaring like a talent show. Chefs tossed raw vegetables into the air in hot pans, breaking them down in matter of seconds like magic tricks. A British chef brushed passed a line-cook and shouted, *"Move out the bloody way!"*

Dirty dishes were taken out the sink and thrown into the dishwasher. Stainless steel counters were wiped down to its original state. It took multiple wipe-downs to get it to a high gloss. Someone shouted, *"Get that order out, NOW!"* The goal was to make sure all the customers ate and drank like kings and queens. Customers should be singing praises to Mrs. Singh the moment she walked through the door. That was the life of the bistro. That was the life of Mrs. Singh. The life every culinary cook wished to have. The dream that everyone in hospitality would kill for.

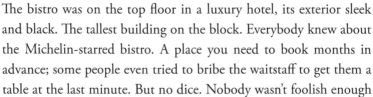

The bistro was on the top floor in a luxury hotel, its exterior sleek and black. The tallest building on the block. Everybody knew about the Michelin-starred bistro. A place you need to book months in advance; some people even tried to bribe the waitstaff to get them a table at the last minute. But no dice. Nobody wasn't foolish enough to risk their job at the bistro. Getting fired would end their culinary career. It would be suicide.

Business professionals staying at the hotel would make U-turns whenever they saw her coming. They didn't mess around with Mrs. Singh, unless they wanted their culinary passport revoked, preventing them from eating at exclusive restaurants all over the world, for free.

The security guard jogged over to the elevator to press the button for Mrs. Singh. He knew she hated touching buttons. She was a germophobe. She carried sanitizer everywhere she went. They rode up in silence. The red numbers flicked up to no end. There was tightness around her mouth, as if she smoked twenty cigarettes a day. She held close to her chest a black leather binder, gold letters running across it, *The Bistro*. A book where she wrote down all her secret recipes, plans and revisions for the seasonal menu. The binder was so fancy, one would think Versace designed it himself.

The elevator door slid open. The security guard told her to have a nice day. She ignored him and stepped off with couture attitude. She ripped off her Chanel shades and assessed the bistro and surveying every speck of dust.

The décor was fierce, just like her outfit. Crystal chandeliers hung from elaborate medallions. Marble white tables and glossy filigree cream wallpaper. Whenever the sunlight hit it, the design looked like it was floating on air.

The tables were filled with customers. The staff looked smart and clean. But she wouldn't tell them that. Of course not. However, Mrs. Singh was pleased to know they were taking full advantage of the free gym membership as one their health benefits. She wanted her staff to look their best. It was great for business.

The restaurant manager flew to Mrs. Singh's side. Godiva gave her boss the rundown on everything that went on at the bistro.

"We're doing well on social media. Our follower count has skyrocketed. We're even trending on Twitter. The new marketing strategy is working. We are posting every day. I made sure to post pictures of celebrities whenever they dine in with us. I also took the liberty updating our website to make it look fresh and new. I ordered more tables for the outdoor patio and portraits for the walls. Reservations are increasing by the hour as we speak. Oh yeah, your literary agent called. It's regarding your manuscript. She was wondering when you think the cookbook will be…"

"Why aren't there white roses on the side tables?"

Godiva's fudgy-brown-eyes looked around frantically at the bouquets, "I could have sworn…I…"

"If I smell gardenias, I'm going to be highly upset."

Mrs. Singh sauntered into the hot kitchen. The cooks moved around like beautiful music, their eyes focusing on making the perfect dish. There were sounds of food hissing away. Cooks flicking sauces in the air, combining exotic ingredients. James Beard awards and Michelin Star plagues hung threateningly over their heads.

"Slice…don't roughly chop… Where did you learn how to chop like that?... In a dark alley on the back of a food truck? Now let me see you julienne those peppers again."

She dipped a gold spoon into a creamy sauce "This needs more garlic." Her tone sharp and quick "This needs more dill. Chop! Chop!"

There'd been casual hookups among the staff: some gay, some straight, some old, some young, some of everything mixing. But they wouldn't dare to show those affections while she was there. She didn't play that. She was old school. Their main focus should be on cooking. Nothing more. Nothing less.

Every cloud of smoke caught her attention. The arch of her back when she leaned forward to taste a sauce had the cooks on edge. The gold on her sari sparkled brilliantly underneath the hot lights. It looked like a chorus of angels sneezed on her. She adjusted the sari on her shoulder and looked over at Anushka, who was stirring a *bouillabaisse*. Mrs. Singh strode over.

"Who are you?"

"The new line cook," Her heart was racing. Mrs. Singh's presence was bigger than life. Bigger than she ever imagined.

"I mean what's your name, child?"

"Anushka, Anushka Black." Mrs. Singh eyed her suspiciously. She took the gold spoon and dipped it into the sauce. She tasted it. Her eyes became hard as rocks. She spat it out in a nearby sink.

"Have you tasted this *bouillabaisse*?"

Anushka tasted it. "I believe it needs more salt."

"More salt?" Mrs. Singh glared at her. "You mean more everything. Start again."

Mrs. Singh strutted away with her sari scraping against the rubber mats. As she existed the hot kitchen, Godiva rushed to her aid with a glass of sparkling water. Mrs. Singh snatched it from her, almost sending her tumbling to the floor.

∽

Mrs. Singh sauntered into her spacious office. The walls were lined with food magazine covers featuring her with arms folded or holding some kind of cooking utensil. Black-and-white photos of France and India hung proudly, like the Arc de Triomphe, Notre-Dame, and the Taj Mahal.

The latest foodie magazines were spread out on her desk. One would think she was a food editor. She enjoyed being on top of the latest trends. Last year, it was the charcoal explosion. Charcoal waffles, charcoal vanilla ice cream, charcoal pasta, the list went on. The Italian restaurants made a killing that year.

Mrs. Singh strode to the floor-to-ceiling window overlooking the city. She glared down onto the street. Watching vacationers drag their luggage into the hotel. She turned her attention to the vacant shop across the street. She saw a moving truck and people carrying items. When Godiva walked into the office to bring her lunch, Mrs. Singh spoke.

"Who are those people moving into that shop across the street?"

"I believe food owners."

"What kind of food owners?"

"Cafe cooks, I believe."

Mrs. Singh scoffed. "Cafe cooks, you say?"

"Yes, it's called the Spice Café."

Mrs. Singh turned around and faced the manager. Godiva was a young woman in her late twenties. She was feeling good after her morning green juice cleanse and hot yoga, hair straight and cut around the face like a Parisian model. She wore a fitted cream khaki skirt and a beige shoulder cap edging to the elbows; two rolls of gold buttons trailing down the middle like a military finish.

"Why did you hire that girl?"

"Anushka? Oh, she's a line cook. She seemed qualified for the position."

"Her *bouillabaisse* is dreadful."

"Oh, my."

"Has she ever been to Paris?"

"No."

"What about Montreal, at least?"

"Not that I'm aware."

"This is my only bistro in Toronto, and you have some bumbling girl in my kitchen?"

"She graduated from Auguste Escoffier School of Culinary Arts."

"That's hard to believe."

"Maybe she's having a bad day."

"There's no room for bad days at the Indo-French Bistro. It's my reputation on the line—not yours. We're still working on earning our third Michelin star. I'm tempted to send that girl's knives packing. I'm pretty sure the Spice Café would love the extra help."

"That won't be necessary. I'll train her."

"*You'll* train her?"

"Yes. I will have her in front of the house until she learns all the aspects what we do here. She can be my assistant."

Godiva's earpiece came to life. A soft voice came in crackling from a waiter. There was a situation in the dining room. Mrs. Singh glared at her. Godiva was happy for the interruption and excused herself to attend to the issue at hand.

Meanwhile, Mrs. Singh sauntered back into the kitchen to observe Anushka, critiquing her every move. Every time Anushka touched something, Mrs. Singh would place it back to its rightful place. Every time Anushka sent out a dish, Mrs. Singh tasted it before it hits the table. Every time Anushka gossiped with another cook, Mrs. Singh would clap her hands for immediate separation.

Mrs. Singh wondered if Anushka was right for her multi-million-dollar business? She knew so little about the girl. This young woman was a mystery. Pretty, yes. But creative? Anushka wasn't the first new cook that Mrs. Singh scrutinized. Everyone goes under investigation in Mrs. Singh's kitchen.

There was more this poor girl needed to learn. There was no room for error. Mrs. Singh would have her eyes on the new cook. Closely.

# CHAPTER 3

I t was grand opening night.

The cafe was going to open within another hour. It wasn't an easy start day for Zola. This morning was crazy. She checked the walk-in freezer to make sure they had everything they needed. She gripped the handle and searched for a box of catfish. Nothing. She moved things around, and still nothing. She jogged to the front where Pierre was hanging pictures.

"Where's the catfish?"

"It's on its way."

"*On its way?* We're open tonight."

"Don't worry. I'll call the guy to see where he's at." He climbed down off the ladder and reached for his cell resting on the counter.

How was Zola going to make her cornmeal catfish bites without catfish? Suddenly, a pile of dishes crashed to the floor. Zola jumped in fright and dashed to the back to see what happened.

The white dishes she bought yesterday, laid in a million pieces. She couldn't believe this was happening. Earlier, one temporary cook burnt the sweet potato pies to a crisp. Now this. What's next?

Today was turning into a nightmare. Could her luck get any worse? She stared at the broken plates on the floor, resembling her frantic nerves. She buried her face in her hands. Her confidence crumbling like an over-baked-dry-cake. Maybe she was in over her head. She was a former waitress opening her own café. Was she out of her god-damn-mind? Maybe she wasn't cut out for this kind of responsibility.

Meanwhile, Pierre called the delivery guy. He was running late; stuck in traffic. Pierre decides not to tell Zola, it would only freak her out. He went back to hanging art created by Black, gay, and local artists. He thought it would be a fair exchange to use their paintings to decorate the cafe and promote locals.

After he finished, the cafe looked like a classy art gallery eatery. It was the mood Pierre was going for. A few tables were set up in the back. They wanted to keep the space open and inviting. Since this was a soft opening, finger food would be served standing up, also to encourage the customers to check out the artwork.

∽

The night had arrived. A live band was playing. The line was wrapped around the block with hungry customers. People were eager to experience something new. There were some people breaking away from the queue because of the long wait, but others filled in the gaps quick. A few were corporate types mixed with vacationers, hipsters and college students.

Zola was a ball of nerves. The temporary crew was tense. Some were feeding off her energy. Everything was set up and ready to go. Pierre opened the door. Some customers gave congratulations while others rolled their eyes at the long wait. Sizzling meats and clinking utensils added to the ambience while crab cake bites were brought out as samples.

Pierre took the role of maître d' and Zola, the head chef. The drinks were flowing, and more food samples were right behind.

Aromas of collard greens and fried catfish and savory stuffed pastries attacked everyone's senses.

Zola peeked out the kitchen door to see how everything was going, and there he was. Wrapped up in black. Looking like midnight. Black hair and silky lashes appeared glossy underneath the dim lights. His espresso truffle eyes studied the artwork on the walls as if they were sheets of music.

Zola kept watching from the door. She thought she looked a hot mess. Flour marked her slim black dress. She tries to brush it away, but it was being stubborn. She looked back up. His eyes searching the café, taking in every imperfection, Zola thought. His hand ran along his jawline, accentuating the five o'clock shadow that made him appear like dark smoke. He looked as if he spent his days at exclusive spas and VIP gyms drinking power juices. He didn't see her spying from behind the door. She was shielded by the thick crowd. The only reason Zola could see him because he was so tall. She loves tall men.

Zola wondered his name. His favorite song. His favorite meal. She wanted to approach him. Say hi, at least. Ask him if he was enjoying himself. Ask him how he liked the food without tripping over her words like an idiot.

As she snaked through the crowd, two beautiful ladies approached him. They looked like personal stylists or interior designers. The ladies were so pulled together, Zola thought. She watched them engage in a casual conversation. Zola wondered who they were. Was he a polygamist? Three people hooking up was becoming more common these days. Times were changing.

Zola watched from afar, behaving like one of the customers. The ladies touched him playfully on the shoulders. Not provocatively, but knowingly. They surrounded him as if they were protecting a golden child.

The witnessing of this closeness made Zola's heart drop down in her chest. But that wasn't the only thing she heard crashing down. A pile of dishes clattering to the floor in the kitchen once again. She rolled her eyes and threw her hands up in the air.

# CHAPTER 4

**M**rs. Singh arrived at the bistro.

She sat across from two people around her age. They were a lovely couple. She wanted to know more about their daughter. She had found their matrimonial ad on an Indian website and invited them to brunch.

They were eating crushed potatoes pan-seared in duck fat, along with tandoori rabbit over saffron rice, and charred vegetables. Tall glasses of prosecco sat on the table untouched.

"Does your daughter cook?" asked Mrs. Singh, her voice tight and haughty. Her face was moody, as if chocolate couldn't melt fast enough in her mouth.

"Oh, yes! She knows how to cook very well. I taught her well. She even knows how to prepare vegan and vegetarian meals. I hate to say this, but she's a better cook than me. I'm a bit jealous." Mrs. Chopra chuckled. Her eyes were a warm brown, like maple syrup. Sweetness exuded from her chubby cheeks.

"Is your daughter shy?"

"No, no, no, you shouldn't assume such a thing. My daughter isn't shy at all. She's a sweet girl. She's anything but shy."

"Well, that's good to know," said Mrs. Singh. "My son is well traveled. The last thing he needs is a quiet girl. He needs a talkative one. Someone that can hold his interest. So, where is she? Where is this daughter of yours?"

"She's here."

Mrs. Singh wore a face of confusion.

Mrs. Chopra rocked back and forth to gain momentum to lift from her chair. Her sari clung to her big frame like an old pillowcase. Her husband gave a look that said *that's all mines*. Mrs. Singh made a disgusted face. Mrs. Chopra hurried back with a big smile.

"Here she is my precious daughter."

A young woman appeared in white; she tried to camouflage the stains of butter and wine from her day's blunders. Mrs. Singh thought this was some kind of a sick joke. She didn't know Anushka Black was the daughter of Mrs. Chopra. The last name totally threw her off. Maybe from a failed marriage, something Mrs. Singh rather not associate with. It could bring down her good family name. But she must admit, Anushka's face was very pleasing.

"I think I've seen and heard enough for today. If you could excuse me." She rose and fetched her driver.

Anushka looked confused. Did she offend? She had told her mother this was a bad idea, why did she even go along with it? But her mother didn't listen. Mrs. Chopra thought since her daughter worked for the most influential woman in the world, why not take a chance in introducing her daughter to Mrs. Singh's eligible son?

Anusha felt like running in the bathroom and crying.

∽

Mrs. Singh sat in the car. Watching people revolving in and out of the hotel doors. The summer's festivals were in full swing and the hotel was picking up. That means more money for the bistro, and more exposure. She thought Anushka was a charming young woman. She wasn't too sure about the brains, though. And her family's limited access to money was worrisome. The Chopra's made some good investments and suddenly became rich. But not close as wealthy as Mrs. Singh. If she goes along with this match up, how would she explain this union to her circle of friends?

She chastised herself for her lack of research on these people. She felt fooled. Tricked. Bamboozled. She got too excited when she read their profile. All this talk about French lessons and dance recitals and frequents trips to the mountains in Vancouver. During lunch she was dismayed to learn they only had one maid.

She stared out the car window and clucked her tongue at the new café. It looked rustic and miniscule in contrast with her bistro. The more she stared, the more curious she became about its existence. She saw some activity that caught her eye in the cafe. Familiar faces. Her heart skipped a couple of beats. She absentmindedly touched her necklace. She squinted. Too make sure she was seeing what she saw. Her son. In that horrible cafe, engaging with what appeared to be a gay man. There were light touches and laughs. She saw enough and waved a hand at the driver to go.

There was one thing she must do: get her son married…and fast.

# CHAPTER 5

**P**ierre arrived at work with a big smile.

A wave of spices assaulted his nose the moment he strode into the cafe. Zola was frying chicken soaked in buttermilk. Spices and grease were seeping into the walls like marination. Ingredients were laid out on reclaimed oak. Flour was dusting the floor, where a plop of melted butter and chocolate lay, evidence of the morning baking.

Pierre sauntered into the kitchen. Zola dipped a chicken thigh into buttermilk and then massaged it in a bowl of flour, its consistency feeling like feathers between her fingers. Memories of playing in the sand on the beach as a kid came to mind. Pierre steals a wing from the cooling rack and bites into it.

"This chicken is slap-yo-momma good." Pierre took a heavy bite again, skin crackling like a dark secret, meat tender against the edge of his teeth, the flavors rolled round in his mouth like tiny waves. Before taking another bite, he dipped it in a honey garlic butter sauce which was made in house.

"I thought you had enough meat last night," Zola teased.

"Gurrrl…last night was everything and then some."

"I know. I heard."

"Oops, were we too loud?"

"A little."

Pierre looked embarrassed.

"So, who was the lucky guy?"

"This guy I met a few weeks ago."

"You mean, the two men?"

Pierre shook his head up and down, and a canine smile swept across his chestnut face.

"Both?"

"Gurl, I wish."

Zola was somewhat relieved. She hoped it wasn't the one she had her eye on.

"Wow, you move fast."

"Gurl, one minute we were watching Netflix, then bam! Our clothes were coming off like hot lava."

They laughed.

"Sounds like you two hit it off…are you going to see him again?"

"Monday, Tuesday, Wednesday, all days throughout the week, if he will allow it."

The conversation was so juicy, Zola had to take a seat. They sauntered to the front of the cafe and settled at a table. They weren't open for another hour, which was enough time for Zola to get all the details. Every hot thing Pierre spilled out of his mouth made Zola gag on her coffee. She was laughing so hard that she almost fell out of her chair. She suddenly wanted a man of her own. Someone that made her feel good. Someone who could make her feel like a woman. Someone who could make her morning breakfast with a sweet kiss on a side. She couldn't remember the last time a man touched her with possibility.

Zola offered Pierre a bite of the red velvet cake she baked. He averted his eyes, not wanting to ruin his figure for his mystery man. He wanted to stay in top shape for their next rubble in the sheets. Pierre checked his phone to see if he had any missed messages. Nothing. He slumped back in his chair and looked back at Zola.

"So, Miss Thing, how does it feel to finally have your own cafe?"

"You mean *our* cafe." Zola still couldn't believe she had the guts to open it. If Pierre hadn't promised to partner with her, she probably would have never done it. But now The Spice Café was finally theirs. "I keep pinching myself thinking I will wake up soon."

"It's no dream. You made it happen."

"Do you think we can do it? You know, run this baby?"

"If you keep cooking chicken like this, we will be owning the block."

Zola laughed. "Thanks for partnering with me. I don't know if I could've ever done this without you."

"No problem, hun, what are friends for?"

Zola paused for a moment. "Pierre."

"Yes."

"Promise you won't freak out."

"What do you mean don't freak out?"

Zola shook her head, regretting even opening her mouth.

"It was a media frenzy this morning."

"That's a good thing, right? That means the grand opening was a success."

Zola groaned. "They think we are exploiting illegal immigrants... from Haiti."

"Why in the world would they think that?" Pierre saw the world shattering in Zola's eyes. He had an inkling the bistro across the street had something to do with it. They been spying on them ever since they opened. The look on Zola's face scared him. He couldn't let them ass hoes kill her dream. The last thing they needed was a scandal on their hands before the café could ever take off.

"Listen, don't stress over this. This will blow over." He rubbed her hand. "Let's think about how we can improve our sales. Maybe I could ask my mystery man if he knows anybody that can help us get the word out there to help generate our business. He seems pretty connected in the streets. I remember him mentioning his boy is some kind of food critic...that's why they were checking out our cafe a few weeks ago. You would have known that if you weren't so antisocial."

Zola smacked her lips. "What's his name?"

"I believe his name is Darshan...and straight."

"I hope this isn't a ploy to get me on a date again."

Pierre laughed. "Girl, it was only that one time. Besides, you needed some spice in your life. A little rendezvous wouldn't hurt once in a while."

"Fine! I'll meet up with this guy if he agrees."

"Great! I'll pass the word along to my mystery man and see what he says. In the meantime, go get your hair done. Can't have you meeting his friend looking like you just rolled out of bed."

She smacked his hand playfully, and self-consciously touched at her messy bun. Ever since they open, she put all her time and energy at the café. She definitely was interested in meeting someone new, maybe this Darshan guy. However, she didn't let it show on her face. Maybe this review could be the turnaround that the cafe needed. Or maybe this review would put them farther down the rabbit hole. She prayed it wouldn't be the latter.

# CHAPTER 6

**M**rs. Singh was forking into a mixed bowl of fruit.

The dragon fruit was cut into cubes with perfect edges. Next up were sweet melon and mango balls; nicely rounded and plump. Watermelon triangles couldn't be ignored, also cut to perfection. All glistening in a pale blue bowl. Did Mrs. Singh appreciate the knife skills that went into her fruit salad? Probably not. The mango juice dripped down the gold fork as she chewed. Each bite was sweet on her delicate tongue. It made her think vacation. Being on an Island would be nice right about now. Nothing but an endless sea of tropical trees bearing exotic fruits, surrounded by gorgeous blue water sparkling like tiny diamonds. *Hell! Why not.* She would go tonight. First, she would have to move around some dates.

When her two daughters came into the office, they were all smiles and giggles, hair flowing down their backs like international super-models. Saris hanging off their slim bodies like fabulous bridezillas.

"The Spice Café was a smash hit, Mother. You should have seen the men there at their grand opening. Doctors, lawyers, executives, YouTube celebs. They were all there."

"Is that so?" Miss Singh forked another juicy cube of dragon fruit into her mouth, making her tongue red like a serpent's.

One of the daughters slid her hip onto the glass desk. Her sari was bright yellow, and her jewelry glistened like French butter. She crossed one thin leg over the other, revealing gold stilettos. She reached over and plucked a cube of fruit into her mouth.

"And the Pierre guy, what a cutie. Too bad he's gay."

So, Mrs. Singh's hunch was right after all.

"What about the girl!?"

"What girl?"

"There's a girl that owns the cafe."

The daughters looked at each other in confusion, foreheads knotted like a ginger root.

"I'm sorry, Mother, we don't know what you're talking about. We didn't see any girl."

Mrs. Singh wagged her fork in their Botox faces. "Don't you two tell me you didn't see any girl. I know what I saw. There's a girl there too."

They shrugged.

"Perhaps, Mother. But you should've come. It was a great time."

"I have a business to run…in case you two hadn't noticed. Instead of gallivanting over there to that measly place, you two should be here helping your dear old mother. I hope there weren't any photographers there. I don't want our good name associated with that shack."

"Measly place? It's rather charming. Rustic, even."

Mrs. Singh sucked her teeth. "If I see any glorifying statements in the media coming from you two about that slum, I will serve your heads to the customers." She forked another piece of dragon fruit into her mouth.

The daughter sitting across from her said, "Mother, don't worry. They won't top us at all. I'm pretty sure that place will come and go like the others. Their food has flavor, I'll give them that, but our food has more sophistication."

"You better be right. Last thing we need is competitors. Our sales dropped ever since they opened, stealing our hotel customers. Who knew they wanted to eat peasant food?" Mrs. Singh clucks her tongue "From what I heard, sounds like this cafe has stirred up quite a buzz."

Her daughter adjusted the yellow slash on her sari. "I'll give them a couple months. The people will get bored eventually. I mean, how many people have we run out of that place already? Like, fifteen? So many that I lost count. No one is a match for us. Once the Spice Café closes for good, the space should be turned into a pet shop."

"A pet shop? In front of my bistro? I think not!" Mrs. Singh stabbed a mango and shoves it into her mouth. One of the sisters could have sworn they heard their mother's jaw crack. The sisters took this as their cue to leave.

Mrs. Singh sunk back in her chair. A dark, twisted part of her wanted the Spice Café to fail, crumble to the ground. She wanted to remain on top. But her food was becoming outdated said a few online reviews. The younger generations weren't dining in fancy restaurants anymore. They wanted something fast and quick. Something new and exciting. Good thing her son had taken over the business and turned their Indian bistro into a fusion place. Now, she was back on top. People loved the change. She would soon receive her third Michelin star. She could smell it.

She rose from the chair to shut the door. The constant clinking of the pots and pans grated on her nerves. She needed to think clearly about how she was going to bring down the Spice Café. Thinking about how she could improve the bistro's menu to make it more interesting. Before she closed the door, someone caught her eye. Anushka. They made eye contact. Mrs. Singh wondered was she eavesdropping on the conversation. What has she heard? She hoped this nosy girl didn't hear anything incriminating, or anything usable to sell to the tabloids.

She cut Anushka an icy glare before closing the door.

# CHAPTER 7

**H**eat invaded Pierre's face.

When he received a text from his mystery guy saying *Are you free tonight?* Pierre almost lost his freak'n mind. A warm rush surged through his body. He kept forgetting homeboy's name, but after tonight he won't. He will remember every syllable.

After his shift ended at the café, he went straight home. He lit scented candles and smoky incenses. After he finished, his place smelt like a Buddhist temple and a French bakery.

He went into the bathroom. He splashed water on his face and gargled with minty mouthwash to wash away the oniony sandwich he had for dinner. He sprayed on some sweet cologne and threw on some jeans that showed off his curves.

Zola was working late at the café. She thought it would be a good idea to extend the hours to make extra money and pull in new customers. Besides, it was her turn to close. Pierre offered to stay longer to help out but she suggested he leave to get some rest for tomorrow's opening. Now he doubted he would get any rest at all.

The mystery guy strode into the apartment. It took him all of twenty minutes to get to Pierre's place, which was a new record. He looked around the small space, taking in everything, perhaps trying to pick up clues to see if another guy been over to smash. He spoke very little and Pierre asked very few questions.

Pierre figured he was the down-low type. The kind that doesn't disclose any personal information. The kind that deletes all his incoming naughty text messages. The kind that messes around at night. The kind that Pierre liked.

There was swag in his walk; some people would mistake it for arrogance. His long curly hair drove Pierre crazy. It was pulled back into a messy bun. The air in the room thickened like a delicious pot of stew when they sat beside each other on the sofa. A glass of water and wine was denied, so that only meant one thing next.

Hours later, heavy breaths were let out, stomachs were rising and falling quickly. Handprints were left on the white walls. They fell onto their backs, laying in a haze of sweat. Pierre learned his name was Marquis.

Marquis's eyes flung open after he caught his breath. He started to look around the bedroom, taking in Pierre's likes and dislikes. His whiskey eyes landed on Pierre's culinary certificates hanging on the wall, then to his desk, where a Caribbean statue sat, then to his bookshelf, reading titles by authors he didn't know.

Pierre suddenly felt self-conscious. He felt exposed. He wished he had switched off the lights. But when Marquis rose from the bed, he took it all back. Praise the lord the lights were on. *Hallelujah!* He watched Marquis shimmy back into his black Versace boxers. His butt as firm as peaches. His boxers hugged him like an Egyptian god.

Even though Marquis's body was lean, there was a nice mixture of muscle and fat. He wore a thin gold chain around his neck that contrasted beautifully against his brown skin. A faded red string was wrapped around his wrist, betraying his heritage. One full sleeve of roses and butterflies danced up his arm. On the side of his torso was a chopping knife tattoo, with the word chef in the blade. Pierre watched him strut into the bathroom, leaving behind a delicious smell of Belgian chocolate, sweet rum, and black smoke.

Minutes later, whispering could be heard from behind the bathroom door. Pierre moved closer to hear. He even didn't see Marquis take the phone inside. Pierre closed his eyes to concentrate on the words. But nothing was coming through clear. Pierre wondered who he could possibly be talking to. Perhaps a wife? Girlfriend? Or a gay lover? Or was he involved in some illegal activity? These questions never came up in their pillow talk. It was obvious Marquis didn't like to talk about his personal life. He was hesitant telling Pierre his name. Pierre was too tired to make sense of it. It wasn't like they were dating. Or were they? Pierre wondered if he was open with his sexuality. He knew very little about the man who just banged his brains out to the middle of next week.

The bathroom door swung opened. Marquis looked like a meal and a snack all wrapped up in one. Pierre wanted him to stay longer and perhaps go for another round, like last week. He cooed for Marquis to stay. The thought enticed him and challenged his everlasting sex drive. He knew he would be frisky again within another hour. His manhood looked as if one touch it would spring back to life. But he had to bounce. Whoever he spoken to had him on the move.

"Who were you talking to?"

"What you mean?"

"You know, in the bathroom."

"Oh! That was work."

He placed on his shoes without sitting down. Every muscle in his back and arms moved with purpose. His dark butterscotch skin still glistening from the hot sex. Pierre had a strong urge to lick him, just to see if he actually tasted like the flavor.

"You had fun?" Pierre asked, the moment he said it, he wanted to take it back.

"Oh yeah...I had fun... When are you free next?"

Pierre thought for a minute. *He wants to see me again.* He was thrilled. He was bubbling inside. But he played it cool. He didn't want to come off as easily accessible. He must play this right. He wanted him to stick around a little longer than all the others. The sex was amazing, and his body was chewing gum for the eyes. He already became aroused thinking about his next visit.

"Um...I don't know... I'm very busy at the cafe."

"Oh, I see. True."

"Since we're on the subject...do you mind talking to your boy to see if he would like to interview us for his magazine?"

Marquis thought for a long second before replying. "I can ask him."

"Thanks...any help is much appreciated."

"No problem, man."

Pierre noticed something was on his mind; he paused at the doorway with one arm left undone outside his black shirt. One dark nipple stared at Pierre, begging him to take another taste.

"I heard the media was at your restaurant. Didn't y'all get enough exposure?"

Pierre suddenly froze. "Who told you that?"

"Man, my ear is always in the streets."

Pierre felt embarrassed. "It was just a big misunderstanding. That's all."

"I gotcha you, boss. Don't worry I have Darshan get in contact with you."

Marquis left. The café only been open for a month, and they already had a scandal on their hands. Pierre hugged his pillow. It smelt like Marquis. He was like a good bottle of wine; he left a lingering finish. The scent took Pierre's mind off the café's drama.

As he grips the pillow tight, he caught something from the corner of his eye. He noticed a chocolate-colored business card with rose-gold letters written across it lying on the bedroom's floor. He got up to pick it up. It read, *Indo-Infused French Bistro*.

He flipped the card over, and Marquis's name was on it, titled executive chef. Pierre tried to figure why the man he just slept with had his name on their competitor's business card. He tossed it in the bathroom's trash and thought it must be another Marquis.

He plopped on the bed and squeezed his pillow, taking in the smell of smoky chocolate and sweet rum. *Damn, he smells so good,* Pierre thought. His eyes shifted back to the business card in the trash. He wondered about the name written on the card. It couldn't be the Marquis he knew. He rose from the bed again, retrieved the card, and studied it. There was a number. He dialed the number, and a woman answered.

# CHAPTER 8

**A**nushka **stumbled into** work late.

She interrupted a crew meeting. She froze in place, holding her Starbucks latte made with almond milk with one pump of white mocha, and a pump of sugar free vanilla syrup. Something Godiva putt her up on.

Food was laid out on the table. Roasted salmon submerged in a honey apricot glazed winked on a white plate. Truffle and foie gras sausages lay sliced and charred with seasoned vegetables. Poached pears flambéed in cognac and lavender were drizzled with chocolate sauce. Bottles of champagne and white wines were popped open like a joyous affair. Servers, busboys, hostesses, bartenders, and chefs all sparkled with renewed energy.

All eyes were on her. *Shit!* She didn't get the memo about the food tasting. Mrs. Singh shot her a glare that could've made Anushka burst into flames. Anushka quietly sank into a seat, trying her best not to make a sound. Marquis slides her the roasted salmon to try. She tastes it and it was salty and sweet. Sampling and drinking all these gourmet foods made her feel important. The Toronto International

Film Festival was right around the corner, and the celebs were staying at the luxurious hotel. That means, their menu had to be on point. They were preparing the best menu possible and best seating arrangements. Mrs. Singh spoke.

"This is going to be our biggest year. We have to be on our A-game. The royals will be in town dining with us. Where should we sit Meghan and Harry?"

"They did a movie?" a waitress asked.

"No, someone played them in a movie," replied Marquis.

"We can sit them next to Drake."

Mrs. Singh sucked her teeth.

She looked at her notes in *the book*. There was tightness all around her mouth. She had on a silk black jumpsuit tapered at the ankle, with floral jewelry. Her hair was up in a French twist, showing off her elegant neck.

"Have we decided on the menu?"

Everyone looked around the table. Nobody had anything to say. Mrs. Singh was starting to look displeased with everyone's lack of imagination. She rolled her eyes at the dead silence. There was a cough somewhere in the room, eyes flung to Anushka. She wasn't the one that coughed, but now she felt obligated to say something smart and clever. She had missed most of the taste test, but she spoke anyway. Some thought it was suicide. She cleared her throat.

"What about tandoori lobster infused with ginger and black garlic? It could be for the adventurous palate. Or sweet potato curry with mussels for those who're trying to watch their figure, or roasted rabbit in a saffron risotto for the traditional?" Mrs. Singh flips open *the book* again and started jotting down the ideas. "…and for appetizers, deep fried goat cheese garnished with fennel leaves, or escargot in a creamy butter garlic sauce. And every table should get a complimentary basket of brioches, served with truffle butter made from Parisian cream. We should keep the menu concise and smart, no?"

Everyone looked around the long table. Mrs. Singh scoffed, bit down on her artsy black glasses, and nonchalantly said with a shrug, "That could work."

Marquis spoke: "What about duck confit on a bed of…"

"Duck confit!" exclaimed Mrs. Singh. "Groundbreaking." The dismissal made Marquis slouch back into his chair.

After the meeting, Anushka was training under Godiva for front house. They were short on staff and Anushka couldn't afford another mistake in the kitchen. But before Anushka started, she wanted to apologize to Mrs. Singh for her tardiness. She walked to her large office as if she was headed to the guillotine block. Some crew members looked at her as if she had lost her freakin' mind.

She appeared at the open door. Mrs. Singh was leafing through *the book*, scrutinizing each page of all the top celebrities that going to be at the restaurant after the Film Festival. She made it a point to visit every important person's table as often as possible.

When Anushka stepped further into the cavernous space, she smelt buttery croissants, melted chocolate, and expensive French coffee. A rack of designer clothes stood off in the corner for an immediate outfit change for important interviews and special occasions. It was rotated every week with the latest hot fashions. Anushka stared in awe at the beauty of everything, and realizing it was her first time standing in her boss's office. The space was so formidable, it made her feel small and insignificant. She thought about turning back, coming was stupid, but before she could they made eye contact.

"Mrs. Singh, I just want to apologize for…"

"Just don't let it happen again," she said turning back to her binder, and leafing through the pages.

"I won't. I promise."

Just before she was about to walk away, Mrs. Singh spoke again.

"And Anika…"

"It's Anushka."

Mrs. Singh eyed her for a minute. "What do you know about the Spice Café?"

"The food is horrible. Over-priced and over-spiced. Not my cup of tea."

"My daughters paid a visit to their grand opening, and they rather had some good things to say about the cafe. Are you calling my daughters liars?"

"Not even. Not even close."

"Because if you are…" Her voice became expensive and terrifying.

"It's just that my taste is sensitive to spice. That's why I love working here. There's a balance between flavors."

Mrs. Singh glares at her some more, analyzing her up and down. "Do you know anything else about the cafe?"

"There's a woman that owns it. People in the neighborhood calls her CHEF. It's like her nickname."

"Is that right?" Mrs. Singh rose from her desk and sauntered to the floor-to-ceiling window and looked down at the cafe. She watched deliverymen unload summer vegetables into the shop. Mrs. Singh recognized it was the same delivery company she used for her organics and grass-fed produce. She assumed the cafe was doing well. Her thoughts were interrupted by Anushka.

"Am I free to go?"

She waves her away then called her back again.

"And Anika…. take *the book* to Godiva's office. "

❦

Godiva had overheard their conversation and dangled a pair of gold stilettos in front of Anushka and snatched *the book* out of her hand.

"Are you crazy going into Mrs. Singh's office wearing Orphan Annie shoes?"

Anushka speed-walked to keep up with Godiva. Once they reached her office, Anushka noticed it wasn't as big as Mrs. Singh's. No windows. No white walls. No air conditioning. No accolades.

No family pictures. Just a dusty printer, a desk stacked with a mountain of cookbooks and a mini refrigerator that barely worked. The air smelt like cigarettes and generic coffee. Godiva closed the door behind them.

"You really fucked up this time."

"What do you mean?"

"Coming in late."

"I spoke to Mrs. Singh. Everything is fine. We're totally cool. I told her it wouldn't happen again."

Godiva took a seat behind the desk and rubbed her temples. "It shows that you're not reliable."

"I am."

"Look, I'm trying to build you up. You might have to take my position someday as restaurant manager. This isn't a joke. You will have some big shoes to fill once I'm gone. Kindergarten is over. You're in the big leagues now. So cut the bull."

Anushka paid no attention to her mini rant. She was too busy eyeing *the book*. She wondered what Godiva was going to do with it. She watched Godiva open to a delectable page, pictures of beautiful desserts with chocolate ganache and glazed fruits. Anushka was suddenly in the mood for molten lava cake. Her mouth started to salivate with every flip of a page. She leaned forward to have a closer peak. Recipes were listed on the side. She unconsciously touched *the book* and Godiva waves her hand away as if she was some pesky insect.

"What's so important about that book?"

"This is Mrs. Singh's seasonal menu markups and other unclassified information."

Anushka leaned over again.

"Don't touch." Godiva carefully flipped to another page "It also has the new bistro details."

"The new bistro?"

"Yes, Mrs. Singh is planning a trip to Paris to open up a new bistro."

"Paris!"

"Yes. Paris…and keep your voice down, don't let the whole bloody world hear you. Besides you might have fucked up your chances of going."

"Just for coming in late?"

Godiva sighed deeply and pops a chocolate truffle into her mouth to calm her nerves. "Mrs. Singh only travels with the best team that she can rely on, and you proved not to be one of those people."

"When is she going to Paris?"

"That's top-secret."

"Is it in that stupid book? Let me see it."

She reached for it. Godiva closed it and slipped it in the drawer.

"What's the big deal? Why the hush-hush? It's just another restaurant."

"It's THE restaurant. All the food critics, food celebrities, fashion gurus are going to be there. This grand opening will be in every food magazine that exist; food bloggers will talk about it for weeks, even months, even centuries."

"No shit." This sounded too good to be true. A chance for Anushka to be recognized. A chance for her to go to Paris.

"Yes shit…so stop slacking off and check your ego at the door, along with your unopened emails."

"Are you going?"

Godiva shrugged.

"I might have to stay here and babysit you guys to make sure nothing burns down."

"If you're chosen to go, who are you taking?"

"Not you." She laughed.

Anushka folded her arms tight.

"I just thought you would take…you know…. Marquis…"

Godiva popped up from her buttery leather chair and made sure the door was closed.

"Don't mention his name."

"Mrs. Singh doesn't know you two are seeing each other?"

"We're not seeing each other. It was just a fling."

Anushka didn't buy it.

"Look, Anushka. If I could take you, I would. You might be scheduled to stay here. I have no control over who stays or who goes."

"But I speak French."

"I know, it's very impressive. But still, look at it this way, this can be your big break, you know, to be in charge of the kitchen in case I go. That's why I'm trying to mentor you."

Anushka thought about it, trying to see the bigger picture. She was right. This could be her big break. Her time to shine. But Paris sounded much, much lovelier. She wanted to rub elbows with every food celebrity there was. The moment was so close, she could taste it. Her in Paris. Her schmoozing with Mrs. Singh's son. She would be the talk of town. Every foodist would know her name. She could see it now, her pictures plastered on every food magazine.

Her dream was to have an honorable career, a successful handsome husband, and fame! Oh yes! fame. The image of her and Mrs. Singh's son strolling underneath the Eiffel Tower made her scream inside with excitement. That's what she wanted. She wanted it all.

She wanted to prove to her parents she wasn't some fuck-up. She was a girl with a plan. She was going to stick to it. She wanted to keep everything air-tight. Let people think she was an idiot, but she was no fool. Soon she would be on top. Everyone will know her name.

❧

Later in the evening, Anushka was eating dinner in the dining room at the bistro. There was a small rush, but nothing the crew couldn't handle. Being an assistant manager wasn't so bad, telling the waitstaff what to do was pretty easy.

Godiva strides towards her, gold heels clicking on the polished floor. She walked with such importance that it demands attention of the waitstaff. Anushka sat up straight when she approaches her table.

"Duck confit, roasted garlic potatoes and a chocolate souffle, all at once?"

"Too much?"

"Not if you're preparing for war."

Before Anushka could take another bite of her dinner, Godiva snaps her fingers to have it removed.

"Hey! What's going on? I wasn't finished."

"If you're going to work your way up to the top, you have to eat smart. You must make better choices, Anushka. You don't just represent yourself; you represent me, you represent the company. From here on out, I want to see more organic vegetables on your plate.... Lots!"

"But what if I don't want to become slim like everyone else here."

"Anushka, you have no choice. Your job depends on it."

"What you have there anyway?"

Godiva was so disgusted with Anushka's dinner that she almost forgot why she came.

"This is the wine list for the Film Festival. I'm going to need you to memorize it before the event."

"I already studied the wine list online."

"This is a new wine list."

Godiva hands it to her

"Oh, this isn't so bad."

"Don't be so naive Anushka, these too."

She dumps leather black folders onto the table ranging from wine, cheeses, to important influencers who were attending.

"I have to know all these by next week?"

"It's important to know everyone that is attending. This is going to be a big night for us. There can't be no slip ups."

Anushka tries to think what all she knew about wine. She knew that prosecco and white wine goes best with fish and chicken. She knows red goes well with dark meat like beef and lamb and anything gamy. However, she was horrible detecting flavors in wine. She instantly thought she was the wrong person for the job. But Godiva stressed since she was a cook and the assistant manager, she needed to the know the place inside and out.

"Where do we keep all these?"

"In the wine cellar."

Anushka was puzzled.

"You're telling me no one shown you the wine cellar?"

Anushka shook her head.

Godiva rolled her painted dark eyes up in the air. "Follow me"

They rode the elevator to the basement. The lighting was dim. Godiva swiped her passkey and the automatic doors slid open and light spilled onto their faces. Anushka's eyes lit up. Everything had their own section. Big round cheeses were stacked on modern shelves releasing a nutty-sweet saltiness. Cheese makers sliced into the creamy mass with steadiness like open-heart surgeons. Workers wearing white coats moved with purpose as if they were curing world hunger. Dried meats hung on big stainless-steel hooks and wines went in all directions from vintage Cabernet Francs to expensive champagne, all with winning gold labels. Anushka's eyes still hadn't scratched the surface of the catalog.

"All this belongs to the bistro?"

"Yes, and whoever Mrs. Singh wants to share it with. The front house staff only come down here if necessary. Everything usually gets delivered by the workers down here. It almost function as its own entity."

"What's over there?"

"That's the room where Mrs. Singh keeps all her designer clothes after they're rotated out of her office from week to week. They get sent back to the designers after use."

"Can we have a look?"

"Sure but make it quick."

Godiva picked out a few outfits that suited Anushka's frumpy physique, some were two sizes too small and needed to be let out.

"Thanks for letting me keep some of these."

"It's for front house wear only until you could afford your own."

Anushka nods.

"Are we done here? I have a kitchen to run."

They made their way back to the dining room. The bistro was picking up. Anushka grateful that Godiva gave her expensive clothes to wear, especially for the Film Festival. She hadn't had a clue what to wear before she obtained these beautiful garments. Clothes that required her to eat tons of leafy greens.

Memorizing the new wine list was daunting. So much to learn in just a few days. *Fuck!* She doesn't know if she could pull it off. But she will try. This was her chance to prove herself. She couldn't mess up. She couldn't show she was a phony that enjoyed eating dhal with roti in her pajamas, instead of duck confit and stuffed brioches, dressed in stilettos.

She was going to live up to Mrs. Singh's expectations. She couldn't let her down. Most importantly she couldn't let herself down.

# CHAPTER 9

"**Y**ou the head chef at the bistro?"

Pierre was pacing back and forth in his small apartment, staring Marquis in the face. The temperature in the room had suddenly skyrocketed. He was trying not to flip out on the guy who's been giving him the best sex of his life. But he was tired of these low-down-lying-guys. He took a deep breath, trying to remember some long-forgotten meditation techniques.

"I can explain."

"Yes, please do."

"But first, how about you sit down?"

"I think I'd rather stand."

"How did you find out?"

"I have my ears in the streets." Pierre smirked.

"True, true," Marquis managed to say.

"So, I'm waiting."

"I hate seeing you like this, man…please have a seat so we can talk about this."

Pierre considered him for a second or two and then sat on the sofa.

This wasn't what Marquis expected when he came over. He was tricked. Bamboozled. He thought he was going to get some of Pierre's sweet cakes. He thought wrong.

"Yes, I'm a chef there."

"Why hadn't you told me?"

"I didn't know it was a big deal."

"That you worked across the street from me and that you're our competitors…um…yeah."

"Is that what you're upset about?"

"No. It isn't."

"What is it then?"

"Why the bistro making false accusations about the Spice Café exploiting illegal immigrants?"

"*Bruh*, I don't know what you're talking about."

"Yeah, right, Marquis, you know exactly what I'm talking about, the press showing up at our cafe."

"Dude, it was in the news. Besides, the whole block knew about it."

Pierre groaned. "I don't know, Marquis. I don't know if I can believe you. It all sounds so fishy. Why were you on the phone whispering in my bathroom the other night?"

"Dude, I told you that was work. Nothing more."

Pierre side-eyed him. "Look Marquis, I'm not playing games. This is my livelihood we're talking about here. Either you tell me what's going on, or you will have to leave."

Marquis weighed his options. He really liked Pierre, and his pheromones were screaming from the roof top. Pierre would know if he sampled him. Seasoned to perfection just the way he liked it. But Pierre wasn't having none of it. Marquis didn't want to leave. He drove all the way from Mississauga to Scarborough, an hour-long commute. *Fuck!* Even longer during rush hour traffic. He couldn't leave without those sweet cakes lingering on his lips.

"One last chance, Marquis, who was it?"

Marquis took a deep breath. For a second it looked like he was going to break. But he refocused his attention on the floor, hiding his eyes as if to prevent the truth from leaking out. He didn't want Pierre's glare imploring him to speak. Pierre was running low on time, energy, and patience. Getting the truth out of Marquis was like foraging for black truffles in a dark forest. This was the reason why he didn't like messing around with guys younger than him. Too many games. They were only good in bed, that's about it. Marquis had a lot growing up to do. Pierre guessed his age had to be around mid-twenties. Marquis tried to sit provocatively to distract Pierre from the heavy conversation. But it didn't work. Pierre's eyes stayed on his.

"Well, since you're not talking, I will have to ask you to leave."

Marquis reluctantly rose, towering over Pierre while he remained seated. Marquis had a sudden urge to shove his tongue down his throat, along with something else. He started to get aroused. A bulge formed, taking on a life of its own. He tried to readjust himself, thinking about unattractive things to calm it down. But being around Pierre, that was hard to do.

Pierre stole a glance at his manhood. He imagined the vein expanding, gathering all weeks' worth of frustration from his tired limbs, taunting Pierre to test his oral skills, perhaps learn some new ones. Pierre dragged his eyes away; he was going to stand his ground. He meant business. He couldn't let anyone damage the café's represen-tation, not even Marquis. Something about him just wasn't right. He believes he was hiding something. But didn't know what. Marquis tried to think of something to rescue the evening but couldn't.

A few minutes after he left, Pierre heard his phone vibrate. It danced on the coffee table as if it was possessed. He looked down, and there were texts from Marquis. Back-to-back. Apologies. Pleading to come back. He was now on the 401-freeway heading home but more than willing to turn around. Pierre didn't respond and tossed the phone to the other end of the sofa.

He never wanted to see him again.

# CHAPTER 10

A month ago, Anushka received the call of her life.

It was from the bistro. She was at home in her town-house, sitting on the sofa watching her favorite movie, Bollywood Hollywood. She couldn't count how many times she watched it.

She was happy to receive a call back. She had applied a few months ago and thought she didn't have a chance.

She graduated at the top of her class. Some family members thought her education was basic. A culinary degree was nothing to brag about, especially not in an Indian household. A medical or engineering degree, yes. Add on a Ph.D. in English, even made things sweeter. The more degrees, the better.

One day, her mother had popped up at her old job. She was working as a waitress. Anushka was clearing tables after a team of soccer players celebrated a win. Her mother clucked her tongue. She didn't have to say it; her expression said it all, but she said it anyway. *Why are you doing this, na? Your father and me didn't work our fingers to the bone so you can become some cook!*

Whether her parents liked it or not, she was taking the culinary route. She enjoyed cooking. It was what she loved. It was her life. Everything she done was out of the norm in her family. She even got married outside her culture. It wasn't anything planned. It just happened. Did she regret it? A little. It crushed her mother's poor heart. To make matters worse, she eloped. Then her marriage failed. But now she must make things right with her mother. She must marry a Singh. That would send her mother over the moon. She didn't bother switching back to her surname. Hell! It was one thing she'd rather keep. It looked good on resumes.

"Hello?"

"Anushka Black?"

"Yes, speaking."

"This is Godiva, manager at Indo-French Bistro… Do you have time for a quick phone interview?"

"Of course." She was screaming inside.

"Great. I see you attended Auguste Escoffier Culinary Arts."

"That's right."

"Have you ever worked in a French kitchen before?"

"No, but I've worked in an Indian restaurant. Your bistro is fusion, correct?"

"Yes, it is. But knowing some French cooking techniques helps a lot for this position."

"I'm a fast learner."

"I see you graduated at the top of your class."

"Yes."

"And won a few cooking competitions. We need someone like that on our team. Why don't you come down to the bistro so we can talk more, lets say tomorrow at 10:00 a.m.?"

"That sounds perfect."

"Great! See you then."

⁓

The following day, she arrived at a tall, black, building. It made her feel so small. She wore black pants with a floral top, and ballerina flats. Her hair was newly cut in a smart bob.

Godiva met her at the door of her office. They shook hands before taking a seat. The air was stuffy, and the lighting was moderately dim.

"Thanks for coming."

"My pleasure."

"Let's get this show on the road, shall we?" Godiva stared at her resume. "It looks like you worked in two kitchens."

"Yes, I left on good terms. The first job was in India, the other in Vancouver."

"You get around."

"Well, I was born in India, and Vancouver I left after a nasty divorce. Now I'm here."

"Why are you interested in working at our bistro?"

"Well, I'm Indian. I love cooking Indian food and learning the ins and outs of a French kitchen would be great experience."

"This isn't a place to learn. Your first day here would be like taking a crash course test. Would you be up for the challenge?"

"Yes. Totally."

"Do you know Mrs. Leena Gandhi?"

"Who?"

Godiva rubbed the bottom of her face. "Mrs. Singh? The woman that owns this bistro?"

Anushka felt like an idiot. She didn't take the time to remember Mrs. Singh's full name as she was perusing their website last night. She had to reel this baby back in.

"Oh, Mrs. Singh. Yes, yes. I know Leena Gandhi Singh. I was having a brain hiccup."

Godiva eyed her suspiciously. "Do you speak French?"

"*Oui.*"

"Good. What's your favorite French meal?"

She thought long and hard about French onion soup—nah, too cliché. Too simple. She made one up.

"I love Boeuf Bourguignon, accompanied by a cheese soufflé."

"Good, good. But we don't cook beef here. I hope that's okay."

"Oh yeah. That's fine."

"How soon can you start?"

"As soon as you want me."

Godiva rose and gave Anushka a quick tour of the kitchen. Copper pots and pans hung in a roll on the wall. Anushka noticed deep fryers, broilers and sauce stations. Cooks stood around with sharp knives hacking into root vegetables and summer fruits. Bakers were slipping puffy dough into greased pans and placing them into wide convectional ovens. She sauntered passed their windows and watched golden cakes and breads balloon into fabulous eats. Her eyes were locked on Godiva and the chaos coalescing around them. She felt like a bystander. An intruder, watching all the hidden secrets coming together to create the perfect dish.

They walked past a huge walk-in cooler. Anushka only wondered what rich ingredients lay behind the stainless-steel door: organic goats' milk, garlic butter, herb cheeses, infused sausages, sea urchins, caviar, artichokes, leeks, imported white truffles.

She couldn't believe this was going to be her new job. A job that will make her feel important, a job that will give her some sense of existence. She definitely saw herself working there.

∽

Anushka called her parents the moment she got home from the interview. They were happy for her new position at the bistro, but her mother didn't understand why she wanted to work in a hot kitchen full of egotistical men. Her mother wanted her to get married. To a SINGH! Now that was news. Anushka waved away her mother's notion. She didn't need her meddling in her romantic affairs. Her parents were well-off; they made their fortune through good investments. However, Anushka's family wasn't as blessed with inheritance as the Singh's.

Her mother couldn't drop the conversation about Mrs. Singh's boy. She wanted to set everything up. She told her only daughter to leave everything to her. Anushka didn't argue. She didn't have the energy. Besides, she didn't want to kill her buzz on getting the job of her dreams. To have the Indo-French bistro printed on her resume would get her inside every restaurant kitchen in the world. Or getting Mrs. Singh as a referral could rocket her to celebrity status.

Yes, her parents had enough money to buy her a bistro. They actually offered. But who would come? Who would grace her tables? Who would know her name? She didn't want to spend time building an audience. That was boring. She would soon have her own bistro, bought with her own money, attracting every superstar from around the world.

∽

The Film Festival was here. The bistro was filling up with men in full black suits and ties and women in long shimmering gowns, all showboating in entitlement.

Mrs. Singh greeted the customers graciously at the door, touching everyone as if they were delicate art. Godiva and Anushka were pinned to her hip like supermodels. Both wearing champagne-colored dresses and encrusted hanging earrings.

They whispered important people's names in Mrs. Singh's ear, especially if they were food bloggers or social media stars. Mrs. Singh couldn't be bothered remembering internet sensations, it was too many of them to keep up.

When everyone was seated, Godiva strutted around the restaurant to make sure everyone was comfortable and served promptly. She blessed everyone with a courtesy smile. She was prepared for tonight, even dreamed about it. She felt she was in her element. Being around so many affluent people and talents made her feel fabulous.

Anushka almost didn't make it tonight. She had such a bad hangover from all the wine sampling from the day before. Pairing wines with all different types of cheeses and meats. She woke up drunk and dazed. Her body weak and limp. If she called off, she knew Godiva would've had her head on a spike.

A few customers waved down Anushka and placed in their orders. Anushka wished she had carried a pen and paper. How was she going to remember everyone's orders in this chao? She tries to memorize their order, by repeating it over and over to herself as she beelined to the kitchen. She didn't know she was waiting tables too, for Christ's sake, why didn't Godiva tell her this would happen? Godiva supposed to be shadowing her so tonight would go smoothly, to save her from making a complete ass of herself.

Before Anushka could go into the kitchen to place in the order, someone else pulled her to the side. Two actors needed to be seated. She looked around the dining room for a vacant table and found one overlooking the city.

Tonight, had to go smooth, she kept repeating in her mind. It was her mantra. This was her chance to redeem herself; show Mrs. Singh she was reliable and not some fuck up who doesn't know how to boil an egg. She glanced over at Mrs. Singh gliding around the room like a curator in an old castle.

Midway into dinner, the muscle in Anushka's thigh started to cry out in pain. She also had a sudden urge to take off her stilettos and massage her tired feet. Godiva's chocolate brown eyes zeroed in on her leaning against the wall. She immediately beelined towards Anushka without missing a beat.

"What the hell are you doing?"

"Just a cramp in my leg."

"Well, shake it out and get back to work. We have a bistro to run. Don't let Mrs. Singh see you posted up like some dying wallflower. Now move it. Move!"

Godiva shooed Anushka away like some unwanted dog begging for scraps. Godiva dashed back onto the scene like a ten-year-old girl light on her feet. Rose-gold makeup shimmered on her sunken in cheeks. She counted her calories for months just to look good for tonight, eating nothing but ratatouille salad and slither almonds.

A bartender overheard Anushka's feet pain and slid her a shot of whisky. She tosses it back and let the heat gush down her throat, it coated her nerves like a heavy blanket. She wanted to go hide in the bathroom until the night was over. But she knew that wasn't an option.

Food was being rushed out the kitchen. Chefs hot and red-faced. F bombs flung silently across the open kitchen. Knives struck chopping boards; pans sizzled on stoves and slipped into hot ovens to be finished off.

Anushka knew tonight would put the bistro back on the map. Everyone knew it. Mrs. Singh has been worried about the competition of the Spice Café, stealing all their hotel customers. Tonight, they will reclaim them back and then some.

The bistro had nothing to fear. Anushka was going to make sure of it.

# CHAPTER 11

**B**itterness hit the back of Pierre's throat.

The café looked different the following morning. It seemed tired and exposed, like a naked woman rising out of bed without makeup. Tables were bare and chairs were empty while the floors remained unmarked by a single customer.

The bistro across the street was generating buzz. The film festival a couple weeks ago had boosted their presence within the city and the community. They were the talk of the town. It was one thing gaining new exposure, but stealing their customers was another.

Pierre watched the bistro employees marched around with signs offering free cooking classes. He wondered if Marquis's shady ass had something to do with this. Maybe he was getting back at Pierre for tossing his narrow butt out of his apartment.

The cafe was quiet. They been open for over a month, and sales had already dropped drastically. No more working overtime. No more changing schedules. No more hiring new help.

Pierre pointed out the cafe's window showing Zola the disrespect.

"Can you believe this? They are giving discounts and free cooking lessons at the bistro."

"Free cooking lessons?"

"Yes. I saw them yesterday handing out flyers *to all our customers.*"

"Now that's low."

"Tell me about it."

"How long you think they're going to keep this up?"

"Until Oprah runs out of money." Pierre placed a hand on his hip and leaned farther into the window.

"Maybe we should go over and introduce ourselves."

"Why? So they can laugh at our expense? I think not."

"Come on, Pierre. We're bigger than this."

"You can mosey on over if you want to. But my black ass is staying here."

A customer came into the cafe, an older gentleman. His hand shook like a broken blender. His skin was as thin as phyllo dough. His eyebrows grew outward like unruly grass. He was their first customer for lunch. Zola brewed him his regular coffee with saffron, condensed milk, and honey, leaving Pierre fuming at the window. The coffee machine screamed to life. Steam puffs in the air clouding Zola's face. She wrapped up a slice of Black Forest cake and placed it in a chic logo bag for the customer. Once he was out the door, Pierre started back up again.

"You know what, Zola, we should do a cooking class."

"A what?"

"Hear me out." Pierre stretched out his arms as if he were going to break into song and dance, eyes bright like glistening pastries. "It will draw people back to our cafe."

"I don't know, Pierre. It costs money; money we don't have."

A black cloud descended on Pierre's thoughts. He didn't see the hole in his plan. She was right, they didn't have money. His brain spun around and around, replaying scenarios back and forth. Cooking up schemes. Flipping them around like runny pancakes refusing to cook.

He stomped his foot in frustration, arms folded in protest. He must find a way to get the people back into the cafe. This time in numbers. He wanted the bistro to take their fancy baguettes and shove them where the sun doesn't shine. *Wait a minute.* He took that back. That could be pleasurable for some. It wasn't over yet. He couldn't let the cafe go under. He had exhausted all his funds. Zola too. He thought about asking for online donations, putting his pride aside. Friends and family were already thinking they were rolling in dough. Some were already asking to borrow money. But in actuality, they were flat broke.

Zola went into the kitchen to check on the food. A box of overripe mangoes stared her in the face. They were used to make a delicious mango mouse. Now they looked like shrivelled-up black truffles. It pained her to toss them out. She'd had enough stressing over the French bistro. She concluded they were the shadiest bunch. She could see right through their tactics. Stealing their customers. How dare they?

She put on some neo-soul music to calm her nerves. Maybe that would bring Pierre out of his funk. The soft melodies escaped into the air. She heard him steaming milk. Perhaps making his favorite, pumpkin spice latte. She donned a clean apron and started baking to ease her mind. She loved baking; it takes her mind off her problems. It was her yoga. Her meditation. She cracked open an exotic spice and instantly she was cool as a cucumber. Butter helped too. She could die in butter. They were like whispering in her ear saying *everything will be all right.* But how would she know that for sure? She needed to talk to someone.

⁂

"Fuck, Zo, are you serious!"

Courtney was Zola's friend. They met when they worked at a high-end Mexican restaurant. Zola got tired of working there and wanted to open her own restaurant, and Courtney was the one that encouraged the crazy venture. Courtney's tall, high-heeled brown boots clicked on the market's floor as they shopped with baskets hanging from their arm like fashionable purses.

"As serious as a heart attack. They are stealing our customers."

"You should go over there and rip their fucking balls off." Courtney flipped her hair in protest and threw a bag of white truffle chips into her basket. "You shouldn't let those fuckers get away with it."

"You sound like Pierre."

"Well, he's right. You can't let them egotistical jerks screw you over. This industry is ruthless, especially on women chefs in a male-dominated industry."

"You used to work at the bistro, right?"

"Yeah, a long time ago, until I got fired."

"For what?

Zola consulted a can of fire-roasted tomatoes seasoned with sumac spice, and then tossed it in her basket.

"She was tired of me flirting with the chefs, especially with the head cook, Marquis."

"That's not a good reason to let someone go."

Courtney shrugged and chucked a pack of butter cookies studded with lavender into her basket, along with a fig-flavored kombucha.

"It took me years to get another gig. No one didn't want to hire me. I was black-balled for a while. Getting fired from the French bistro isn't a good thing. It could ruin your fucking culinary career. But luckily, I had a friend that helped me out. He opened a very small kitchen in Kensington market where all the hipsters hang out. Now I'm working in his kitchen."

"What you think I should do other than snatching their balls off?"

"Host a cooking class. That's a great idea. Throw the dirt back into their faces."

"Um…hello. It costs money."

"Not if somebody sponsors it."

"I will have to think about that."

"Fuck, Zola, don't think, do. These fuckers are out for blood, it seems. I would hate to see your business go under because of these psycho pricks."

"How long did you work there?"

"Long enough." She leaned over a glass counter and smelled a Gorgonzola cheese smothered in blackcurrant jam. A woman working behind it, cut a hefty slice, wrapped it, and handed it off to Courtney. "This Eataly market is amazing. I could live here."

"I know. You should try their saffron coconut milk. So good."

"It gives me heartburn."

"Oh."

"This situation you're in has me thinking. You need to take control of your life. Don't let those sick fucks bully you. They want to see you throw in the towel. You're stronger than that."

"You think so?"

"I know so."

After they finished shopping. They parted ways. Zola watched Courtney walk away with the wind whipping in her strawberry blonde hair. She tugged at her leather coat, heels clicking on the pavement like a Parisian fashion model. Men stole glances at her, and she paid no attention.

She lit a cigarette hanging from her lips. She took a hard drag from it and blew out a body of smoke, dancing up her nose and face into the cool air. Zola imagined her cigarette being sticky with flavored lip gloss by now. A tall man bumped into Courtney, almost knocking her cigarette out of her mouth. It looked like she wanted to deck him a good one. There were some brief exchanges. No phones pulled out. No handshakes. She gave him a smoke, and he strode away. She stomped out her cigarette and hopped on the streetcar. She turned toward the window and waved.

# CHAPTER 12

Darshan walked into the Spice Café.

A waitress with dreads spotted him and escorted him to a table. She didn't have a clue he was a revered food critic. She handed him a plastic menu and recommended a couple of items. She came back with sweet yams smothered in melted marshmallows and crunchy pecans, along with smoked Cajun fish over a bed of creamy grits, and fried okra.

Darshan tasted everything and jotted down notes on his phone. He was going to judge the food on its merits, not letting his feelings for Zola interfere with his work. The *Gourmet* magazine only published the best restaurants. He snapped a few pictures of the dishes and Bohemian feel décor.

The waitress assumed he was a food blogger. Therefore she was extra courteous, her smile wider than usual. He asked to speak with the owner or the manager. His face and body language unreadable. The waitress stumbled away as if she was in some kind of trouble.

A few minutes later, Zola emerged from the kitchen. She used the bottom of her apron to wipe the flour off her hands. Her hair was pinned up in a loose bun. Rebellious strands escaped and sought refuge on her face. She didn't have time to hit the salon this week. She wanted to look her best for the interview, but she was tied up with the shop.

She shook Darshan's hand, surprised that he was the food critic that attended the grand opening. He was more beautiful up close than she ever imagined. He smelled like fine champagne and hickory smoke.

Darshan followed her into the kitchen. Fresh garlic cloves were being smashed with the blade of a knife, its sharp smell perfuming the hot air.

A cook was cutting collard greens and adding them to a large pot where bacon fat was rendering. Another cook was chopping something unrecognizable to Darshan. A man covered with tattoos was coating catfish in cornmeal and giving it a good shake before tossing it in hot grease. It sizzled and crackled like fireworks. The workers wore regular clothes as uniforms. Zola checked a few dishes before sending them out. The energy in the kitchen was much calmer than the hustle and bustle at the bistro. Zola was showing him a new world. A world he was beginning to appreciate, but he didn't let it show on his face.

"What do you call this?" He pointed inside a large pot.

"That's black-eyed peas and neckbones."

"Neckbones?"

"It's a neck of a turkey. It gives the beans a lot of flavor."

She gave him a taste with a wooden spoon. The meat dissolved quickly before he could chew. He let the flavors and spices seduce him. She gestured him over to the dessert station. It hosted a slew of tarts, pies, cookies, cornbread muffins, and decadent cakes. All resting on cooling racks.

Zola popped a chocolate brownie bite into his mouth, laced with saffron and Madagascar vanilla. She watched the flavors travel from his mouth to his sparkling dark eyes. He gave no sign that he loved it or hated it. Since he arrived, he kept her in suspense.

Before he took leave, she gave him a slice of peach cobbler pie, on the house. A dessert that Darshan never had. The cinnamon spice flamingo-danced up his perfect nose. If Darshan wasn't so stuffed, he would have devoured it right there.

When he got outside, Darshan grabbed his phone out of his pocket and took a few more pictures of the cafe. He replayed the interview sound bites, and deemed he got everything he needed that could change the fate of the Spice Café.

# CHAPTER 13

*Y*ou *want exposure. I'll give you exposure!*

Pierre held his phone in his hand, trying to decipher the meaning of the text. Was this some kind of a sick joke? It was from a blocked number. He thought it had to be from Marquis or his hooligan cooks. They'd started to get on nerves. Marquis was the only one who knew they wanted publicity for their cafe. Pierre was sure he was behind this. He didn't understand why Marquis was doing this crazy mess, but he was going to find out.

Pierre marched to the bistro, arms swinging as if he was in the military. The décor was smart and elegant. Pierre instantly smelled sweet-dirt coffee and French butter. The interior was a flawless depiction of Paris. The windows were floor-to-ceiling, they were so clear one would swear nothing was there. The sunlight hitting the crystal chandeliers made them appear like freezing rain.

A hostess wearing a black turtleneck, black tights and stilettos approached him at the door. Her gold eye lids were straight out of a high-fashion magazine. Godiva surveyed Pierre's attire; he wore jeans and a white T-shirt, marked with chocolate. She almost denied him entry, until Marquis appeared out of nowhere and beelined towards him.

He escorted Pierre to a nearby corner, they were shaded by a big potted plant that blocked all stares and looks.

"What are you doing here, and how did you get past security dressed like that?" Marquis combed the length of Pierre's body.

"Why the threats?"

"Huh?...bruh, I don't know what you're talking about."

"I'm tired of your lame ass games, Marquis."

"Listen, can we talk about this later? This is really not the place."

"Oh, but it's always the right place and time to put me on blast, right?"

"Bruh, I'm sorry for what happened, but I really have to get back to work."

"Who's your boss?"

"What?"

"The owner of this piece of crap."

Pierre's eyes darted around the restaurant. He knew Marquis wasn't the owner. He looked too young and childish. The customers had started to stare in their direction. Pierre was creating a scene. He didn't care, but Marquis did.

Marquis pleaded for him to chill out and to have a seat. Pierre thought for a second and sat at a window table overlooking Lake Ontario. Yachts could be seen at a distance. Marquis left and came back with a bottle of champagne. He poured Pierre a hefty glass, and they both watched the gold bubbles dance to the top. Marquis disappeared again.

Pierre watched him melt into a flurry of egomaniac chefs. Someone shouted out, *your onions are too dry, do it again!* Big rubber mats squeaked beneath their heavy feet in haste. Fingers struck brass pots and pans fanatically. Suckling duck was being butchered and swordfish being filleted. Pierre thought Marquis looked smart in his chef whites. The black bandana on his head gave him an edge.

A few minutes later, Marquis reappeared with a piping hot plate. His biceps looked as if he had carried a lifetime of heavy trays. Pierre kissed every part of him with his chocolate eyes. Marquis sat the plate in front of him, grilled scallops in a yellow curry sauce with Japanese mushrooms, with specks of pink peppercorns and white truffles over saffron rice laid underneath like the ocean floor.

Pierre's stomach growled. His body was already betraying the Spice Café without taking a single bite. Marquis stood by, waiting for a verdict. Pierre looked up at him and back down at the food. He took a bite, eyes closed. He believed good food demanded complete submission. The warm sauce glided down his throat. White flesh against the edges of his teeth, meat slicing like butter. Suddenly, flavors opened across his tongue like a blooming flower. One petal at a time. Cinnamon. Earthiness. Lime. He wanted to talk, but the flavors held his tongue hostage for a few more seconds.

"This is…this is delicious," Pierre said reluctantly.

"Really, man? That means a lot coming from you. Listen, don't worry about paying for the meal, it's on the house." Marquis jogged back into the kitchen without saying another word.

Pierre liked the kind gesture. But that still didn't answer his question about the elusive text message. He knew he couldn't stay mad at Marquis; he was too damn cute. He couldn't remember the last time a man cooked for him. But why did Marquis cooked for him? Was he guilty of something? Pierre couldn't figure out what was going on. But if Zola found out that Pierre was eating at the bistro, she would have his head on a chopping block.

Before leaving, Pierre noticed a middle-aged Indian woman staring at him from across the room. He wondered what her deal was. She ate her food slowly, not taking her eyes off him. This made Pierre uneasy. His phone vibrated in his pocket, making him jump.

He read the text: *Can I see you tonight?*

# CHAPTER 14

S tudents were trickling into the cooking class.
They were excited to be in the kitchen of *Gourmet* magazine.
They felt like real chefs in a real culinary kitchen. They were eager
to learn. Some were hoping today's dish would bring their families
together, others impress dates and lovers. They all chose a workbench
made from smooth oak wood, the color of butterscotch.

Zola stood at the front of the class. She was grateful that Darshan
asked her to host a cooking class at the *Gourmet*. She grabbed at the
opportunity. He checked on her once every other ten minutes to
make sure she had everything she needed. She looked up at the clock
mounted on the wall. It was almost time to start. Nerves were starting
to get the best of her, she had never done anything like this before.
But she planned on knocking it out of the park.

The meats were laid out in bowls over ice, like: crab legs, scallops,
shrimp, and chorizo sausage. The *Gourmet* had nothing but the best
ingredients. Instead of black truffles, they had white. Instead of white
salt, they had black. She loved the variety of options. It was like being
in a specialty shop.

Pierre came in support but decided to be one of the students. Being the center of attention wasn't his thing. Public speaking freaked him out. He thought it would be a great idea to pretend to be a student to fill up the class, just in case the turnout wasn't that great, but it was a success.

He saw Marquis come into the class with a beautiful woman on his arm. Pierre wondered if they were an item. Marquis wore a surprised expression when he saw Pierre.

Everyone took to their stations. Class was in session. Knives striking boards. Black garlic perfuming the room. Pierre felt Marquis search-lighting him from across the room. He was suddenly happy he lost five pounds last week and decided to wear his skinny jeans. He knew he looked sensational in them. Marquis left his station to speak to him.

"Hey, man."

"Why are you here, Marquis?"

"I was invited.'"

"So you could steal our recipes? Our customers weren't enough, I see."

"Bruh, it isn't like that. We've been doing cooking classes at the bistro off and on. We only do it a few times a year. But listen, I didn't come over here to talk about that. I came over to ask why you didn't answer my texts last night?"

"For a good reason."

Zola cleared her throat to cease the chattering. She was now frying onions, black garlic, and spiced sausage in a big pot with olive oil. A heavy wave of aromas spread throughout the spacious room.

"Whoever that girl you with should be the one keeping you warm at night." Marquis looked back at Godiva chopping away at the workstation as if she had made this dish plenty of times in her life. She felt their stares and looked their way.

"That's my colleague."

"Why does she keep staring over here?"

"She is?"

"Yes."

"Maybe she recognizes you from the Spice Café. But back to my question… Am I going to see you tonight?" Marquis leaned on the workbench, eyes sparkling like glistening caramelized hazelnuts, they made Pierre's heartbeat like an African drum. Zola was now adding corn and okra to the pot.

"Maybe."

"Come on, Pierre."

"Look, Marquis. I can't forget what you've done. And you should have told me you worked at the bistro. I mean, why the secrecy? And what was up with the whispering on the phone in my bathroom? How am I supposed to trust you?"

"Does Zola know?"

"No, she doesn't know you work at the bistro. But if she did, she'd probably kick you out this class."

"I'm telling you, bruh, I had nothing to do with all that crazy mess that's been going on at the cafe. I swear."

"You know what, Marquis, why don't you go back to your date."

"She's not my date."

"That's what you say."

"It's the truth."

"Finally, you're telling the truth now, eh?"

"Look, am I seeing you tonight or what?"

Zola was now adding the crab legs into the pot and warned the class not to overcook them or the meat would shrink, and that the scallops should be added last so they wouldn't dry up like apricots.

"Let me think about it."

Marquis pushed off Pierre's workbench in frustration and strutted back to his station where Godiva showed off her creation. He looked slightly defeated. But his cockiness was still intact. Pierre didn't know why he kept entertaining his antics. Zola told him time and time and time again to leave such knuckleheads alone. But he couldn't. If she only knew how good he was in bed.

Pierre liked Marquis for sure. But he felt like Marquis was hiding something. He wasn't open with his feelings. They barely spoke about food or what they did outside of work.

The class was packing up to leave. Zola was telling people to come by the Spice Café and try their Sunday's special: Poutine gumbo, which she uses peppery Cajun fries, thick cheese curds and smoked sausage. The students shook her hand one by one, as if she was some kind of priestess that saved their lives. Darshan stood by, thanking everyone for coming.

While Pierre waited outside of the building for Zola, he saw Marquis and the beautiful bombshell head towards his yellow Ferrari parked out front. He didn't know Marquis drove such an expensive car. Godiva stared back at Pierre and grinned. Lips as red as lobster tails, and legs as limber as a gazelle. Marquis didn't see him leaning against the building, too involved opening doors for his new bae, Pierre thought.

Before they pulled off she shot Pierre another glance.

# CHAPTER 15

"**H**appy birthday, old man!"

Marquis slapped Darshan on the back. They were posted at the bar. Anushka was standing with a group of girls draped in fine jewelry.

"What can I get the birthday boy?" asked Marquis, now ensconced between two beautiful ladies. Before Darshan could reply, Marquis snapped his fingers at the bartender and ordered him a beer. The bartender robotically popped open the beer and shoved a wedge of lime into its neck. She wore a face that read, "Night student. Rent due next week. Don't fuck with me." Darshan tipped her generously. She smiled and glared at Marquis, who only licked his lips at her big bountiful breasts.

Anushka saunters up to Darshan and planted a glossy kiss on his cheek. She wished him a happy birthday. Marquis felt jealous of the affection and thought it was time to order a round of tequila shots. Everyone chanted and tossed back the shots, which burned on the way down. A rush went straight to their heads, faces twisted in ugly lines. Marquis shouted something nonsensical over the thundering music while smacking down his empty glass like an unruly guest. Anushka let down her French twist and grabbed Darshan by the hand to dance.

"Have you been to Paris?" she asked Darshan, hanging on his neck while her hair brushed along her shoulders. Her voice was as dark and flirty as the eyeshadow she wore.

"A few times, mostly on business."

"I always wanted to see Paris. It looks so magical on TV, and when you write about it in your food articles, it makes me even more excited about going. What do you say we go together someday?"

Suddenly, there was awkwardness between them. Darshan excused himself to go to the restroom, leaving her to dance with three other girls from her clique.

When he got back, she was dancing on a guy. He didn't know how to feel about it. He looked at the bar and saw Marquis talking to Zola. Excitement flooded his face. He hoped she would come. He mentioned the party to her after the cooking session at the Gourmet. He contemplated inviting her, thinking she would be too busy with the cafe.

"Zola! You made it."

"I wouldn't have missed it for the world."

He leaned in for a hug. It felt good to haul her into his arms. She smelled like cinnamon and peaches mingled with avocado oils. He figured she must've come straight from the Spice Café.

"Sorry I'm late." She handed him a gift bag with blue dots. "This is also a little something for having me host at the *Gourmet*."

"Would you like anything to drink?"

"Too late, bud, I got her one." Marquis winked at her with two girls pinned to his hip, once again. The ladies were impressed he was the head chef at the most famous bistro in Toronto. This was Zola's first-time meeting Marquis up close. Pierre failed to mention he was bisexual. She should have known. All Pierre's sexual encounters always been bisexual and bi-curious men. He said they were fabulous in bed but made lousy boyfriends. She wondered how Pierre would feel to find out Marquis was here cuddled up with two girls. She thought to text him the scoop but knew it would only upset him. So, she slips her phone back into her handbag and looked at the excitement around the bar.

"Darshan, you dirty dog, you didn't tell me you were interested in this beautiful human."

Zola blushed.

"She's a vision to behold." He leaned an elbow on the counter and seductively molested the straw in his drink. His dark eyebrows twinkled against his cinnamon complexion with a thick layer of lust.

"I think I've seen you once before, I work at the Spice Café."

"The Spice Café!?" He didn't recognize her without the long apron, crazy hair bun and sweat trinkling down her face. She was dressed in an oatmeal-colored dress with bell sleeves. Her black hair cascaded down her back and over her eye, her skin looked as smooth as apple-butter. Marquis instantly shoved the two girls off him and checked his phone for Pierre's text. *Nothing.* The girls looked confused and went to the dance floor.

Zola started to feel strange around Marquis and directed her attention to Darshan. "You hadn't opened your gift." He sat down his beer and dug into the bag. It was a charcoal-grey scarf that accentuated his dark eyes.

"I love it."

Anushka wrapped her bangled arms around Darshan's neck and yelled, "There you are!" She planted a sloppy kiss on his rugged cheek. "I thought I lost you." Zola looked at the show playing out in front of her like a bad Bollywood movie. Darshan was trying to untangle himself from Anushka's embrace. She wouldn't let go. Her claws were hooked on him like a crab to a barrel. She seemed tipsy. She had a laughing tickle in her speech. She looked at Zola and rolled her eyes as if she was trash that needed to be taken out.

Marquis took this opportunity to slide closer to Zola. "So, how's the business going at the cafe, and how's Pierre?" Zola had the urge to toss her drink into his face. How dear he ask about Pierre's well-being. Pierre deserved better. Not this, and neither did she. She ignored his questions and left. Before Darshan could stop her, Anushka wiggled down on Darshan to the music and came back up. Once he managed to tear himself from her grip, he turned to Marquis with death in his eyes.

"What did you do? Where did she go?"

"Who?" he said, uninterested.

"Zola. That's who."

"Oh! Her. She mumbled something about opening the cafe in the morning." One of Anushka's friends was back playing with Marquis's silky long curls. He welcome the touch.

Darshan stormed outside, bumping a few people along the way. He peered through the dark night. She was gone.

~

Music spilled out onto the streets.

Instead of going home, Zola decided to meet up with Courtney at a nightclub. It was a few blocks down from the bar where Darshan was hosting his birthday party. She couldn't believe she thought she had a shot with him. She didn't understand why she was tripping anyway. He wasn't her type. She preferred chocolate any day.

Once inside, Zola was assaulted by colorful flashing lights. The music poured in her ears making her body tremble. Before she sat down, she heard "Chef! Chef!" She spotted Courtney's crazy ass at the bar, looking fierce in a shimmering pale gold dress. It looked sensational on her in the dim light, which made her appear like an expensive bottle of champagne. Her blond hair was cut shoulder length and spiraled, with hazelnut highlights. She was stepping in feathered stilettos.

Zola made a beeline for her. Courtney ordered her a much-needed martini and placed it in her hand. They strutted toward a cozy booth in the middle of the club.

The music became soul-snatching. The crowd broke out into an eruption of clapping and foot-pounding. A sea of hands went up in the air. Courtney raised both hands in the air, not wanting to feel left out. Zola laughed. A tidal wave of hands was now in the air. It looked as if everyone was possessed. Everyone was having a good time…and the drinks were flowing.

Zola caught a good-looking man staring their way. He was across the room, beer in hand. Courtney also noticed the admirer; she broke out her compact mirror before the guy approached their table. He was wearing dark denim jeans and a fitted black tee. His dark hair was tossed around as if he just ran his hand through it. His eyes were a forest green. His eyebrows were set heavy against his creamy coconut complexion. He asked Courtney if she would like to dance. Courtney told Zola, "Bye, girl."

Zola was left to fend for herself. She was enjoying the music until someone came up behind and interrupted her groove, causing her to spill half her drink on the table. He apologized for making her jump. She reached for a napkin and patted herself dry.

"Can I get you another drink?"

He was tall, dark, and handsome.

"Sure, I mean, I guess," she said, slightly lowering her head out of embarrassment, but she was slightly annoyed at being startled. He came back with two drinks.

"How did you know I was drinking an apple martini?"

"Lucky guess." He slid the green concoction closer to her and ran his thin fingers through his dreads.

"Thanks for the drink."

"No worries. The pleasure is all mine." He took a swig from his beer. "So, I heard you've been looking around for me?"

Zola choked again on her martini. "Excuse me? Don't take this personally, but I don't know who you are."

"Okay, okay. You can play coy if you want to. But I know the truth." He grinned. "My colleague was trying to set us up for the longest."

"Your colleague?"

"Yes, Courtney."

She was going to kill Courtney. Zola shot a glare from across the room. Courtney giggled and gave a light wave. Zola smacked her lips in retort. How dare Courtney butt into her personal life? Now she wished she hadn't come at all. The fast music changed to something slow, dulling down as if submerging into a thick, rich sauce.

"You want to dance?"

"I don't dance."

"Come on, I'll teach you some moves."

The dance floor was packed. Zola looked like a fish out of water. People were grinding and swirling their hips. Zola thought about sitting this one out, but Hakeem took her hand and wrapped them around his long neck. The lights were brought down more, turning Hakeem's dark chocolate skin a midnight blue.

Zola felt silly and laughed. But he stayed intense and steady. The people around them faded into irrelevance. Some people watched and tried to mimic their moves but couldn't master the passion. He pulled Zola closer to his hard, lean body. She smelled the masculinity of his cologne mixed with the soap that he uses. She was suddenly drawn to him like a plant in a dark room drawn to a slither of light.

Fast music was slowly emerging, pushing its way back up to surface, urging dancers to pick up their pace. The lights flashed like crazy. Everything was sensory overload once again. People were jumping up and down as if they didn't want the night to end. Courtney was nowhere to be found with the heartthrob she met minutes ago.

Hakeem and Zola stepped apart, leaving confused space between them.

# CHAPTER 16

**P**ierre smelt like heat, flour, and dirty cups of coffee.

The café was closed. He wanted to sink his tired bones into a chair. But the buzz in his pocket brought him back to life. It was Marquis. He knew who it was without looking at his phone. Marquis was the only one who text this late at night. Pierre thought it was him apologizing for the umpteenth time. Pierre was exhausted after a long day's work, was he really in the mood to fool around? His feet were pounding. He couldn't wait to go home and soak in a hot bath. He was going to ignore the text, let Marquis suffer some more. Then he thought it could be Zola wanting to tell him all about her romantic night with Darshan at his birthday party. She probably needed a 101 crash course on being a slut. Pierre had coached her a few times how to use whipped cream and strawberries to seduce a man. He said it worked like a charm. Their next lesson would be using a grapefruit.

Pierre whipped out his phone from his pocket, and his eyes almost popped out their sockets. Nude pictures of him and Marquis. Shame and horror played Double Dutch on Pierre's face. Marquis sexing him up at night behind the cafe. Their faces wild and animal-like.

A look that only comes with a situation that is completely different from normal everyday life. This couldn't be happening. Pierre felt the cafe walls closing in on him, squeezing him to the last drop.

Why did he ever listen to Marquis? *This will be quick. No one will see. You know you want this. Stop acting like you don't. C'mere and taste this creamy seduction. Don't be scared. It doesn't bite. Come touch it.* And Pierre did all those things. He couldn't resist. Marquis's manhood rose to the occasion like a well-mixed soufflé. That's why Pierre liked him so much; Marquis didn't waste time.

They touched each other madly. Marquis wanted to take Pierre's raw ingredients and make something exotic. No hair on Pierre's body delayed Marquis's attacks. Pierre was caught up in a web of dark lashes. The diamonds in Marquis's ears sparkled in the dark night, beckoning Pierre for a hungry taste. Their bodies melting into one, releasing aromas of spices from a long day's work in the kitchen: Ginger. Turmeric. Mustard seeds. Truffles. Saffron. Fennel. Cinnamon. Peppercorns. All mingling together until they became their own scent. What a crazy night. A night that lingered in Pierre's mind for days.

There were rapid knocks on the window. Pierre's shoulders shot up like hot toast in the toaster. It was Marquis, looking to have another rumble in the dark. Pierre unlocked the door, and Marquis slid in like a smooth criminal. His skin smelled like French butter, expensive cheeses, sweet rum, and black smoke. Marquis looked around the cafe as if to make sure the coast was clear. His hazel eyes suggested they try something new. Perhaps pouring warm liquid chocolate on one another and licking it off. Marquis pulls Pierre into his arms, disregarding Pierre's wilted appearance. Before Marquis lifted his shirt past his stomach, Pierre shoves the phone into his chest.

"*Bruh*, what's this?"

"Naked pictures of us."

"How did those get on your phone?"

"I don't know, you tell me."

"Hey, if you wanted to take pictures of my baguette, all you had to do was ask." Marquis blushed twenty shades of cinnamon. "I'm down for video too, you know…and since we're on the subject, can I record you too?" Marquis's smile whipped up in a frenzy, like a speeding train waiting to smash into Pierre.

"No, Marquis. Somebody sent me these."

"Maybe it was that nosy partner of yours."

"Zola?"

"She seems like the type that likes a *ménage à trois*." He darted around the cafe. "Where is she anyway? Tell her to come out, no need for her to be shy. I should've known you two were some freaks."

"Look, Marquis. I'm not playing with you. Do you have any idea who took these pictures?"

"Nah, bruh."

Pierre felt like he wasn't getting anywhere with Marquis. Getting answers out of him was like fishing on a moonless night. Zola wouldn't spy on them. How ridiculous for Marquis to think so. He wondered if Marquis had one of his boys take the pictures. He was obviously a freak by nature.

It was so quiet, the alley cats could be heard yowling and fighting. Pierre realized he still had inventory to put up. Crates of tomatoes sat in the corner, waiting to be refrigerated.

Marquis's cinnamon complexion turned the shade of creamy milk chocolate in the moonlight. His eyes were pleading for Pierre to loosen up. Take a chill pill. He wasn't worried at all about the nude photos. It only excited him. The pictures were blurry anyway. Who would know? Pierre saw his points. His face was blocked by Marquis's toned arms. But it was still an invasion of privacy. It was too risky to do it again.

"Nothing is going down tonight, Marquis, until I get to the bottom of who sent these pictures. You must understand, this could damage our business at the cafe, and you not being upset concerns me." Pierre folded his arms. "If these pictures leak out to the public, the cafe is done, and you don't have nothing to worry about because it didn't happen at your precious bistro."

"Listen, man, I'm going to leave. Obviously, you freaked out over those pictures."

"I am, and you should be too."

"Trust me. I am."

"You have an interesting way of showing it."

"I've been told."

Before Marquis left, he turned around and said, "Can I ask you one thing?"

Pierre nodded.

"Do you mind sending me those pictures?"

"Get out, Marquis!"

# CHAPTER 17

"**L**unch today, Cinderella?"

The sun was screaming in Zola's face the following morning. She was yanked out of sleep by the sound of her phone. She opened her heavy eyes and reached for it; it was like reaching into deep space. She felt dried, roasted, and chewed up. Her head was spinning from all the apple martinis last night.

She licked the inside of her mouth and felt like death. Hair like cotton candy. Voice thick like waves crashing against rocks. High-quality mascara smeared under her eyes like war paint. She couldn't remember much of last night. Her thoughts were rearranging fast and furious. *Who could this be?* She cursed herself for having too many drinks. She looked at her black heels lying sideways and upright in the middle of the room, staring back at her as if it had a story to tell. Pillows were knocked to the floor. She tried to ignore the pounding sensation behind her eyes so she could think clearly.

Once she realized who it was, she wondered how Hakeem got her number. Was she that wasted she forgot she'd given it to him? She clenched the white duvet, trying to recall everything. Darshan huddled up in the bar with some chick. And Courtney hooking her up with some hot guy from her workplace. *That's right.*

She looked back down at the text message, debating whether to reply. She thought about how arrogant he was that night and how disgustingly attractive he was too. She hated his guts, yet she wanted to know more about him. Who was he? Where did he lived and where was he from? What did he do for a living? A plethora of questions raced through her mind, skyrocketing her head spinning once again. She thought about her past failed relationships. The guys she dated were users and abusers. Men were dogs. All of them. She had sworn them off. Maybe becoming a lesbian wasn't a bad idea. Hell! Maybe becoming pansexual wasn't a bad idea either. Who was she kidding? She loved men too much. She looked back down at the text and replied, *What time?*

～

The sun was the color of thick lemonade, and the clouds were the color of fresh cream. Hakeem and Zola took a ferry over to the Toronto Island. They sat in an open field. Zola eyed the picnic basket he was carrying, feeling hungry. He unearthed fresh fruit, fried plantains, oxtail smothered in onions and peppers, and jerk chicken smoked on a fire pit. Zola's stomach rumbled. He opened the carton of fruit first and fed her a fat strawberry. She bit into it and red juice ran down her chin dripping on the grass. He helps her clean up with a napkin.

"The word has it you own a cafe?"

"Yes. That's right." She hoped that was all he heard. She wasn't in the mood to explain all the shenanigans that'd been going on at the cafe.

"So… is it true you been smuggling illegal immigrants at your workplace and poisoned several people?"

Zola gasped. "Who told you that?"

"Word travels."

"I'd rather not talk about it. But to let you know, the food poison thing never happened and the exploitation situation is a big fat lie."

"If you like, I could call up some people if you're having trouble. Did you see my shirt?" He stretched it out so she could see the print #BLMTO. "We can form a protest against anyone harassing you. We gotta stick up for our Black businesses." This made Zola smile, but she didn't want anyone to get hurt or go to jail. She would never forgive herself. Besides, it hadn't gotten to that point. She didn't even know who placed the false report. She and Pierre were only going on a wild hunch that it was the bistro.

She watched Hakeem snake his fingers through his dreads; each seemed to contain a fiber of rich intellect, cultural connection, and historical pride.

"That's okay. I can take care of it. But thanks."

"If you say so. You have my number. I know how tough it is to run a business. It isn't easy. I invested into two restaurants. One here and the other in Montreal."

"Why Montreal?"

"Because that's where I'm from, but I'm originally from Haiti."

She thought it was interesting he was from Haiti, because she was accused of exploiting Haitians at her restaurant. She wondered if Hakeem knew about this small detail in the accusation. If he did, he didn't allude to it.

They strode to the beach. They were the only ones there. A light breeze brushed against Zola's face, making her feel beautiful and vibrant. The sunlight shimmered on the water making golden specks. Being on the beach was what she needed to reset her mind.

"I can't believe I've never been here before. It's so peaceful."

"Yeah, I come here sometimes to visualize my dreams."

"Oh yeah, what are they?"

"Do you really what to know?"

Zola looked away, fearing he might say something she might

regret hearing. When she turned back, he was taking off his shirt and pants. Her hand flew to her eyes.

"What are you doing?"

He bolts towards the open water without replying, kicking up sand along the way. The waves picked up and crashed harder into the big rocks, as if they were up for a good challenge. He gestured for her to join him, and she put up a hand to say no thanks.

She strode closer to the water and sat. She folds her arms around her knees. The cold waves licked her feet, making her shiver. She wasn't at all a good swimmer. She remembered having her mother pull her out of swim class by saying her daughter was allergic to chlorine. She was happy to be placed in home economics, where she discovered her love for cooking.

Mr. Hot Damn emerged from the water. Zola's cheeks turned red. Endless droplets rolled down his tall frame, accentuating every perfect muscle. Tattoos snaked up and down his arms. For a moment, Zola forgot how to breathe. She pulled in a heavy breath that tasted like lust and frustration. She was all eyes and no blinking. It felt like her heart would fly out of her chest. He was so freaking hot. She tries to simmer down by turning the other way.

He placed back on his pants and flopped down exhausted, smothering his feet in the warm sand. A dog drops a stick in front of them. The dog came out of nowhere. Zola threw the stick into the water. The dog madly took off after it, crashing into the waves like a crazy beach goer. The owner appeared and whistled the dog in his direction.

Hakeem wrapped his arms around his date. The sunset highlighted his face. He was handsome. Not model handsome, but regular guy handsome. Zola buried her head into his strong chest. He smelt like musk and roasted chestnuts. She leaned into him willingly. The attraction was so strong it was overwhelming. This was dangerous territory. She had sworn off men. However, she couldn't resist keeping Hakeem at the edge of her world. He found a way to pierce right through it. His embrace felt so good, and so needed. Zola could feel his rapid heartbeat. The rhythm soothed her into a further embrace. She tries not to let the sound of the waves drown her judgement. She won't allow this situation to go any further.

He wanted to spoil her, take the sadness out of her eyes. Tell her how much he was enjoying himself. Tell her things that he hadn't shared before.

They watched the sunset and a fleet of boats drift. The sky bled pink, purple and blue until it all melted together into a simmering darkness.

Mathis Bailey

# CHAPTER 18

A **dark figure dressed** in black stood outside the cafe.

The moon was perfectly round and white, like a dinner plate. Shops were long closed. The intruder's shadow stretched on the pavement. A faint light from the streetlight barely penetrated the cafe's darkness.

The intruder snuck through the back door, which was propped open. The intruder had smoothly placed a small rock in the door when an employee threw out the trash at the end of the night.

Now the intruder switched on a penlight. Moving skillfully, like a snake. Dark slicing through darkness. Rummaging around. Tossing back chocolate truffles. Melting instantly on the tongue. Eyes shot up with pleasure. Boxes of wine sat in the corner, stacked high. The light landed on labels of spices: cacao powder from Tahiti, cinnamon sticks from Sri Lanka, nutmeg from Indonesia. Now the intruder was in the mood for hot chocolate. The intruder suddenly thought *why not?* The stove was switched on. Cream poured, simmered, rose syrup, cinnamon, saffron, and cocoa powder added. Grated nutmeg on top of the froth. The scent was orgasmic and therapeutic. Tiny sips taken. Layer upon layers of flavors, texture like cashmere coating the tongue. So delicious.

Noise could be hard in the alley. Heavy footsteps falling on black pavement. Someone rustling around. Sounded like more than one person. The intruder freezes. Eyes darting this way and that way. Paranoid as fuck. The movements stopped.

The walk-in refrigerator door was now pulled open. A burst of cold air rushed out. The intruder shivered. Mini crystals of ice on the walls. Tomatoes, cilantro, parsley, blocks of butter, eggs, and meats.

More noise was heard. This time laughter. A giggle, perhaps. Drops of items falling to concrete pavement, making a clattering sound. The dark figure froze. Then the noise stopped, and the dark figure moves again like a shadow in the night. Flour and sugar were tossed in the air. Cake smashed on the floor. This was fun. Lots of fun. Too much fun. Imprisonment entered the intruder's mind and then vanished. The thrill was arousing. The cafe was scoped out weeks ago. No security cameras were found.

Cabinets were opened and searched. Spices were moved around. The dark figure wanted to break some cups and plates. But that would make too much noise.

The office door was locked. *Shit!* Who knew they would be so smart as to lock it? The intruder stomps a foot in protest. This must be another way into the office. The intruder started to look around. There must be a spare key somewhere. Every shop had a spare key hidden.

Drawers were checked: pencils. Chocolates. Paper clips. Batteries. Mini staplers. Old receipts. The intruder saw a cigarette lighter and got nefarious ideas. Should the cafe burn to the ground? Should it be on the morning news? The intruder imagined the billowing flames screaming up the hickory-colored walls. The bar and portraits suffering a silent death. Turning the Spice Café into Hell's Kitchen. *Oh, yes!* A slippery grin swept across the intruder's face. But this could cause the whole block to catch fire. That wasn't good because there was a corner coffee shop that made the best vegan wraps. That would be sacrilege, the intruder thought.

No key was found. No secret recipes scattered anywhere. The intruder cursed and slipped out through the back door, evaporating into the night like boiling water on a hot stove. Nothing taken…only leaving a trail of chocolate truffles.

∽

Pierre stormed into the bistro, bumping into servers and guests. Godiva tried to stop him as she stiletto-sprinted across the room. But she was no match for his speed.

He spun around in the kitchen. A cacophony of sizzles, slammed oven doors, chopping of knives and boiling water flooded his senses. Cooks wearing impeccable clean aprons were carefully tweezing vegetables onto porcelain plates. They looked as if they were classically trained in France for many years.

Pierre's eyes darted around for Marquis. He didn't see the scumbag. He was about to leave until he overheard someone say Marquis was on the roof having a smoke. When Pierre found him, he was taking a long drag from a cigarette.

"You bastard!"

Marquis was caught off-guard. His eyes were wide open when Pierre approached him with heavy steps. He immediately clicked off his phone and stomp out his cigarette.

"Bruh, what the hell?"

"Someone broke into my cafe and trashed the place."

"Should you be talking to police instead of me?"

"Confess, Marquis, you had something to do with it."

"Keep your voice down and no. I didn't. Why you keep accusing me of this shit?"

He reached deep into his pocket and lit another cig. The end burned bright red. He sucked in a long drag and pushed smoke from one side of his mouth.

"What's the deal Pierre? …Is this all about me loving on the ladies?"

"Don't change the subject, Marquis. You texted me in the middle of the night wanting to come over. I blew you off. You got upset and trashed my place of business. Admit it. How can you be so childish and destructive? I'll bet you had your hooligan friends to help you. Was it Darshan? What did he do, hold the door open for you? Kept the coast clear? Y'all some twisted fucks."

Before Pierre could walk away, Marquis put out his cigarette and pressed Pierre against the door. Heat was radiating between them. The sweltering sun increasing the intensity. Marquis's breath smelled like tobacco and mints… Pierre's spiced lattes.

"What are you doing?"

"I know why you came over here."

He pressed harder against Pierre; their blood vessels could be felt, pulsating like thunderbolts. Marquis looked like a lion that needed to be fed and put to sleep.

Pierre's judgment was clouded. He felt too animal to talk. He felt the roughness of Marquis's callous hands; a lifetime of working in a hot kitchen. Pierre wanted to eat Marquis alive, devour him whole. Taste his spices. Taste his heritage. Taste his past and present. But he must stand firm.

"Marquis, this isn't no game."

"Alright man." Marquis backed up slowly, readjusting himself as if he was putting away a loaded gun. "Your loss." He smirked with sarcasm curled up in his voice.

He went back into the restaurant, pots and pans clinking like a mad symphony. Pierre was happy he wasn't pressure further into another salacious scandal. He had no idea that Marquis was such an exhibitionist. It was scary yet thrilling.

Marquis still refused to confess anything. Pierre pulled his phone from his pocket and stopped the recording. The only thing he captured was that Marquis was a hormonal freak, and that wasn't a crime. He concluded he needed to stay away from Marquis. But how could he when Marquis was only a few feet away from the Spice Cafe, and packing all that meat? He was tempting. But dangerous.

When Pierre arrived home that evening, he took a long shower. He was exhausted from cleaning up the mess at the cafe. He took pictures of the damages. Zola filed a police report. Pierre knew they weren't going to do nothing to catch the perps. He also knew this has the bistro stink all over it. Zola talked about installing surveillance cameras. It would mean spending more money that they didn't have.

After smothering a yawn with his hand, Pierre's five-year-old laptop swirled to life which felt like a century. Buttercup licked her fur beside him on the sofa. He searched for the Indo-French Bistro. All five-star reviews. Not one wavering star, until now. He clicks one-star. Was he going to use his real name, you ask? Oh, yes sir! They'd messed around with the wrong one.

*Pierre Du Pont Jackson 1 star*

*Zero stars if I could give this bistro. This place is overrated and overhyped. The food was awful. I ordered the butter chicken risotto. It tasted like glue and rocks. It was unseasoned and overcooked. The rice almost chipped my tooth, and the chicken was the size of peanuts. And the white truffle shavings tasted like sawdust.*

*The spiced tuna tartare was despicably salty. When it touched my tongue, the meat vacuumed the moisture from my mouth, leaving me looking like a shriveled up black truffle.*

*The dessert wasn't no saving grace. The saffron crème brûlée*

*looked like it had the bubonic plague. Top was burnt to a crisp
and filling was crazy thick. I ordered an espresso to dislodge the
lump from my poor throat and even that tasted like dirt.*

*This place is nothing to write home about. The only thing I can
think of to explain this travesty is that they must've hired new
cooks. If so, their knives need to be sent packing. Better yet, the
place needs to be shut down. I am never going back.*

Pierre posted it without hesitation. He reread it a few times, and
he liked what he wrote while tossing back a mouthful of wine. Just
three minutes later, a message popped up.

*Indo-French Bistro*

*We are sincerely sorry to hear about your experience at Indo-
French Bistro. We take our patrons' complaints very seriously and
get to the root of them. Please visit us again, we will comp your
next meal. Thanks for your review, Pierre Du Pont. Hope to see
you soon.*

"There she is!!! The infamous chef!" shouted a young bartender as
Anushka sauntered into the bistro. She was wondering what he was
yelling about. He was cleaning a glass cup while wearing a silly grin.

"What are you talking about, you fool?"

"You didn't read the review?"

"What review?"

He jumped over the marble counter and jogged across the room
toward Anushka. He moved with as much vigor as if he had never
endured injury in his life. He located a tablet and brought up the
review. Anushka read it with studied focus. Her eyes grew big as
rocks. She looked up at the bartender, who was still grinning from
ear to ear.

"How did you find out about this?"

"Godiva put me in charge of the customer complaints. She's thinking about making me an assistant manager on your days off."

"You?" Anushka stifled a giggle.

"Yes, me… Godiva said I'm smart, organized, fast, and well put-together." He stood up straighter, like a lieutenant in roll call.

"Has anyone seen this review yet?"

"Not to my knowledge."

"Maybe because it's still early morning."

"Perhaps."

"Why did you call me infamous?"

"Because you were the one in charge of the risotto and bread baking this week, right? You also were managing the dinning room that evening while Godiva ran arrands for Mrs. Singh."

Anushka groaned.

"So, it's your head that's on the chopping block."

"Over one online complaint?"

"The last time a person filed a complaint on a staff member, Mrs. Singh canned their ass."

"But how does she know the customer isn't making this stuff up?"

"Believe me, she knows. She has her way in finding things out. I don't know how she does it."

"I'm not worried… I'm not going to let one little review shake me up."

"Who said anything about one?"

Just before Anushka walked away, he showed her pages of bloggers reposting the review, others adding their spin on it.

"This can't go viral. Is there anything you can do to help?"

"I can think of something, but it might cost me my promotion, let alone my job."

"I need this job as much as you."

"If I help you out, would you go out on a date with me?"

"No."

"How come?"

"You're too young."

"I'm twenty-three."

"Exactly my point."

"What I gotta do to get you in my arms?" He stepped forward as if to take the prize. She pushed him back.

"Just get the review taken down. Please."

"Okay. Okay. I have a friend that might help. He's good at hacking websites."

"When can he do it?"

"Today. He works from home."

"I need it done now. We can't waste another second."

He put his hands on his slim waist and said, "I'm on it."

Anushka sauntered away wearing stilettos, gold leggings tapered at the ankles, and a cream chiffon kameez. She ruffled at her bangs after taking off a chunky white hat. Her gold bracelet glistened in the morning light. She was working front house today and she was looking sensational. She wasn't going to let one lousy review ruin her day.

She thought about Pierre. She didn't know his middle name was DuPont. But she knew it was him. She remembers Marquis mentioning his name a few times at the bistro. She also recalls the police coming to the bistro asking questions about recent break-ins around the area. Marquis claims he hadn't seen anything. However, he seemed nervous.

After the police left, he was shouting at everyone at the bistro. He was on edge. Some would say he was always like that. What do you expect from a French chef? Anushka knew he was bothered and wanted to know why. She could read body language well. Whatever was bothering Marquis, she wasn't privy to. Whatever it was, he wasn't saying.

# CHAPTER 19

**D**arshan started writing the article for the Spice Café.

He was in his small office at the *Gourmet*. White walls were devoid of pictures. No framed master's degrees proclaimed his brilliance. They were nothing but distractions.

He revised line after line, crossing out words left, right, and center. The article had to be perfect. He felt bad about what happened at his birthday party at the bar. He didn't mean to neglect Zola. He wanted to give her his undivided attention, but Anushka got in the way.

He shooed away anyone who came into his office. Interference wasn't on his agenda. He couldn't wait to see Zola's face when she read this article. Once he finished, he sat back smoothly in his leather chair. He saw his boss walk past his office and yelled out, "Mr. Smith!"

Darshan hit "print," and papers shot out the printer. His boss turned on his heels and tapped his foot on the hard floor. He was an older man with a ring of gray hair. He had an apple-shaped torso that was disproportionate to the rest of his short body.

"Read this!"

"This better be good, Mr. Singh." He perused the article with glasses perched on his nose like a college professor. He made a disgruntled sound. Darshan didn't know if it was good or bad.

"So, Mr. Smith. What do you think? Is it good for our fall issue? I can't think of a more perfect season for comfort eats, other than winter, but who wants to go out in the cold?" He chuckled.

Mr. Smith gave him a look to show he wasn't amused. He shoved the article into Darshan's chest. "Our columns are already full for fall. Try sending it to a publication in Scarborough." His boss was so close that Darshan smelled instant coffee and cheap corner store pastries on his breath. Begging wasn't Darshan's strong suit, but he pleaded until his boss relented.

"Fine, just quit your whining. I'll see what I can do. I'm not making any promises. Email me the article. I'll pass it along to the copy editors. But don't make me regret it." Darshan thanked him profusely. His boss gifted him a nasty glare before walking away.

# CHAPTER 20

"**C**an you trust him?"

Pierre and Zola were making cakes at the Spice Café. They separated eggs into a large bowl. Empty egg cartons were littered all over the counter, and spilled flour blessed the floor once again, while sticky butter clung to their black aprons.

"He seems like a nice guy, Pierre."

"I don't know. There's something about Darshan I just can't put my finger on."

"Pierre, you are paranoid, and you have every right to be after all the mess that's been happening around here, but I appreciate your concern. I don't think Darshan will write a bad review to put us further down in the hole."

"How can you be so sure?"

"I'm not. But what choice do we have?"

Pierre shrugged and thought about Marquis and his affiliation with Darshan. They weren't up to no good. He thought they were out to get their recipes and shout them down. Now Pierre knew why restaurants didn't last long on this block. The bistro was a vulture stealing every good recipe it could find.

"Just watch your back, Zo. I know you like him...it is written all over your face."

"How we easily we forget about Marquis."

Pierre smacked his lips. He slept with Marquis, but he regretted every minute of it. If only she knew half the things he knew.

"What's up between you two anyway? I haven't seen him around the Spice Café or at the  apartment."

"We're taking a break. But listen, Zo, just keep a look out for any shadiness, that's all I'm saying. You're deserving of love. Real love. Nothing fake and phony like what I've been experiencing lately."

Zola pensively took a sip of her coffee, considering every word. Maybe she should stay single and focus on the cafe. Drama was the last thing she needed. But who was to say Darshan was any of that? Pierre was just letting off steam from whatever happened between him and Marquis; it had nothing to do with her. She was more than capable of deciding if she should see Darshan tonight. He had texted her out for dinner. She said yes. She was over what happened at his birthday party. She didn't understand why she was taking it so personally anyway. It wasn't like they were together. Darshan said he had something important tell her. She wondered what the surprise could be.

While Pierre placed the cakes in the oven, Zola's phone buzzed in her pocket. She went into the corner to check. Pierre looked at her from the corner of his eye. She didn't want him to see the smile painted across her face. Butterflies soared in the pit of her stomach. It was him. The words were like music to her eyes.

*Hope to see you tonight.*

⁓

Darshan was excited for his date with Zola. He couldn't mess this night up like the last. Not this time. Not ever. Not on his watch.

He scrubbed and cleaned surfaces in his penthouse. He made sure everything was perfect. He even ordered in a fresh bouquet of black roses for the side-tables. Why black? Because he liked to be different.

He had special news to share, that she would be on the cover of the new fall issue of *Gourmet* magazine. It wasn't due out for another month. He couldn't wait to see her face.

His phone buzzed on the kitchen counter. He hoped it wasn't Zola cancelling. He checked the text message, and it was Anushka. She wanted to see him to apologize face-to-face for getting wasted on his birthday. He texted back *no worries, all is forgiven*.

He sauntered into the bathroom, took off his shirt, and jumped into the walk-in shower. The water pounded onto his body like tropical rain.

After he dried off, he strode into the living room with a towel wrapped around his waist, chest hair slick against muscle. From the corner of his eye, he saw Anushka sitting on the sofa. She popped a mini chocolate-coated-strawberry into her mouth, which was sat out for Zola. The sweetness of the fruit sparked heat into her green eyes.

"Hey! How did you get in here?"

"Your mother gave me the key."

"My mother?"

She giggled. "Yes. Don't look so surprised."

"Why would my own mother give you the key to my apartment?"

"She wanted me to drop off *the book*."

Darshan followed her eyes toward the coffee table hosting a bouquet of black roses where *the book* rested.

"Thanks for dropping that off, but you must leave now."

"Is this how you talk to the woman who gave you the best night of your life?"

"Look, Anushka, we both were messed-up that night. We did things that we shouldn't have done."

"I don't believe you. It seemed like you rather enjoyed your birthday gift."

"Look, I'm expecting company. I will have to ask you to leave."

"Oh, you mean that Black chick you're dating. I guess us brown girls aren't good enough for ya?"

She strolled over to Darshan. His black chest hair still wet and glistened in the moonlight that drew Anushka toward him like a moth to light. She was so turned on that she could scream. Her lips were painted red, and her silk kimono felt sexy against her smooth skin. The fabric was so thin, it looked like one blow could send it flying across the room. A dragon printed on it set off her wild eyes. If her hair was up in a bun, she would have looked like a French supermodel.

She caught her reflection in a mirror and liked what she saw. The darkness of Darshan's apartment made her appear slimmer than she actually was. She stabbed a chocolate finger on his chest, leaving faint smudges. She smelled like expensive European perfume, like musky rose.

"You're not being nice."

"What do you want?"

"What I want?"

"You must be here for a reason."

"Don't act like you don't want me to be here."

She nibbled on his neck. He tasted like sweet spices. She loved being close to him. He pulled her away and told her to leave again. She stumbled back; ego still intact. She grabbed her purse off the sofa and kissed him on the lips for good measure. He didn't resist. She giggled again before exiting his penthouse, leaving behind a delicious scent.

He was relieved that she was gone. He looked down at his watch. Zola would be there any minute. A black button-up shirt hung on the bedroom doorknob. He put it on and looked himself over in the mirror. He was ready for tonight. He hoped Anushka wouldn't be back.

⁓

Zola took a private elevator up to Darshan's penthouse. She was totally impressed. How many guys had she dated that had their own private elevator? None. She started to wonder how much money Darshan made at the *Gourmet*. She knew it was a well-known magazine, but *damn!*

She knocked three times, and he answered immediately. He looked stressed. It took a minute for him to recognize her. He looked down both hallways before letting her in. She thought his behavior was strange.

"Are you okay?"

"Yeah, I just had some unexpected company."

"Should I come back later? There's a coffee shop down th…"

"No…no. You're good." He forced a smile, which placed Zola at ease. He ushered her in like a true gentleman. Her heels clicked on gunmetal-gray wood floors, anticipation rising with each step. She wondered where the night was going to lead them.

She took a seat at the dining room table. He went into the kitchen to add the finishing touches to the meal.

She looked around his penthouse. Soft music was floating from hidden speakers. It was her first time being in the home of a writer. The decor reminded her of a five-star hotel in upstate New York City. Uncomfortable-looking black sofas sat against clean white walls. Open-face black cabinets hosted white plates and cups. State-of-the-art gold lamps torpedoed downward over a marble counter. Potted plants with big green leaves peppered the corners. Funky art books hung out on tables. One portrait had Darshan shirtless, chest splashed with black paint. His eyes were closed, his lashes looking like Persian silk. A tatted hand clung from his bottom lip. The piece was getting Zola hot and bothered.

Darshan thought tonight was going smoothly, despite Anushka showing up. He couldn't believe she used his mother as an excuse to barge in his place. Why would his mother trust her with *the book* anyway? A book he had privilege of flipping through a couple times. He didn't believe Anushka one bit and was convinced one of the concierges was tricked into believing she left something behind. He regrets messing around with her. They both had a few too many. He made a note to return *the book* to his mother tomorrow morning in one piece.

He took his mind off Anushka and placed it on Zola. She was important tonight. He liked what she had on, a cream dress, standing in the tallest knee-high black leather boots. Her black hair was draped down her back, a look that celebrities would pay thousands to achieve and maintain.

Darshan wasn't hip on fashion, but he assumed Zola had on Chanel or Kate Spade, and he only knew these designers because of his sisters. He complimented how beautiful she looked. Her cheeks caught fire. Unaware to him, she had on her favorite black bra that gave her an extra boost of confidence.

"Would you like some help in there? Perhaps a woman's touch," she joked, peering over her shoulder, stealing a glance into the open kitchen where he was doing all the chopping, blending, and sauteing.

"You just sit tight."

Good enough for Zola. She settled back into her chair, enjoying the wonderful smells of dinner being prepared for her. Zola took a smooth sip of her wine. The bottle seemed to be from somewhere in France. It was delicious. Her attention flew to a collection of family photos on the side table. One was Darshan as a young boy. Straight black hair lapped over his dark eyes, standing between two beautiful young girls with braids running down their backs. A tall dark man stood behind them. Zola asked Darshan about the guy. He simply said his father; he didn't seem keen on talking about him, so she left it alone.

Darshan placed a plate in front of her. He sat down and reached over for the bottle of wine to refill their glasses. He looked handsome. His dark eyes against the candlelight reminded Zola of fire burning too hot.

"*Bon Appetit!*"

Zola looked down, and her appetite suddenly morphed into disapproval. "What is this?" she asked. She thought the dish looked like a pile of rice with gravy, something she would serve as a side dish at the cafe.

"It's a French take on butter chicken. Instead of chicken, I used rabbit. Instead of ghee, I used French butter. Instead of heavy cream, I used crème fraiche. It's a family recipe. I hope I got it right. My first time making it. Try it. Let me know what you think, chef."

"Are you sure you're not leaving anything off this plate?" she asked inquisitively, peering over the kitchen counter for any sign of morsels of food that resembled a drumstick.

Darshan laughed and was delighted to expose her to something new. "It's Indian food with a twist. Just try it, you might like it."

Zola tried to recall having Indian food. Nothing came to mind. She hesitantly toyed with the rice before forking it into her mouth. She chewed it thoughtfully. The rice was kissed with butter, saffron, cumin seeds, and roasted cashews. She forked more. The reaction on her face shot up higher and higher. The shallots gave the sauce a delicate touch. Darshan's eyes became intense underneath the candlelight while he waited for a verdict.

"Wow! This is good, Darshan. So rich and creamy."

"I'm glad you like it." He smiled "You had me worried there for a moment."

"What spice am I tasting?" Zola chewed slowly, as if she was trying to put together a jigsaw puzzle of flavors. "I would love to learn how to use it in my food. I'm always looking for ways to fuse other cultures in Southern cuisine. That's what the culinary world needs, you know. Fusion."

⁓

Anushka walked into her townhome on Bayview Avenue. The neighborhood was littered with fancy cafes, specialty stores, and innovative coffee houses where a bunch of baristas wore black shirts with tattoos snaking up their arms. Her parents thought she should be living somewhere like Upper North Forest Hill, where the houses were bigger. They didn't understand why she decided to live with common people, even though her townhouse costed more than million dollars.

She thought about Darshan as she sat on her pink sofa. A black cat jumped onto her lap. The cat's eyes glistened in the dim light as Anushka thought *How dare he toss me out of his penthouse?* The cat purrs as if responding to her question.

She thought about sending Mrs. Singh a text, telling her how rude her son was tonight. Then she stopped herself before texting. What the hell was she doing? They weren't girlfriends or sorority sisters who gossiped about the hottest men in Bollywood. She retrieved her laptop from the bedroom. Max followed in moral support. She waited for the computer to come to life and clicked on her fake email account. She started writing.

Dear. Mrs. Singh

I hope all is well. What I'm about to say isn't for the faint of heart, so brace yourself.

I have suspicion that your son, Darshan Singh, is involved in questionable activities with basic cook Zola Washington, the owner of the Spice Café. There's maybe talk about a possible business venture between the two, and you don't want the food bloggers to get a hold of this information. Can you imagine the headlines? Indo-French bistro turns into a chicken shack. Oh, gosh!

Mrs. Singh, do not let your son destroy three generations of hard work. Reclaim your family's legacy. Please be aware I'm as concerned about your son's future as you are. I'd hate to see him pass up an opportunity to run the family's empire over some flighty hole-in-the-wall-diner.

I warn you to dissuade Darshan in this crazy undertaking and convince him to reconsider these plans he's kiting around so proudly, before he ruins the family's legacy for good. Please, with all your power, try to stop him from making the biggest mistake of his life.

My apologies if this letter rattles your spirit. But news travels fast in the culinary circles. I wanted to tell you before it reaches your delicate ears. I'm doing nothing but looking out for the Singh family. I know you helped build the family's dynasty. This is much admired.

I wish I were sending you good news, like an innovative delicious recipe for your fabulous restaurant or some exotic vegetable that the grand chefs are keeping under wraps. But that isn't the case here. I couldn't stand by and watch this deception without saying anything. I hope you understand.

Please take care of yourself.

Anonymous.

⁂

Darshan led Zola out onto the balcony after dinner.

Ebony bamboo mats felt relaxing underneath Zola's feet. Darshan flicked a switch, and mini balls of fire appeared around the balcony, pitched on black wooden sticks. The flames made the night even darker. Zola was amazed at the display. She sat on a swing sofa and cradled her wine.

She took a sip and tasted dark cherries, dried plums, mulberries, and rich chocolate. All the flavors exploded in her mouth like a long, dense, French kiss. She took another lingering sip and felt her heart settle peacefully within her chest. Bright stars fought to be seen over the fire. Sailboats drifted in the distance on Lake Ontario.

"Who knew Toronto could be so beautiful at night?"

Darshan assessed the view as if looking at it for the first time.

"Yeah, it is." He sat beside her. He was so close that Zola could smell his aftershave mingling in the night air. She sensed something was cooking inside of him. Something simmering. She could read his body language like her favorite book. She embraced herself.

"Are you seeing anyone, Zola?" The words exploded from his lips as if they had been waiting to be released from a dark place. He suddenly wanted to suck the words back in. Zola's heart went higher in her chest. "If I'm being too forward, just let me know, because…."

"No, no, no, I don't mind. I'm single." Their new vulnerabilities caused their bodies to become uncomfortable. Darshan was hunched over his knees, while Zola slouched on the sofa. She tasted her mother's words in her mouth. *Zola, it's time for you to find a man who makes you happy. You don't want to grow old and alone like me.* "To be honest, Darshan, I'm not looking for a relationship. I mean, I just came out of one…a bad one…and I just opened up a restaurant…and I just moved here and…"

"This isn't a proposition, Zola."

Zola's phone buzzed in her purse. It was Pierre.

"Sorry, I have to take this." He was closing the cafe tonight. She was worried that something might have gone wrong. She rose and walked inside the penthouse for some privacy.

She came back ten minutes later.

"Is everything okay?" Darshan asked.

"It was Pierre. He just had a little scare."

"Has something happened?"

"I don't know. He wouldn't say."

They fell silent. Suddenly, they heard a faint commotion on the street below. A drunk guy had bumped into a homeless man. A few aggressive words were exchanged. A shaken fist rose in the air.

Darshan and Zola chuckled at the insanity, a sound that was thicker and richer only because they were joining each other. But reality slipped back in like slow-reacting poison, gradually destroying everything that they thought was secure in their lives.

Zola was grateful for the comedic relief to avoid a confession that she might regret. The night sky was changing into an outrageous darkness as if trying to provoke deep secrets out of distant lovers. Darshan thought about telling her about the fall issue of *Gourmet* magazine, but decided to hold back on the surprise; he wanted her to share the special moment with someone she loved or cared about, perhaps with Pierre. All he knew, it wasn't him.

# CHAPTER 21

Sunlight filled Mrs. Singh's spacious office.
The window view always impressed visitors. Mrs. Singh had
pushed forward the family's name to new heights. So, you can imagine her face when she opened her email. Her heart dropped.

She reread the email over and over until she took two painkillers.
This must be a sick joke. No way her only son was leaving the family
business. She thought about calling Darshan to see if it was true.

She paused before dialing his number. If she got involved, it
would push him further into his crazy endeavors. She'd better stay
out of it. He would soon come to his senses. But she also noticed him
spending too much time with that Zola girl. Mrs. Singh thought she
was only after the family's money and name to skyrocket her little
cafe. She was no different from every other woman that came into her
son's life. She needed to find a distraction for her son. She hoped he
had taken her up on her offer on running the new bistro in France.

Her coffee on the glass desk was getting cold. She even didn't see
Godiva bring it in. Was she that bent out of shape? Yes. She was. This

news worked her nerves to the core. She couldn't take it anymore; she picked up the phone.

"Hello, Mother."

"Darshan, did I catch you at a bad time?"

"I was in a meeting, but I can talk. Is there anything wrong, is everything okay?"

"Yes…no…I mean…it's regarding the new bistro in Paris." She rose and strode to the floor-to-ceiling window. She stares down at her platinum heels. "See, the thing is, darling, I'm not able to fly, at least not for a couple of weeks. I got that eye surgery done. I'm going to need someone to go and speak to the media and present the grand opening."

"Say no more. I'll do it. When are you planning on coming?"

"Three or four days after you."

"Don't worry, Mother. I have this under control."

"I know you do, dear."

"Is there anything else?"

She cast her eyes to her nails and toyed with the sapphire that displayed her wealth.

"Yes, there's this one thing. Have you given any thought to my proposal about running the new bistro?"

There was a moment of silence.

"I'll do it. My boss at the Gourmet thinks it will be great for me to write in Paris. He said it will benefit their Parisian readers and French enthusiast."

"Oh good!...Has that Anushka girl delivered you *the book?*"

Darshan fell silent. The sound of her name made him cringe a little. He felt horrible tossing her out, but she had no right to come to his penthouse unannounced.

"About that. She said you've given a key to my place."

"Yes, I did."

"Mother, why would you do that?"

"I don't trust in leaving it with your incompetent concierge, so I told Anushka she could place it on your coffee table near those dreadful black roses. Inside *the book* has all the markups for the new bistro. I hope it got there without incident."

"Yes…but…"

"Good. It's nice to know she is capable of doing something right. I hope the lock on *the book* is in fine condition."

"Yes Mother."

"Wonderful. It shows she's trustworthy. How'd the evening go with Anushka?"

"Evening?"

"Oh, Darshan, what happened?"

"Nothing. I had plans that night. You should've told me she was coming over with *the book*. I probably would've treated her a little nicer."

"Darshan, you don't return my phone calls, and you know I don't text. Besides, it was a last-minute decision; she was going home that way, so I didn't see any harm. By the way dear, I met her parents. They were charming, simple-minded, but good people nonetheless."

"I have to go, Mother."

He knew where this was heading.

"All right, darling."

After they hung up, a smile swept across her face. She thought her plan was going to work. After spending some time promoting the new bistro in Paris, he wouldn't have time for anything else. It would be enough to get him busy and keep his mind off that Zola girl and whatever nefarious business ideas she had cooked up her sleeve.

Mrs. Singh melted back into her chair that looked as if it was custom made from some advanced planet. She entertained the idea of sending Anushka with Darshan to Paris. Maybe their romance could catch fire there. Maybe he would find her more agreeable in a romantic setting. Mrs. Singh's lips formed in a straight line in thought. How could she make this plan even more brilliant? How could she create a fantasy that was the perfect recipe? Her fingertips tapped on the desk.

She brainstormed every angle, like she was creating a fabulous dish. She could fly out Anushka for a few days to help out at the new bistro. But she wondered if Anushka was ready to be cooking amongst the top chefs in the world.

∽

There was a knock at the door. Mrs. Singh looked up from the *Food & Wine* magazine. Anushka set her lunch on her glass desk. She glanced sweetly at the vase of fresh white roses that Godiva had ordered this morning. Mrs. Singh loved fresh white roses but didn't show any appreciation for how it got from the florist to her office.

On her plate was roasted rabbit stuffed with white asparagus and expensive cheese. She was happy it wasn't chicken; she hated chicken. She found it boring. She grew up eating chicken and always wanted something different. Something that could excite her appetite, like pheasant and duck. She found those meats sumptuous. More flavorful. Anushka came back and poured her a glass of champagne. Mrs. Singh didn't mind a good glass of champagne anytime of the day.

Anushka was working front house today. She made sure everything ran smoothly before leaving the floor. She was dressed in fitted black pants and a long-sleeved black top. Her hair was snatched back into a smooth ponytail, and she stepped in leather boots. Black encrusted Mediterranean earrings swung from her ears. An Indian shawl was wrapped around her neck like a goddess.

Anushka wondered if Mrs. Singh had read her disturbing email yet. She gave no indication that she had. She looked cool as a cucumber. She was so hard to read at times.

Mrs. Singh examined Anushka up and down. Slicing through her. A smile ghosted across her face. She liked what she saw. Not the frumpy girl she met the first day. She didn't look like someone who worked on a greasy food truck in a dark alley. Good riddance! She was finally getting it. Putting your best face forward was the way to go. Mrs. Singh could actually see her being the face of the new bistro. But it was risky. She could cost her a Michelin star. Mrs. Singh had promised herself she would only hire the best team.

Maybe Anushka should show up on Darshan's arm in Paris to generate buzz for the new restaurant. People like a salacious story, give the media sharks something to talk about. *Who's the mystery girl with Mr. Singh? Is she his bride-to-be? Is she the inspiration behind Paris 65?* Maybe she was ready. Maybe she *was* ready for Paris.

# CHAPTER 22

Zola was meeting Darshan at Queen's Park.

He had important news to tell her. She wondered what it could be. The grass was soft beneath her feet as she waited on the bench. The sun was struggling to come out from thick clouds. The air smelled like green and dirt. Joggers and walkers were scattered everywhere, and dogs played fetch with their owners while they unconsciously trampled over used condoms from last night's indecent activity.

Darshan arrived and sat close beside her.

"So why did you invite me here?

Darshan took a deep breath and leaned forward on his knees. "I plan on going to Paris."

"What? For how long? Why... When? How come?" A sour taste stung the back of her throat.

"It's pertaining to family matters."

"But I thought you loved Toronto."

"Well, I really don't have much going on here." Zola wanted to say that wasn't true. *You have me*. But she stayed silent. "My family is always traveling these days; one minute they are in Singapore, next London, then India. I rarely see them. I feel like I've been stagnant." He paused and toyed with the threads on his wrist. He took in a long breath. His dark expressions were suddenly running hot. "Zola... would you like to go...you know...to Paris...with me?" The words rumbled from his stomach up the throat, pushing through his body as if tired of being ignored. The words were out there in the worst possible way. He didn't bother to sell her on it with all the buttery desserts piled high in French bakeries.

A thousand words hung in the space between them. The question weighed heavy on Zola's shoulders. It felt like a million invisible walls closing in around her with no escape. There was a lot to consider. Did he really expect her to drop everything and go across the world? Who was going to run the cafe? Who was going to do all the business dealings? Answer all the calls, send out emails, do interviews, cooking segments on the morning news, opening and closing. Would Pierre be down with all the responsibility? Opening a cafe was her idea. She was the one that kept everything in working order.

She was fond of Darshan, but did she like him enough to put her business on pause? *Paris!* He said *Paris!* A Southern Black girl in *Paris!* Hell! Moving to Canada still felt adventurous and exotic to her. She promised herself that this year she would take more risks. See and do more things outside her comfort zone. It was plastered all over her New Year's resolutions vision board. Romance wasn't on there.

If she didn't say yes, she would never see his gorgeous face again. Those perfectly smooth dark eyebrows. Those expressive eyes. Those sexy ears. She had beautiful words all lined up for Darshan, but a few worst ones jumped ahead.

"I can't, Darshan. I have a lot riding here. It's a wonderful idea, though. I mean, gosh! Paris!" she cried out. "That's around the world, and I even don't speak French. What am I going to do in Paris?" She paused and toyed with the idea of living in Paris. It seemed incredible to her. Relaxing at cafes spilling out onto cobblestone streets. Drinking chilled champagne on summer days and Parisian hot chocolate on cool nights. All while watching street vendors handmake crêpes and baguettes that she could eat at any time.

But not knowing anyone and speaking the language frightened her; she didn't want to depend on Darshan for everything. She felt her independence was being compromised. Working since she was fourteen, driving since she was sixteen, obtaining her first apartment since she was eighteen, all a huge accomplishment. Now, owning her own restaurant was a big deal.

She was used to men taking advantage of her kindness, and Darshan didn't seem like that kind of guy, but she couldn't take any chances. She still hadn't healed from the ashes of her last relationship, the one she still hadn't told Darshan about. But he sensed she had been hurt in the past.

"I understand, Zola. No more needs to be said."

Zola suddenly felt bad. She felt she had ripped his heart out, seared it to a crisp and served it to a pack of hungry wolves. She wasn't sure what to say. She didn't want to play with his emotions by saying something she really didn't mean. The silence was so thin that it was breakable. Despair colored the air around them. There were tears in Zola's eyes, but she blinked them away so quickly, Darshan thought he only imagined it.

"We can still stay in contact, Darshan. I mean, we have all this fancy technology these days. We could Skype, which I do all the time with my mom and friends back home in Atlanta. We shouldn't think of this as a goodb—" Her lips suddenly became inflamed. His lips were slightly chapped against hers from the light breeze. His fingers slipped across her cheek like a warm river. She felt like butter in a hot skillet, melting into a rich foam. She was bubbling. Sizzling. Her heart turned over in her chest like a dog receiving a generous belly rub.

His warm breath feathered across her face, creating a new sensation, reminding her how cold she'd been emotionally all these months, turning down guys left and right. The longer they kissed, the filthier it got. She loved it. The kiss was better than she thought it would be. She could taste hints of spice from the red cinnamon gum he chewed minutes ago.

Darshan pulled away and looked deeply into her eyes, searching for something, anything, to let him know she wanted him. Nothing. He stroked her cheek once again and left.

⌒

Daylight burned through Zola's bedroom.

Zola's face baked into the pillow. Her alarmed sounded in her ears. Hair wild. Breath sour. Limbs ached. She fought against opening her eyes. She had to open the cafe today. However, all she wanted to do was eat an unholy amount of chocolate and do some mindless online shopping while watching Mukbang videos.

The solitude of the room ate at her soul, bringing back all the years of loneliness. She wondered if she made the right decision. Maybe reading a book would take her mind off things. Nope. She wasn't in the mood. A cocktail of emotions raced through her like a freight train that refused to stop. The guilt consumed her like fire. Darshan laid out his heart, and she shoved it back into his chest. But he must understand where she was coming from. Right? Her livelihood was at stake. The Spice Café did not care that a wrecking ball had crashed through her life. Darshan was leaving. What was she going to do in Paris anyway? She didn't even speak French. Hell! She barely spoke proper English. And he wanted her to go to Paris. She shook her head. She couldn't be having her head in the clouds. She had a business to run. She couldn't be bothered with Paris. What was in Paris? Nothing she wanted to see, that was for sure. She knew it was Pierre's dream to see the city. But not hers. Okay, okay, she played with the idea of going to culinary school there, but that's about it.

She strode into the living room. Pierre was in the kitchen cooking up a storm. Sausage patties were frying in the pan, eggs cooked in onions, green peppers, and chives. Roasted potatoes smothered with cheddar cheese and smoked bacon. Crème fraîche hung out on the sidelines for good measure. Dark roast coffee percolated away... sounding like music to Zola's ears. The campfire aroma pierced through her confused fog enough to help her grasp her surroundings.

She wondered if Pierre got lucky last night with Marquis. He was in a good mood. He was usually setting off the fire alarm. She strode over to the sofa, and Buttercup jumped on her lap. Zola patted the cat lovingly. Birds chirped outside the window. She had an urge to shoo them away. Nothing was chipper about her life. She tried to unravel her tongue from the walls of her mouth to say good morning.

"Oooh, Zola, you look like shit."

"Thank you, you're so kind."

"What can I get you? Coffee? Eggs? A hairbrush?"

"Coffee."

"Coming right up."

Zola smothered a yawn with her hand. She watched Pierre moving around the kitchen. The kitchen was old-fashioned; they had discussed updating once the cafe picked up. Zola somewhat liked the old rustic look anyway. Pierre wanted a fancy back splash with a big white farm sink.

She thought about telling Pierre about Darshan's plans. Leaving everything behind, including her. She couldn't find her voice to tell Pierre how much she fallen for Darshan. If she decided to go to Paris, would Pierre be cool in running the cafe without her? She couldn't abandon him on a sinking ship. This could ruin their friendship and partnership. She must see something through in her life. Dropping out of college was something she regretted. Not having kids at a youthful age was another thing she regretted. The restaurant was falling apart. She felt like she was at her wit's end. Pierre handed her a cup of strong coffee.

"Zo, you don't look too good. Maybe you should take the day off."

"No way, you've been opening for the past few days. I can't have you keep bailing me out whenever I'm feeling under the weather. I will push through it. You can still come in the evening, though; besides, some cute guy you've been flirting with has been looking for you." Zola took a lingering sip of her coffee as if she had hit checkmate.

"Bitch, you don't play fair."

"I never do."

Pierre hadn't told Zola about the nude pictures of him and Marquis, or the accusations of her taking them. However, he didn't believe for one second that she snapped those photos. But he had to know for sure.

"Have you been taking nude pictures of me and Marquis?"

Zola almost choked on her coffee, which burned the back of her throat. The coffee turned into tar in her stomach. "Excuse me?"

"Someone sent nude pictures of us on my phone."

"Oh my god, Pierre! Why would you think I would do something like that?"

"Well, they were taken at the Spice Café."

"Pierre! At our place of work."

"It was actually in the alley." He said it like there any consolation.

Zola groaned. She buried her face in her hands.

"We don't need this type of publicity right now, Pierre."

"I know. I told Marquis it can't happen again."

Hearing this made Zola feel a little better. But she wondered who took the pictures.

"So, no leads?"

"None. It's weird."

She wondered if this was connected to the immigration exploitation thingy, or the break-in. Was somebody trying to blackmail them? She didn't need this right now. She didn't look forward telling anyone about her financial troubles. The bills that she was avoiding on her office desk. Not even Pierre. She handled all the books; Pierre handled the front of the house. She thought about the prospects of her cafe falling into bankruptcy. Her stomach turned into knots. Maybe taking a long vacation wasn't a bad idea after all.

～

"You're going to Paris!"

Pierre's eyes and ears perked up like a wild fox. All he could think about was all the fabulous French wine and Frenchmen that she was going to be surrounded by; and there was only one Eiffel Tower he was interested in seeing and being under.

The last few lingering customers left the cafe with their stomachs bloated with spiced fish and fried green tomatoes and okra, hanging over their belts, declaring an imminent return. It had started to rain. Fat raindrops resembled leopard prints on the windows against the night and streetlight. Pierre locked the door and turned back to Zola, who was wiping down the tables and collecting empty wine glasses.

"I know, right?"

"You lucky trollop. I can't get a guy to take me down the street."

"What about that stud that took you to Jamaica?"

"Gurrrl, he just wanted these beefcakes." Pierre stuck out his tongue and started to twerk like a seasoned contestant on *Dancing with the Stars*. Zola smacked his little fanny with the dishtowel and laughed. "But for real, he wasn't trying to put a ring on this."

"It didn't look that way to me. No man sends a bouquet of roses to someone's workplace if they aren't serious. Now give me the dirt, boy...and don't leave out details... Just because I'm not one of the *children* doesn't mean I can't enjoy a good nasty story. I promise it will not go further than this cafe."

"If you must know, little miss nosy, we didn't have sex."

"He's too fine for me to believe that. People around here talk. Be careful who you share your business with," she said while spraying disinfectant on a table.

"Speaking of Caribbean men, what's up with you and Hakeem? I haven't seen him around here lately."

"What about him?"

"What about him?! Are you mad? The man got skin as smooth as Venezuelan chocolate and a heart of liquid gold. He has his own place. He drives a car that costs nearly as much as this cafe, he's CEO of his own business, he's more beautiful than hot damn! And this hussy says what's about him? Are you feeling okay? Every girl in Toronto would drop their panties for him."

"Not everyone fast like you."

Pierre popped his head up from wiping the tables. He looked like those long neck birds taking its head out of the ground. "Who are you calling fast, miss thang. I have you know I'm not the one grinding on two men at once." Zola laughed and told him to shut his mouth and mind his business. "Now, back to this Indian god that asked you to Paris. I would say drop everything and go. I promise I'll behave myself." He chuckles. "The lord knows you need a break, and if he's willing to pay, why not?

"But he's Indian."

"Excuse me? When did you become a Donald Trump supporter?" Zola sucked her teeth. "Who cares if he's Indian? You could be passing up on something special…okay…okay…. I know I've been giving him hell lately for his connection to Marquis. But I barely know homeboy. I wasn't fair to him, and neither are you. He seems to respect what we're doing here. So, give the guy a chance. I'm tired of you looking at old photos of your ex. Don't pretend like you didn't catch me spying. I see everything you do. It's time for you to move on. He was no good anyway, and you know this. You deserve much better."

Zola collapsed in a chair in thought. "What if I'm too late?"

"Better late than never."

# CHAPTER 23

Hey Darshan,

How's Paris? I'm sending you this email just to see if you're enjoying yourself. I guess I could've sent you a text but just called me old-fashioned. You're so lucky to be in France.. How are the pastries there? Scrumptious, I'm sure.

I've never been to Paris. I've heard it is a romantic place with all its ancient historical white buildings. Please post pictures on your social media soon.

Me, I'm doing fine. The Spice Café is picking up all thanks to you. I saw your review in the Gourmet. Wow! I made the front cover! You should have seen my face. I was so EXCITED! Pierre showed me the magazine at work, and I almost lost my freakin' mind. I let out a scream that almost scared away all the new customers.

Thank you so much for putting my business on the map. Food bloggers and foodie lovers are hashtagging the café as I write this. The tables are filling up quickly; so much that I had to hire more staff!

Well, enough of my rambling. I don't want to bore you with my life. You are in Paris for crying out loud! The land of magic and beautiful people. Enjoy yourself. Don't forget to send me a postcard.

OXOXO Zola

Bonjour beautiful!

I'm thrilled to hear the success of the café. Don't thank me...it was all you. Your food speaks for itself.

I'm staying at a hotel. What extravagances! Lots of gold and high ceilings. The room service is great too. The shower even has a built-in TV. Cool, eh? The pastries are like floating therapy for the mouth. So smooth and creamy. Oops! That sounded a bit erotic. Ignore me. It's been a while. I wish you were here to share this wonderful culinary adventure with me.

The offer still stands.

Darshan

# CHAPTER 24

**H**akeem arrived at the Spice Café.

He looked like a tall fountain of chocolate, almost touching the door. He filled it out like a bouncer at a raging nightclub. He was also known to fill out other orifices.

Zola was expecting him. She strode out of the kitchen. She had changed out of her kitchen clothes and into something more relaxing. She no longer looked like a cook or chef, maybe a yoga instructor instead. She wore black tights and a beige top. A few customers trickled in. Some ate today's special, which was gumbo and fried alligator bites.

All morning long, words were marinating on Zola's tongue. She knew exactly what she wanted to say to Hakeem. This was the hardest thing she had ever done.

They sat at a table. His long body seemed like it was too big for it. Zola was slightly turned on. She couldn't believe she was going to jeopardize this relationship that could lead to great sex and more. Pierre thought she was crazy without test-driving the goods first.

"Thanks for coming."

"No problem."

His eyes darted around the cafe. This was his third time dining inside. His eyes shot open when he saw a photo of Zola framed on the wall. "Hey! That's you." He pointed to the cover of *Gourmet* magazine. "You're famous!"

Zola laughed. It still hadn't hit home yet that she was on the most popular foodie magazine in North America.

"Yes, that's me."

"That's crazy."

"Yeah, it is."

Pierre brought over two cups of coffee and a two slices of carrot cake made with buttercream icing and Madagascar vanilla. Hakeem took a bite. The cake melted first, then the frosting, taking turns like two lovers tumbling between the sheets. It was the best dessert he had ever tasted. He deemed it better than his mother's. The cakes and pies were a hit at the restaurant. Zola couldn't keep up with the demand and had to order more ovens and staff.

"Hakeem, I invited you here to talk about—"

"How much you in love with me?"

This joke made it harder for Zola to spit it out. Hakeem leaned backward in his chair with legs spread open; they looked like bookends for the table. She was boiling all over once again. Who was she kidding? He was totally her type. The type she normally went for. Timberland boots and dreads. She started to doubt saying anything at all.

"Hakeem, I'm taking a break."

"A break from what?"

"From everything… I'm going on a vacation."

"Where to?"

"Paris."

"*Yo!* Paris?" He blinked wildly. "I didn't know you were blowing up like that. Are you thinking about opening up another cafe over there or sumthin'? Maybe you need company for protection." He leaned forward salaciously. Zola swallowed hard, cursing herself for how fine he was. She was going to leave this chocolate fountain all behind without even bathing in it. Pierre was right; she was crazy. Her mind flung to Hakeem's assumption of opening a French cafe in Paris. The idea dazzled her.

"I'm actually going to see a friend." The words felt like cayenne pepper on her tongue.

"A friend, eh?" He sunk back, sizing up the situation, placing two and two together like a mathematician. His brain heard the words, but his heart refused to accept it. "What if I don't want you to go?"

"What do you mean?"

"What if I want you to come to Montreal with me. I have a house there. You will get all the relaxation you need." He winked.

The temperature was rising in the Spice Café. Heat raced up her neck and down her spine like an electric current. Hakeem was making this hard for her. The memory of him shirtless on the beach, showing his happy trail, excited her again. She looked at the maze of vines bulging under his dark skin looking like a road map to great sex. She wondered where else on his body they were prominent.

Why did Hakeem want her to go to Montreal with him? What was going on? These men pulling her in all directions. France and now Quebec. Who knew Frenchmen were so passionate about their women? This had never happened to her before. Did he read between the lines? She was going away. Far away. Away from everybody, including him. To clear her mind. To be with another man. Why was he making this so difficult? She shifted uncomfortably in her chair, hoping to gain some common ground.

A bell rang on the counter each time an order was up in the kitchen. The place was running smoothly, all thanks to Pierre, which brought some comfort to Zola. She knew the cafe would be in good hands while she was gone.

"Hakeem, the offer sounds great. Trust me, it does. But I've made my mind up. I'm going to Paris. I need this for myself."

"Is there anything I can say to change your mind?" His voice went flat and lifeless. Zola let the heavy silence do all the talking. He let down his guard. He decided to tell her a personal story. It took her by surprise.

His family sought refuge in Montreal after a nasty hurricane. When his parents applied for Canadian immigration, their forms somehow got lost in the shuffle of other applicants. His parents got sent back to Haiti. Hakeem was born in Canada during the time of his parents' deportation. Since he was Canadian, the officials placed him in child welfare. They said he could stay, but his parents had to go. Separated. Their hearts were broken. They fought tooth and nail to stay in Canada, but the government deported them anyway.

He finished his story, and Zola's heart sank like an undercooked soufflé. Why was he telling her all this? To make her feel guilty for leaving. Was her leaving conjuring up old memories? Or did he know this would be the last time he would ever see her again? Her head was spinning. A part of her wanted to stay and make him happy, to comfort him. Say it was all a joke. It would be easier, right? His vulnerability made him appear sexier. She played with ideas of friendship. But she somehow knew it wouldn't work.

She looked down at his long fingers gripping his coffee cup. If he only knew one touch from his hand would make her forget all about Paris.

Pierre emerged from the kitchen balancing what looked like several different plates. Zola needed the distraction, and it meant money was coming in. She noticed Hakeem's confidence had evaporated; his defensiveness had been stripped away. He looked like a little boy that just lost his kite in a strong wind. There was an organic innocence that swept over his face. Was this a ploy to get her to stay? No, he was breaking down the walls of his past to let her in, stripping the layers off himself to show her who he really was. He trusted her with his secret, with his story.

She prayed for voice of reason to come with banging pots and pans to wake her up to reality. This could not work. She knew she was in love with Darshan. She saw a brighter future. A happy one. A long-lasting one. But did he want the same with her?

Zola watched him drop two fifties onto the table. The bills were new and starchy as if they were printed days before.

No hug. No kiss. No have a good time in Paris. It looked like Hakeem wanted to hit something but didn't. He strode out of the cafe and lit a cigarette and stared long and hard at Zola through the window. She hadn't realized he smoked. *Good thing I didn't pursue anything further, I hate guys that smoked; that would have been a problem.* She tried to find fault in something to ease the numbness she felt. She knew he would have quit if she asked, that was the kind of person he was. She was going to miss him. Zola doubted her decision once again. She no longer trusted her intuition. It always seemed to lead her down the wrong path.

She prayed to God she was making the right choice.

# CHAPTER 25

**H**er bags were packed at the door.

No time was wasted. Zola felt strangely excited. Pierre stood in the living room, making sure she had everything she needed. He couldn't believe Zola was spending a month in *Paris!* with a gorgeous man, a man he wouldn't mind licking and teasing himself. *Bitch!* But he was happy for her nonetheless.

After all was set, she plopped on the sofa, thinking about how blessed her life had turned out. She was lucky. She was blessed to be on the cover of *Gourmet,* have her own cafe, and an all-expenses paid trip to Paris. Could things get any sweeter? She finally felt like everything in her life was becoming full circle.

She wondered what Darshan had planned the moment she arrived. She knew meeting him would feel a little awkward. They still hadn't talked about their first kiss at the park. Was she ready for a relationship? A relationship usually brought nothing but bad luck. She was terrible at it. The moment romance comes into her life, everything seemed to fall apart. She couldn't trust herself with another man. Never! She couldn't allow it. At least not now. She must take things slow. Everything was too good to mess up.

A loud vibration from Zola's phone sent Buttercup into cardiac arrest. The cat sprang into action and scurried underneath the bed, dragging her belly on the dusty floor. Hate radiated from the cat's eyes, itching to claw at Zola's phone and tear it into pieces. She licked her unruly fur to calm her nerves.

Zola's Uber was waiting outside. She kissed Pierre on the cheek and glanced around the small apartment one last time. He told her to be good and to bring him back a French man as a souvenir. She laughed and rubbed her cat on the head. Buttercup purred and jumps into Pierre's arms, as if to get a closer look at Zola before she ventured off on her long journey.

# CHAPTER 26

**P**aris, France was announced.

This was Zola's first time flying first-class. She loved it. She didn't want to go back to economy anytime soon. She was served chocolate-covered strawberries and ice-cold French champagne the entire way there, in her own cubicle! This pampering definitely melted away her anxiety. She hated flying. The turbulence freaked her the hell out. It made her heart pound like crazy. But Air France knew what they were doing. Everything was smooth and relaxing. She would have to thank Darshan once again.

He waited anxiously outside customs. More champagne awaited in his hand. His driver stood beside him, dressed in black. Darshan wiped sweat from his forehead. He didn't understand why he was so nervous. Maybe he didn't want to fuck up again and face rejection.

Darshan rolled back his sleeves and consulted his watch. Her plane had landed an hour ago. He tried to envision what could be going on behind those frosty glass doors. This was Zola's first time in Paris, and he didn't want anything to go wrong. He had to fight the urge to go behind the doors to find out what was going on. He hoped she wasn't being harassed. Customs could be a pain. All the extra questioning. All the intimidation. He could think how many times he been through the scrutiny.

Then he saw her. Relief and excitement washed over him. He popped open the champagne right there and poured her a glass. The fizz went to her head. She couldn't believe she was in another country, halfway around the world. He saw her struggling with her luggage and helped by swinging one carry-on over his shoulder and handing the other to the driver.

∽

It was a glorious day, warm and sunny. The puffy clouds couldn't look even more perfect against a wide-open blue sky. Windows down, the sweet smells of fresh-baked breads and buttery desserts stacked high drifted into the black town-car. Darshan wasn't hungry, but Zola's stomach spoke differently, and she wanted out. Now!

The driver pulled over to a wide boulevard lined with trees shading cafes and their bistro tables and chairs. Darshan's hotel was only a few blocks away. The beauty of the city chased away the fatigue of travel. Zola peeled herself from the leather seat and let the intoxicating smells guide her down the narrow cobblestone streets.

The air was heavy with history. She took in the seventeenth-century stone buildings, some running the length of the road. The elegant sound of French being spoken floated from sidewalk cafes. Zola was so excited and taken back with sights and smells that she almost tripped and bust her head. She savored old-world charm like good wine. This was her first time traveling outside of North America, and she loved it. She wanted to kick herself for not doing this sooner.

Exploring cafes and specialty shops was on top of her list of things to do. The Parisian boutiques looked like holiday stores on steroids. The windows overflowed with one-of-a-kind items. She sauntered past a cafe and gawked at tarts topped with candied violets, rose petals, and glazed strawberries. They were so beautiful, they needed a *Do Not Eat Me* sign.

A middle-aged woman with high cheekbones and pineapple-yellow hair standing behind a stall smiled at Zola, hoping she would try her artisanal sandwiches.

"*Bonjour!*"

Darshan greeted her back in French, "*Bonjour, Mademoiselle.*" They spoke in rapid French before ordering. Perhaps Darshan was showing off his French, Zola thought. It was sexy. She wanted to jump his bones right then and there. She didn't know he spoke the language so fluently which he later explains he studied French in Montreal.

She gawked at all the rustic sandwiches. Tomato and basil with mozzarella, smoked salmon with capers and cream cheese, roasted ham with double-aged cheddar. Everything looked so scrumptious, she didn't know which one to choose.

However, she went with the smoked salmon because the meat looked like layers of beautiful pink ribbons. Darshan got the tomato and basil. The woman heated the sandwiches on a grill, which sizzled to everyone passing by delight. She then wrapped them up in white paper.

Zola took a big bite. Her eyes rolled to the back of her head. It was the best sandwich she had ever tasted, and she was never big on sandwiches. Today she'd been converted to a sandwich lover. Crusty, chewy bread: the aroma seemed like it was baked minutes ago. Each bite of the sandwich crumbled nicely in Zola's mouth. She suddenly felt bad for her waistline because she knew this was going to be a passionate food affair.

# CHAPTER 27

**P**ierre received a mysterious text: *Meet me at the bistro.*

Butternut squash stuffed with spiced meat and rice could be smelled from the cafe. Pierre pulled the meatloaf out of the oven and let it cool. He washed his hands and placed an employee in charge while he left for his rendezvous at the bistro; he figured it was Marquis that sent him the text. He didn't understand why Marquis was using another number. But he didn't care; he just wanted to see him. It'd been weeks since they saw each other.

Godiva remembered Pierre from his last visit. She stood guard, anticipating another attack on the crew. She had her finger on the walkie ready to page security until Pierre told her he was meeting someone. She reluctantly checked his name on the reservation list; a gold necklace ran down the middle of her apple-shaped breast, they were so perfect and round it looked as if she just left a surgeon's table. Her chocolate eyes fluttered when she saw his name.

"Follow me." Godiva's ponytail swung as they ascended the staircase that led out to an open rooftop patio. Pierre been up here before but didn't know this luxurious greenhouse existed…hidden away behind foliage.

There was an Indian woman at a table wearing chef whites. Her skin was the shade of sweet ginger. Her hair was up in a French twist. Pierre was confused. Where was Marquis? He suddenly was annoyed that Marquis wasn't the one who sent him the text.

"Pierre. It's nice to finally meet you. They say the best way to get to know a cook is to dine with them. Please have a seat."

"I'm sorry, who are you?"

She giggled behind a white napkin before placing it in her lap. Her oversized black shades hid her blazing green eyes. She leaned forward, cleavage spilling over unapologetically as she took off her chef coat.

"Marquis hasn't told you about me?"

Pierre twisted his face for recollection.

"Men!" She pouted. "Please, don't stand. Sit."

She reached for the bottle of champagne and pours him a glass.

"What are we celebrating?

"Us finally meeting."

It sounded like an offer Pierre couldn't refuse. The champagne looked playful and mysterious underneath the shadows of plants and sunlight. The glass was chilled to his liking, imploring him to take a sip. As he sniffed the notes, the bubbles tickled at his nose like giggling queens. It tasted like the golden sweet of summery flowers, spring melons and sour apples, and winter snow.

The space around them was a canopy of cherry blossoms and dark vines twisting and knotting on brick walls, shading them from the summer's sun. Beneath Pierre's shoes was old red cobblestone that gave the patio an historical ambience. Soft, chic French music floated into his ears, a song he had never heard before, a language he barely knew but urging him to hum along.

A waitress came with their menus.

"Oh! Try the pheasant and mushroom roasted in saffron butter. It's divine!"

The waitress came back with a basket of brioche and French butter that looked like tiny cheesecakes on a small white plate, and presented Anushka with a salad that looked like a fucking flower arrangement from Malibu; the meat underneath was sliced thin, like gorgeous leaves. The waitress set the plate before Anushka as if she was someone of importance.

The French music, laughter, and clinking of gold cutlery against white plates could be heard faintly in Pierre's ears. Aromas of caramelized soufflés and cakes being pulled out of hot ovens could be smelt all around. Everyone looked as if they had five degrees in fine arts.

"So how is life, Pierre?"

"Why am I here?"

"Gosh, men love to rush."

"Sorry to cut to the chase, but I have a cafe to run. Could you please tell me what this is all about?"

"This is about you and that slutty partner of yours."

Pierre's mind was flickering between confusion and offense. "Marquis?"

"No, silly. You and Zola."

Pierre sat up straighter. "What about Zola?"

"She's intruding on some dangerous turf. She needs to back off." The waitress came back and placed their food on the table. It smelled scrumptious. But Pierre couldn't eat. He needed to get to the bottom of what she was saying.

"What do you mean?"

"She will never be accepted into the Singh family. She needs to stay away, or things will get ugly."

"Is that a threat?"

"Pierre don't take this personally…this is not your fight. It's a losing battle if she pursues Darshan. He's Indian, she's Black. He's a chef. She's a cook. He's rich, she's poor."

"You're not exactly swimming in money neither. I mean, you work here."

She laughed and leaned forward onto the table. Her perfume smelled like rose tea, and her breath: chocolate mints.

"That's what you think."

"Darshan's a writer. Not a chef. Why do you care so much about him anyway?"

"She didn't tell you?"

"Tell me what?"

She laughed darkly.

"Darshan is the executive chef at Indo-French Bistro. He's left for Paris this week to open another bistro. He recruited all the top chefs here to help. Marquis being one of them. He packed his gold knives and left. No kiss on the cheek. Just gone." She pouted. "Can you believe that? Leaving me here to run this dump." She frantically looked around to make sure no one heard her mini rant.

Pierre's ears were burning. He couldn't believe the information she was spewing from her pink lips. Darshan was the executive chef at Indo-French bistro? He was rich? He'd flown to Paris to open another bistro? Did Zola had any idea she was vacationing with a tycoon? Or did she have a hidden agenda that Pierre didn't know about? Was she throwing in the towel at the Spice Café? And Marquis, did he plan on moving to Paris without telling him? What was going on? A sense of betrayal ate ravenously at Pierre's skin. Everybody was having a big orgy in Paris without him. His food was getting cold. The black truffle pungency no longer attacked his nose.

"How do I know you telling the truth?"

"Pierre, you can believe whatever you want. I'm not here to convince you one way or the other. Take the information as a gift."

"Look, I don't know what you have against Zola, but she's capable of making her own decisions."

Anushka'd had enough of this discussion. She dug into her Chanel purse and tossed pictures and letters onto the marble table. Pierre's eyes grew big like puff pastries. Humiliation smacked him in the face once again. He and Marquis entangled like a well-seasoned pretzel. Naked. Anushka smile moved slowly across her face like molasses running down a stack of thick pancakes. These pictures couldn't see the light of day. Pierre gathered them up urgently.

"It was you!"

"Isn't that a Department of Health violation?" Her smile became dark and rich, eyes melting like dark lava chocolate, her voice sustaining its sweet quality. "You two were amazing. Bravo. If this restaurant career doesn't work out for you, I know one that will, online." Pierre face shot up in horror. Did she have video too? "And if Zola doesn't watch it, she will be finding herself working on a food truck hawking her crab cakes."

The Detroit in Pierre wanted to give her a good ol' cussin' out. But he refrained.

"Are you blackmailing us?"

"Call it brown-mailing, but you call it whatever you want to, sweet cakes." She smiled, taking a sip of her champagne. Pierre had heard enough. He rose and took everything with him, including his meal to go. There was no way he was letting this hundred-dollar food go to waste.

He needed to text Zola as soon as possible.

# CHAPTER 28

F at chocolate covered strawberries rested on golden plates.
Darshan's open-concept penthouse suite was opulent. The
high ceiling was rose gold. The big windows brought in a lot of natural light. Every room hosted a bouquet of cream and peach roses
in crystal vases. Fuzzy bottles of champagne sat on ice in gleaming
bronze canisters. Pictures of Parisian monuments hung proudly in
each room encrusted in gold frames fit for a royal palace. Filigreed
wallpaper shifted in the sunlight as if it wanted to fly into the air.
Every nook and cranny gave Zola's neck whiplash.

"If I'd known you were living like this, I would have come a
lot sooner."

Darshan chuckled. He placed her things in the room. He suggested she take a nap to shake off jet lag. She didn't even know what
jet lag was. But sleep sounded like a good idea.

Zola rose out of a beautiful fog at night. She reached for her phone
and couldn't believe she slept for eight hours. She experienced the
best sleep of her life. It still felt like a dream. But wait! Was it a dream?

The Eiffel tower sparkling outside her window reminded her she wasn't dreaming at all. It glittered like an undying star, its glow highlighting the centuries-old buildings in the night.

Darshan strode into the bedroom. He wanted to ask if she was ready for dinner. Zola sat up against the tall headboard, knees close to her breast. She looked at him admiringly. His eyes were as dark as hidden secrets. She peeled back the cream sheets, inviting him in. The moment was too beautiful to have all to herself. He shed his clothes, leaving on his black boxers.

As her focus faded into ecstasy, his sharpened into midnight. He studied her terrain as he crawled toward her like the Indian sun over a cold desert. He moved with a predatorial grace. The lines in his back and arms came alive from the dusty orange glow floating in from the French windows. Her sex helplessly softened against the fabric of her panties. The heat in his eyes matched the hunger in her own. Black chest hair was slicked against whisky skin like a beautiful dance of flames. His nipples were the color of expensive wine. Sweet saliva coated Zola's mouth, begging for a taste.

A cool breeze was chased out the room by hot air when Darshan pulled Zola into his arms. The arch of her back rose slow like honey. He smelled like a warm blanket pulled fresh out the dryer, with a hint of dark spice.

She took his tatted hand and placed it down below the sheets. His touch hit like fiery amber to her folds. She moaned. Her leg muscles clenched then loosened. Her body felt a million times more sensitive. She was simmering. The room spun. She saw the Eiffel Tower going from bright gold to a pale dullness. Gold flakes lifted off her skin. His touch felt soft and warm. She gasped for air. They kissed. He devoured her mouth and tasted the remnants of sparkling champagne and sweet strawberries. He feasted on her lips, making her the object of his ravenous hunger. The gold glow of the Eiffel Tower seemed fuzzy in their periphery. Everything seemed swollen on their bodies as they dove deeper into each other. Zola's nipples throbbed, after Darshan get finished with them they would look like black truffles.

Watching his body from the ceiling mirror made her eyes sparkle. She needed this. Zola had been without it for far too long. She hoped all this would mean long romantic showers together on Sunday mornings, and lazy sweet kisses in public places.

His manhood kissed her folds. Teasing. Pressing. Caressing. Outlining every agonizing inch. A condom was lying on the dresser. Their minds were too far gone to grab it. Were they about to go without it? Oh, my! He twisted her nipple while dragging his tongue across the valley of her breast, teasing them as if he was tying a double knot on a cherry stem. A tsunami of heat slammed over her body, over and over. She dug her nails into the bedspread, bracing herself for what was about to come.

He slipped inside, parting the doors to paradise. Her eyes flung open. His chest and biceps flexed hard, cocooning her like a solar eclipse. Time stopped. Galaxies were exploding behind their eyes, soaring on an illusion that they couldn't identify. They lost all sense of time and place, as if the calendar had somersaulted several times throughout the night.

Their bodies were simmering. Their mouths were inches apart. She felt the rapid beat of his heart beneath her hand. So eager. So hungry. So full of power. The air locked in her throat as he dug deeper; it felt soul-searching. His erection bobbed and jerked within her like an untamed animal enjoying its natural habitat.

Their sex exchanged masalas. Secret recipes. He threw a strong thrust, his eyes burning black, his lashes fanning down toward his chiseled jawline. She could see all the muscles in his neck. The pulse of his orgasm was so intense, it felt like her own. He grunted hard. It felt like birthdays, Diwali, anniversaries all wrapped up in one. Then his silky lashes hooded his eyes. Their hearts stopped threatening to leap out of their chests. A heavy breath was released. He held himself deep inside her until all his muscles became relaxed.

Zola couldn't help to think, *Sweet Jesus, I already love Paris.*

⌒

Wine stained the old pages on Pierre's coffee table.

It was a quiet night. Pierre had shut down the cafe an hour early. His mind was all over the place. He kept thinking about the conversation he had with Anushka. Could he believe her? Could she be trusted? He didn't understand why Marquis hadn't told him about the trip to Paris. *Bastard!* That explained the unanswered text messages. And this thing about Darshan being rich and owning bistros. What the hell? What was going on? Pierre felt like he'd been left out the loop of everything.

Pierre held the wrinkled letters in his hands. The letters were in Marquis's handwriting addressing his mother. They looked like journal entries. *Marquis writes? How bizarre.* Pierre didn't take him for a writer. A person that was so in touch with their emotions. Pierre was confused. He read on. The further he read, the more aggressive the writing became. Buttercup jumped onto his lap, making him lose focus.

He kept reading, shifting from one page to the next. The writing became more intense. More emotional. More aggressive. Pierre's hand flung to his mouth, one shocker after another. Where did Anushka get these letters? How did she obtain them? She must have forged them herself; these stories couldn't be true. Darshan and Marquis were half-brothers? Pierre shook his head; this Anushka girl couldn't be trusted. There had to be some explanation.

If any of it was true, why didn't Marquis tell him? All those nights of them being together, he hadn't breathed a word about his personal life. Did he trust Pierre with his past? Did he think Pierre would look at him differently? Judge him in ways others had?

He wondered if Anushka was at home or at the bistro caressing an eggplant, getting off on exposing people's weaknesses and miseries just so she could move up in the world. Was she doing this to be head chef at the bistro? Was she blackmailing Pierre to get the Spice Café shut down? Was she intimidating Zola so she could have Darshan all to herself? Pierre sensed Anushka had a thing for Darshan. She probably didn't say it in so many words, but Pierre got the message. She'd made herself clear. She wasn't the one to be messed with. But she didn't know who she was playing with either.

Pierre was angry. He gripped the pages. The air got hot. The lies Anushka was spewing, the threats. Divide-and-conquer techniques would not work on him. She would not make him believe Zola was leaving the Spice Café to open shop in France. *Or was she?* Did she know Darshan was the owner of Indo-French Bistro? Was it even true? How could he believe Anushka? She was a liar and a manipulator. He was pretty sure she was behind the Haiti exploitation scandal. He felt bad blaming Marquis. That was probably the reason he didn't trust Pierre with his story.

He had an urge to text Zola. Tell her everything. Tell her she was dating a millionaire. Tell her she was dating her enemy. Darshan was probably in cahoots with Anushka. If he wasn't, why would he keep all this from Zola? Or did she know and decided not to tell Pierre? He couldn't blame her. He didn't tell her about Marquis working at the bistro, either. He wondered what else Zola might be holding back from him.

# CHAPTER 29

"**B**onjour, Monsieur!"
A hotel chef entered the penthouse suite. His stomach round and plump. His face appeared as if it was carved from thick clay. He wore a tall chef's hat and a white coat with his name embossed in gold letters. He was one of the most talented gourmet chefs in all of Paris. He worked at the five-star restaurant on the top floor. He spent all morning creating food that looked like expensive jewels, forged by freezing, pressure, and heat. He could manipulate beets into looking like macarons with a horse radish mousse filling.

Darshan stood barefoot and shirtless, wearing only dark jeans. He held the door open as the portly chef pushed in a golden cart. The room instantly smelled of chocolate, butter, and spice. The chef left as quickly as he came.

Being the son of one of the best restaurateurs in the world could land him great treatment in the finest places. When the news got out that he was staying at their luxurious hotel, security was heightened, and everything was immediately comped. He also had appeared in a few Bollywood movies, and he was already creating a buzz in the

South Asian community in France. Darshan had the ability to turn a mediocre hotel into a five-star.

∽

Zola rose from a beautiful haze, tiny stars fading in her brown eyes. Sunlight blazed into the bedroom. Everything felt like a distant dream. However, the Eiffel Tower winked at her, saying *everything is real, baby.* It felt as if a weight had been lifted, far away from family, friends and worries.

The morning was quiet. The streets of Paris still hesitated to wake up as people clung to their warm beds, warm showers, or warm coffees. She searched for her clothes and found them folded neatly at the edge of the bed. She hadn't realized Darshan was such a neat freak. She was reluctant to remove herself from comfort of the duvet. It felt like soft waves. But something was nudging her up. The air was salty and sweet, like breakfast was being cooked.

She chose not to check emails or text messages to hide from responsibilities back home. Instead, she took a minute to flirt with the Eiffel, its sharp point slicing through the underbelly of thick clouds. Zola gave it a silky smile and took in the perfume of the ancient city.

She suddenly had the urge to call one of her girlfriends to talk about the amazing night she had with Darshan. But that meant she would have to explain why she was in Paris…with a man. She wasn't in the mood for anyone's judgments about her sex life in a strange city. Her actions didn't strike her as promiscuous; irresponsible yes, but it felt like she had known Darshan forever. But were they in a relationship? They had never discussed it. Flirting here and there, that was about it. She wondered if he wanted more than a fling, perhaps friends with benefits. She was cool with it. It wasn't like they were planning a wedding anytime soon. They were two consenting adults, single, free, in Paris. He had rewarded her the best sex of her life; why couldn't she just enjoy it? She tried moving her body, and it was humming from last night's rumble in the sheets. She felt soreness in areas that hadn't hurt in years.

After soaking in the jacuzzi, she wrapped herself in a puffy bathrobe and sauntered into the living room, leaving liquid gold footprints in her wake from the bomb salt. There was warmth in her cheeks. Darshan sat reading emails on his phone when Zola entered the living room. Her hunger curled within her when she saw the assortment of food.

There was quiches, croissants, macarons, tarts, and crusty breads with creamy dips. There was also fried duck eggs drenched in a silky truffle hollandaise sauce, which caught Zola's eye immediately. Everything made from the finest ingredients. So fresh that it would challenge the pickiest eater. Zola was experiencing multiple mouth orgasms as she tried everything. Her eyebrows climbed higher and higher with each bite. She took a sip of the organic cucumber soda that was freshly squeezed and carbonated, in-house.

She looked over at Darshan sitting in a chair, shirtless, grinning. She realized he didn't have any visible tattoos, except the one on his hand. He was gripping a cup of coffee.

"Good morning, beautiful. How did you sleep?"

"You should know." She winked, biting into a chocolate croissant. It had a hint of espresso.

"I hope I didn't get too carry away last night, because you're going to be using your leg muscles again today. We have a big day ahead of us."

"I don't know about that."

"What you mean?"

"With all this food, you will have to roll me out of here."

Darshan laughed. He passed her a chilled glass of orange mimosa, raspberries suspended inside like mini hearts.

"So what's on the agenda, Mr. Tour Guide?"

"Well, first we're going to stroll down the Champs-Élysées."

Zola was confused.

He read her blank expression and said, "We're going shopping!"

Zola screamed like a little girl, jumped into his arms, and landed chocolate kisses on his cheeks.

"Woah! I didn't know shopping gets you this excited."

"What girl doesn't like shopping?"

"Touché."

"What else are we going do in this fabulous city?"

"That's a surprise."

〰

Before they left the Louvre, a skinny man wearing a plaid vest jogged after them. Zola assumed he was a curator of some sort. Nutmeg freckles dusted his creamy cheeks. He asked if they enjoyed their visit. He explained he was conducting a survey. Zola didn't know how to give an honest answer without sounding…you know…American. But she tried anyway.

"It would've been nice if the art had English subtitles. The audio was pretty tedious to use, to keep rewinding it back and forth.

"But *madame*, you're in France."

"Um…you're right, but you're so close to England. I assume there's a lot of British tourists that come visit your lovely museum."

"But *madame*, there aren't any French translations when I visit London's museums. Why shall *we* be any different, uh?" He stared blankly at her as if she had all the answers. Zola didn't respond and just handed him back the audio translator device.

Later, they strode down a skinny cobblestone street, passing a sea of black iron balconies on beige old-world apartments, with splashes of pink and red flowers hanging from baskets. They passed hidden gardens and gorgeous white fountains. Cafes were scattered throughout, looking like works of art. They walked so much, Zola's feet were beginning to pound in her ears. She cursed herself for wearing heels, trying to be cute. Paris slowly faded into night while streetlights sprang warmly into life. Cafes had started to fill up as people got off work to meet loved ones and friends over wine and coffee.

They continued strolling passing statues of emperors, archways and historical buildings, all lit up in a string of old elegance. Zola fought against the cold wind stinging her eyes as she marveled at the beautiful city, holding Darshan's hand. She couldn't believe she was in City of Lights with this sexy man. She had to be the luckiest girl in the world. The night was sweeter than the chocolate rose truffle she popped into her mouth minutes ago.

They were on Champs-Élysées. Bright-lit storefronts lined both lanes of the avenue. Trees were wrapped up in fairy-lights. Zola's eyes sparkled with amazement. They stopped occasionally so Zola could ooh and aah at the merchandise in the window. Darshan wore a look as if he seen it all before, but Zola's enthusiasm made him enjoy it more.

She strode into a music store and saw a few European-edition CDs of her favorite R&B artists and purchased a couple. They reached the high-end stores like Louis Vuitton and Gucci. Fabulous tourists and Parisians walked around wearing designer shades and tailored clothes. They looked as if they skipped breakfast every morning aspiring to be on the cover of *Vogue*.

Zola went into a few shops. She was blown away how expensive everything was. Before walking out of every store empty-handed, Darshan insisted he would pay. She liked that he didn't get bored as she browsed the women's section. He seemed interested and in tune with her movements. She walked away with enough clothes to last her a week in Paris.

They came to the end of the avenue. The Arc de Triomphe stood before them massive and imposing in all its chunkiness, looking like a gateway to another dimension. Darshan suggested they grab a cup of coffee at a corner cafe before climbing the structure.

Zola's legs were exhausted after the first dozen steps, but once at the top, it was all worth the effort. They took in the panoramic view of the sparkling city, spread out like a beautiful blanket of lights and diamonds. Zola felt she was at the center of the universe. She tried to locate their hotel. She squints but couldn't find it. She pulled out her phone and snapped a few shots. She was itching to post one picture, but that would lead to questioning from friends, family, and associates. Her phone and DMs would be demanding her attention, and the only person she wanted to give that to was Darshan. She wasn't in the mood for people asking silly things like: *What you eating? What's that behind you? What's the weather like there? Where is this monument at? Or why you looking so grumpy?* Nope! She wasn't going to engage with social media while she was in Paris. Thanks to Darshan, she could scratch four things off her Paris do-list: The Louvre, Champs-Élysées, Arc de Triomphe, and having mind-blowing sex. Darshan hinted there was one more surprise, and she hoped it didn't involve climbing anymore stairs.

They Uber'ed over to the Eiffel Tower. The tall monument glittered down onto the city, sparkling like crazy, as if she didn't give a damn who she offended. Ornate black streetlights illuminated old historic buildings. Friends, tourists, and lovers lounged on the grass leading up to the tower, some kissing, others cuddling, some enjoying a romantic meal under the comfort of a shaded tree.

Darshan's eyes darkened. Jewel-lights danced in them, making halos. The mystery around them thickened like good pot of stew. He smelled of toasted coconut and vanilla after spraying on array of colognes at a shop moments ago; it played deliciously against his natural musk. Zola didn't think it possible he could look more handsome and irresistible than he did now.

He took a deep breath. His phone beeped and buzzed in his pocket. He ignored whoever was trying to reach. He sank to one knee. Zola gasped. People at close distance looked on with curiosity; some whispered in rapid French.

"Zola Camila Washington. When I first saw you at the cafe, I knew you were the one for me. I feel complete whenever I'm with you. I feel like I can be myself around you. What I'm trying to say is." He reached down into his pocket, relieved that it was still there. He was terrified it might've fallen out doing their hike around the city. He unearthed a velvety black box.

"Will you marry me?"

"Oh my god, Darshan…yes…I mean…are you sure?"

"I can't be even more sure, Zola."

He studied Zola underneath his long lashes.

"Yes, Darshan, I'll marry you…yes…yes."

He slid the ring slowly onto Zola's finger. It was the biggest diamond she had ever seen. The gold band sparkled like expensive champagne. Darshan had spent three months looking for the perfect ring. She kissed him passionately. A church bell rang in the distance. People stood around watching the spectacle, many clapping and screaming out congratulations. Hired photographers came out of hiding and started snapping pictures in a frenzy. Flashes of bright lights danced around them. They looked like high-profile celebrities, and new arrivals wondered what the good-looking couple's claim to fame.

The sky was turning a dark blue. The air became joyous and sweet. The Eiffel Tower glittered like a firecracker on steroids. Darshan lifted Zola in the air and spun her around.

It seemed like nothing could knock them off their high.

༄

Darshan chose a romantic table by the window at a trendy bistro. The place was buzzing with activity under low lighting. A smooth layer of darkness hovered around the room. Each table had a lit candle to set the ambience. People dressed in chic clothing, mostly in dark palettes, spoke over glasses of wine and espresso.

While Darshan left to use the restroom, Zola slipped out of

her heels and pressed the soles of her feet. It felt good to sit down. Darshan was somewhere in the restaurant by now. Perhaps talking to the head chef; he did it everywhere they went. He loved getting the rundown on a restaurant.

Zola texted Pierre the good news. A few minutes later, Pierre replied to Zola's engagement. He didn't sound too enthusiastic: *Seriously?* Followed by *Are you mad?* Next text *I hope it's to Hakeem and not Darshan. We must talk.*

She sat mulling over Pierre's texts. She was afraid to reply. She didn't want anything to bring down her happiness. Whatever concerns he had could wait until she got back. This was her moment.

A glass of French wine kept her company. Zola wondered what was keeping her new fiancé. She saw him disappear into the kitchen, as if he owned the place. She loved his confidence, his swag; it turned her on just thinking about it.

Her stomach began to growl. Darshan told her to order without him. But she was afraid to speak French. Everywhere they went, French was being tossed around like a tennis ball. She received confused looks when she tried to attempt a few French words that Darshan taught her this morning. She didn't want to eat alone, neither. He suggested she try the caviar. Fish eggs? She didn't think so. Then he suggested the saffron risotto. That sounded much better. Her face was still bursting with flames from all the unnecessary smiling from the proposal. Some customers thought she was crazy. Some thought she was some supermodel visiting Paris for the first time, and some wanted to book her for their next shoot.

Zola's mind flung back to Pierre's text. He must've been stressed out with the cafe. She refused to believe he was envious. Or was he? Perhaps he wished he were here schmoozing in Paris with a hot Frenchman on his arm. Darshan wasn't born in France, but he spoke the language masterfully and was half French, so technically he could get a passing grade.

She pictured Pierre sitting at home dateless on a Saturday night with a bottle of cheap wine watching wretched TV with Buttercup on his lap, digging her sharp claws into his thighs. Or swiping faces endlessly on his phone. Pierre had emailed her yesterday. She decides to open it and ignores everything else. The café was running smoothly. Business was picking up because of the *Gourmet* review. Food bloggers had been visiting the cafe, posting their meals on Instagram, Twitter, and Facebook. Their posts were getting an insane number of shares, likes, views, and comments. The morning news even reached out to Pierre to see if he would be interested in doing a ten-minute cooking segment.

Hearing this put Zola's mind at ease. Seconds later, a message popped up. *I hope you're having fun.* It was Hakeem. Her stomach had started to sink. His timing was perfect. Why did he have to come back into her psyche? She flipped the phone over when Darshan approached with two crêpes stuffed with summer fruits and Nutella.

"For my bride-to-be."

Zola couldn't believe she was engaged, in Paris. All within two days. *Slow down, girl,* she told herself, but who could resist those dark lashes?

"Thanks, Darshan."

"Are you enjoying yourself?"

"Too much."

"And just think, you almost didn't come."

"I know. Silly me to have pass all this up." She flashed him the ring.

"Try the crêpe."

"I've never had crêpe before."

"Seriously?"

Zola nodded.

"We don't have crêpes in Georgia. We have waffle houses." She tasted the crêpe with flavors of hazelnut and chocolate and strawberries.

"Now try it with the French wine."

She swirled the glass first to open the bouquet.

"Mmm...delicious...soft and silky, like you."

"Oh, really. I guess I will have to top that tonight."

"Why is this wine is so good?"

"It's from my family's vineyard."

"What?"

"Yes, you heard me right." He laughed. "It's right outside of Paris. We could take a tour there if you like, and drink lots and lots of wine."

"And eat grapes right off the bushes?"

He laughs

"If you like."

"I can't wait. I'll bet its beautiful there. But why France of all places?"

"Like I told you, I'm half-French. My father's family is originally from here. We still want to keep that family connection to France. So, we started a winery here. You can say it's in memory of my father."

Darshan's phone buzzed on the table. He studied the text. Zola shifted in her seat trying to steal a peek while slicing into her crêpe.

Darshan shoved the phone into his pocket. She wondered who it could've been. Doubt flooded her mind. Maybe she was rushing things. She was engaged in Paris to a man that she barely knew. She felt silly, like a young teenage floozy. Who in the hell runs off to another country halfway around the world and gets engaged?

"How's the crêpe?"

"Good. Who was that?"

"Oh, the text? Nobody important."

His dismissive response bothered Zola. It was important to her. If she was going to marry the man she loved, she needs to know everything.

"Does your family know about us?"

The question caught Darshan off-guard. He put down his coffee and grabbed Zola's hand. He chose his words carefully. He didn't want to ruin this perfect night.

"They don't. But I can change that. Would you like to meet them this weekend?"

"This weekend?"

"Yes, you can meet my aunts and uncles on my father's side, and my mother will be flying in. I think it would be a perfect time. They live in Provence. A few hours away from Paris."

Zola didn't know what to say. This weekend? She was thinking more like next year. It wasn't like he was bringing home a girlfriend. He was bringing home a freakin' fiancée. A fiancée he just got engaged to within matter of days. *Oh shit.* His family was going to think she was a lunatic. What did she get herself into? She chewed at her bottom lip as she pondered the question. She had no perception of his family. How would they react to their sudden engagement? Would they be upset? Would they be happy? Would they disown him? Cast them away like Prince Harry and Meghan? Cut him off from family ties and security? She had no idea what she was in for.

Zola always felt nervous meeting anyone's family or friends, especially the men she was dating. It just wasn't her thing. It irritated her when strangers pried into her personal life. Or hearing bougie people solidifying their prestigious careers through party talk. She shouldn't be in this predicament. She was supposed to be running her cafe. She'd sworn off dating ever since her crazy ass boyfriend decided to stalk her all the way to Toronto. He was such a scumbag. How did she ever get involved with him? She was happy that relationship was over. Now she was thrown into a marriage. But she liked the thrill. The suspense. The excitement. The adventure. It felt like Darshan was what she needed.

"So, what you say?"

"Darshan, I don't know."

"I know, I know…all this must be very sudden for you…I'm sorry that I even brought it up. I understand if you need more time to process everything."

Zola slowly set down her coffee cup and swallowed hard. She wondered if Darshan's mother was traditional. An old-school type. How would she feel about having a Black daughter in-law?

"Wouldn't your mother be upset… You know, about us?" Soft French music played in the background, softening their conversation.

Darshan leaned back and rubbed his neck. "She will love you. Because I love you."

Zola looked out the window at the Eiffel Tower, tiny golden halos in her eyes. Darshan thought she looked like an angel. He felt like the luckiest man in the world. He placed a tatted hand on top of hers, and she felt warm inside. The reassurance that she needed. She stared deep into his espresso eyes and said,

"Yes, I would love to meet your family."

# CHAPTER 30

**T**ruffle butter was spread over his body.

Marquis was back home from Paris. He loved the city, but he loved Toronto even more. His apartment was above a Chinese take-out restaurant where the décor was trimmed in gold and everything priced under ten bucks; a place he ate at more often than the bistro.

Before Pierre entered Marquis's apartment, he watched two coyotes tussle over a greasy Styrofoam container in a graffiti-infested dark alley, sending ants into the night air. A lump set in Pierre's throat as he watched the numbers flick up on the elevator. He couldn't believe he was invited over to Marquis's place; it meant their relationship was progressing.

Instead of ordering in, they were in the kitchen cooking chutney sandwiches. Marquis claims his sandwiches were world famous. After potatoes boiled, Pierre seasoned them with cumin and chili powder and salt. Marquis smashed them into disks and fried them in garlic butter.

Marquis slipped and slid around in black Nike socks and shorts.

He grabbed cheap dollar store plates and cups out of a junky cabinet. He kept pulling up his shorts every other second. His curly hair was braided in six sections, three on each side. Sideburns and hairline sculpted to perfection, which caused Pierre to swoon even more. Marquis whipped up a kickass green mint sauce to go on the potato sandwiches. Pierre watched him blend cilantro, mint, and garlic with lemon juice. It tasted stellar on its own.

Marquis leaned against the sink, chomping on his sandwich like a ravenous beast. They ate in an easy silence. Both drank from foggy glasses that made the apartment appear as if it was submerged under murky water. Family pictures and maps of India and France stuck on his refrigerator. A cracked window let in a cold breeze. A blank canvas stood center in the living room. Marquis painted? Pierre didn't know that. He noticed the artworks on the walls, with their unique textures. They were beautiful. Marquis was talented in many areas.

They migrated into the bedroom. Rap music played softly through a system that wasn't visible to the eye and lent the night more possibilities. Pierre offered Marquis a massage. He was totally down for one. He pulled off his shirt and flung it across the room as if it was nuisance to his skin. His lean muscles and long torso set Pierre's body on fire.

The mattress was on the floor. His chef whites were dumped across it, then pushed to the side. The ceiling were trimmed with red lights. An empty bottle of wine hung out in the trash bin while a pile of clothes stood in the corner, bearing witness to what about to go down. It was the type of room that bred dirty secrets. The TV was playing a Bollywood film. Pierre even didn't know Marquis liked Bollywood movies. There was so much he didn't know about this mysterious hottie.

Pierre reached for the truffle butter on the nightstand. He tried not to get any on the black sheets. It seemed like the only nice thing Marquis owned in his apartment. He dabbed the golden cream on his palm and spread it over Marquis's smooth back. It melted into his warm skin within seconds, all the compacted stress evaporating. Marquis moaned. Pierre massaged deeper and deeper; he was known to give great massages, it was his hidden specialty

Pierre slid his hands up the shoulders and down the blade of his back, brushing along his spine. Marquis cursed softly: "*Fuuuuuck.*" The room was wrapped in a delicious silence. Earthy smells permeated the air.

The handwritten letters came to mind. The words. The secrets. The anger. The frustration. Should Pierre bring them up? Would Marquis flip out? The nude pictures didn't upset him, so why should this? Maybe he would laugh it off. Maybe he would be so amused and ask him to read them out loud for kicks.

"Marquis."

"Mmm…whaaattt?"

"I received some…"

"Don't stop, man…it feels good."

The air around them smelled like sweet darkness, simmering in truffle butter. Pierre was suddenly having second thoughts about saying anything at all. Why mess up this sexy evening with Anushka's drama? But he had to know the truth.

"Why didn't you tell me about your trip to Paris?"

"It was a last-minute thing, I hope you're not mad."

"I'm not. It's just that…I had to hear it from somebody else."

"Who?"

"Anushka."

The sound of her name made his body tense.

"I didn't know you two were so close."

"We're not." Pierre took a breath. "She invited me to brunch at the bistro. She told me things that I thought were interesting. Things that I think you should be aware of, like Darshan being the owner and the executive chef at Indo-French Bistro."

"Yeah, man. He is. I thought you knew that."

"No, I didn't. You made it seem like you were the head chef and executive."

"I am!"

"You're not."

"Dude, Darshan is never there. I'm the one that makes all the decisions dealing with that place."

"There's more. Why didn't you tell me that Darshan was your half-brother?"

Marquis froze. All the emotions and tension slammed back into his body. He shook Pierre off his back and stood erect. Pierre crumpled onto the bed like a cheap slut. Marquis's hands were planted on hips with an erection barely springing to life.

"Did Anushka tell you that?"

"She told me a lot of things. She was also the one who took the nude pictures of us. Did you know about this all along?"

He ignored the question. Marquis paced back and forth, scratching the back of his head, as if he was loosening his thoughts. His back glistened like a glazed delectable dessert. Pierre's hunger reignited. Marquis looked so hot mad. He was breathing heavily. Past and present memories piling up on his chest like massive stones.

"She had no right to tell you my business, bruh."

Pierre didn't understand why he was flipping out so much about people finding out Darshan was his half-brother. Then he thought back to those letters. *Yes!* Those letters. He wanted to address them, but caution held Pierre hostage. A breath was stuck in his throat. He had never seen Marquis so upset and had an urged to rub his back, telling him everything would be okay. Perhaps toss in a *take it easy*. But he refrained. Nobody wants to hear that when they're upset.

There was no more questions Pierre wanted to ask. He knew he was skating on thin ice. Pierre rose and collected his things. It was better this way, before things got out of hand. Pierre had a cocktail of mixed emotions, which consisted of spicy, sweet, sour, salty, and bitter. Bitter because Anushka knew something personal about Marquis and he didn't. Spicy because Marquis's sexiness turned him the fuck on. Sweet because Pierre really cared about him. Sour because their romantic relationship could go downhill real quick if this situation didn't turn around. He really didn't want to leave. He wanted to know more about Marquis's past. All his secrets. All the lies. All the deceits. All of everything. Getting to know the wild child in him that could potentially ruin their chances of being together.

Pierre reached the dilapidated elevators. The hallway looked and smelled like an old bar stuck in another decade. The elevator's down button was blackened by age and overuse. It rattled up like a broken icebox. Pierre waited for a moment, hoping Marquis would race out and tell him to come back in, Say things that could make the situation better. The elevator door opened. He never came.

⬥

Wild mushrooms littered the forest floor.

Marquis took Pierre hiking. Why did he let Marquis talk him into it? Pierre shook his head while trying not to trip over a rock or anything that resembled a snake. But at least Marquis was talking to him again.

"I was surprised to hear from you."

"Yeah, man, I needed time to myself."

"What happened the other day? You flipped out."

"Sorry about that, man. It just…"

He looked at Pierre unblinkingly, as if judging to see he was worthy of what he was about to say, but out of impulse he ran and climbed a rocky cliff. Pierre thought he had lost his freakin' mind as he watched Marquis's muscles bulge with each grip, the sun French-kissing his whiskey skin.

Once at the top, he waved at Pierre to come up. This was crazy, Pierre thought. He started climbing up the rocky wall, parts of it threatening to crumble underneath his weight. Pierre regrets eating three slices of pumpkin pie this morning.

Marquis grabbed Pierre by the arm and pulled him up. Pierre was happy he made it without injury. He wanted to kiss the ground. He knew Marquis did this to deflect from the conversation, perhaps hoping Pierre would forget. They continued walking down an open path. Marquis's eyes were glued to the ground as if he was foraging for something he couldn't find.

"So?"

"Yes, Darshan is my half-brother. Happy? The letters you've read was written by me."

"How did Anushka get them?"

He shrugged. "Probably when she was over at my place."

"And why was she there?"

"Look, Pierre, we used to mess around, okay?"

"What?"

"It's over now. She broke things off when she found out I was…"

"Gay?"

"Man, whatever."

"Why is it so hard to tell people Darshan is your brother?"

"Half-brother. We share the same father, who had an affair with my mother while he was married to Mrs. Singh."

The news was so heavy that Pierre hadn't realized they'd stopped walking. The air around them was earthy and pungent from last night's rain. Black squirrels chased one another, scampering up and down massive trees that released a strong scent of pine. Since they'd known each other, this was as much they ever talked. The confused space between them felt new.

"How's your relationship with Darshan's mother?"

"It's distant. But I don't care. I'm pretty sure my face reminds her of the affair. She doesn't say it, but I know. She barely visits the bistro because of me. The only reason why I even work there is because of Darshan."

He kicked a lumpy rock that resembled a truffle.

"Where's your biological mother?"

"Your guess is as good as mine."

Marquis struck another rock with his foot, sending it soaring into a nearby pond, it made a heavy sound that scared off a family of wild birds. He cracked a bone in his neck, planting his hands on top of his head. His shirt hiked up inch by inch, showing a glossy black happy trail down to his boxers.

Pierre tried to shoo away indecent thoughts, they danced around in his head like dirty sugar plums. This wasn't the right moment for playtime while Marquis was sharing something so intimate. Or was it? There were plenty of trees around, and he knew Marquis was an exhibitionist.

"Have you sought therapy?"

"Yeah, man, that shit doesn't work. I'm still fucked up." He threw a rock this time.

"Are you moving to Paris?"

"Why? You want me to stay?" He smirked.

Pierre punched him in the arm. Marquis acted like the blow was strong enough to knock him over. A couple of hikers carrying backpacks walked past eating berries and trail mix from plastic bags, playing music from a small device.

Pierre wanted to ask him about the Haitian exploitation scandal and the café's break-in. Did Anushka put him up to it? He decided to let it go. It was no longer important.

"I'm glad you told me all this."

Marquis was quiet and turned to Pierre.

"Thanks for listening."

# CHAPTER 31

They were on a private jet.

Zola couldn't believe Darshan's family had a home in France. Somewhere secluded outside of Paris. She was a ball of nerves. Everything was happening so quickly. One minute she was single, the next she was engaged in Paris. Darshan calculated the party should be in full swing by the time they reached the castle. Zola almost flipped out when he mentioned castle. His family lived in a freakin' castle? She hoped the dress she brought along was good enough for the occasion. It wasn't often she dined at a castle, in France. Darshan told her all the big people would be there, food critics, top chefs, designers, and celebrities. Zola just hoped she wouldn't be the only Black person in the room.

Another cart came around serving champagne. Zola grabbed a glass of Dom Perignon and a mini bottle to take back to Toronto as a souvenir. Darshan laughed. Zola wore a look that read, *You can take a girl out of the hood, but you can't take the hood out of the girl.*

There was some turbulence. The champagne helped thin out her nerves, but Darshan could sense she was still tense about flying and everything else. He placed a blanket over her for comfort and caressed her inner thigh for reassurance. She melted like butter. The warmth of his touch and the sensation of the booze bear-hugged her insides like a cozy furnace, placing her in a deep sleep.

⌒

They checked into a hotel before heading to the party. While Darshan was in the shower, Zola decided to call her mother to tell her the good news.

"Congratulations, baby. When am I going to meet Hakeem?"

Zola swallowed hard. She failed to mention she was marrying Darshan. How could she word this to her Christian mother without sounding like an impulsive slut? She and Darshan totally skipped the relationship status part and jumped right into marriage. She even didn't have time to post pictures of Paris. She was having too much fun. A part of her was also uneasy about posting pictures of her dating outside her race. What would her Black friends say? What would her family say? *Oh! She lives in Canada now, Black men aren't good enough for her.* That wasn't the case at all.

"Mom, about that…his name is Darshan, and he actually Indian."

Her mother fell silent. "Indian?"

"Yes, Mom, Indian."

"Oh dear, I think you mean Native Indian. You know we have Indian in our blood, more on your father's side, though. His mother was half Cherokee. She had that good hair, you know, god rest her soul. I think it's a blessing you're keeping your father's roots alive. He would be so proud."

Zola sighed. "Mother, I mean, he's Indian…like from India."

Her mother fell silent again, trying to process everything that was being said.

Zola tried to explain that everything happened so quickly. She also failed to mention that she was in France. She wanted to spoon-feed her mother little information at a time. Zola's mother seemed a little hurt that her daughter kept all this from her. Zola apologized and asked for her blessing.

"Of course, baby, you have my blessing. I just wish your father was here to hear the good news, that's all. I hope you'll be happy being married, as I always been. Your father was a good man. I miss him every day of my life." Zola could imagine her mother staring up at her husband's picture mounted on the living room wall.

After Zola hung up, she sent her mother a slew of pictures of the trip in Paris. Her wrapped in Darshan's embrace underneath the Eiffel Tower, smiling like two goof heads.

Her mother said she thought the pictures were beautiful and Darshan a good-looking man. She was happy that her daughter was living her life. She also thought her daughter was so lucky to be in Paris, a place she had never been. A place that never entered her mind to travel to. She couldn't wait to meet her new son in-law. She couldn't wait to tell all her church friends.

Before getting off the phone, her mother preached to Zola to stay safe and try not to go anywhere alone. Zola thought her mother watched too many action movies.

Zola was happy that her mother was on board with her engagement. Now let's see how Darshan's family would take the news.

⁓

Savory reductions and curry sauces aromas filled the *château*.

Every light was on through the tall windows. It was a limestone façade. Around the compound were soaring trees and exotic gardens. Expensive cars were parked in the roundabout driveway. Indian, Canadian, and France flags flapped proudly in the night's sky, looking like an embassy of nations.

The sleeping landscape morphed into beautiful foliage as they drove to the chateau. Castle-like country homes camouflaged behind leafy trees. Wild grass transitioned into manicured lawns and vineyards. The Seine River hugged the compound, looking like a sparkling black necklace.

Zola had no idea the Singhs were so rich. Leading up to the château, massive trees stood erect like soldiers awaiting their arrival. The tall iron gate was decorated in gold flamboyant symbols. It swung open smoothly as if floating on air. The name on top— *Château La Singh*—broke in half and reattached after they entered.

Zola swallowed hard as she looked up at the four-story château, which boasted little cute black balconies. The driver opened her door. She linked arms with Darshan who wore a charcoal black *kurta*. He looked like a prince. This was Zola's first-time seeing him dress traditional.

He escorted her up the porch. If daylight, she would've seen a garden that stretched out for acres with fat butternut squashes, heirloom tomatoes, and pumpkins waiting to be plucked. The garden was used for the new bistro and high-end markets, some vegetables prechopped and packaged with Mrs. Singh's face plastered on the cover.

Zola thought the compound looked like a beach resort. It screamed rich and privileged. A place to raise your children without a care in the world. A home that required a shit-load of staff and protection.

They walked into the château. The foyer was bigger than Zola's whole apartment. A big crystal chandelier hung like freezing rain. She heard laughter somewhere in the house. Her chest was tight; each step made her heart constrict inside. She instantly felt out of place. She wanted to make an escape. Her blood turned cold. Realization set in that there was no turning back. Someone could toss a grenade in the living room, and it wouldn't have caused as much damage as she was about to make.

She gingerly walked down a long hall, passing a kitchen full of top chefs and servers. She couldn't believe her eyes. She heard light footsteps echoing on the marble floors meeting them halfway. Her heart fluttered. She heard Darshan's name being called out in a sing-song fashion, as if he was royalty coming home from a great war.

Mrs. Singh glided toward them. The living room expanded beyond her like a maze at a grand museum. She was dripping in diamonds, and gold bangles jingled on her arm like classical music. Her hair was simple yet elegant. Her eyes combed the length of Zola's body, disapproval written all over her dainty face.

"I'm so glad you can bring your friend."

"Mother, this is Zola. She's my fiancée."

The news shook Mrs. Singh to the core. It was worse than she thought. Her hand flung to her chest. She wanted to be happy but wasn't.

"Oh… Well…Welcome to our home."

A server hands Zola a glass of champagne. She noticed gold flakes floating with the bubbles. As they drifted farther into the château, there were big family portraits hung along the walls. Everything looked so grand. So old. So new. Precious crystals sat behind white-glassed cabinets. Light cream sofas stood on gold-filigreed legs like centerpieces.

There was a long table hosting a few important guests, two sparkling chandeliers hovered above. Zola was happy to see a small turnout. The setup looked very intimate. The women looked like peacocks in their exquisite colorful saris and the men looked equally as fierce.

"Who is this beautiful creature?" asked Darshan's cousin, who owned four restaurants in New York City and Dubai.

"This is my—"

"Don't pester my son with your boring questions," said Mrs. Singh. "Eat. Eat. Eat. Or the food will get cold." She threw her scarf over her shoulder. The news would be a shock to the whole family and to the press, which were present at the table. Mrs. Singh had to find a way to salvage the evening.

The food came out one after another: green, yellow, and deep red curries hit the table. Rabbit simmered in spicy tomato. Tandoori duck in a creamy white truffle sauce with dill to brighten it up. Crab and lobster sizzling in herb butter and garlic. Saffron rice studded with pine nuts and yellow raisins cooked in rosewater. The delicious aromas floated around the room, stealing the show from expensive perfumes and masculine aftershaves.

Anushka was there. She had flown with Mrs. Singh in her private plane, leaving Godiva behind to hold down the fork at Indo-French bistro. Godiva's dream was shattered. She didn't understand how Anushka got the greenlight and she didn't. Anushka felt horrible how things pan out but she was over the moon to be in Paris. This was her chance. Her chance to win Darshan and blow the reporters over with her charm and wit. She was wearing an apricot sari with bangles to match. She looked at Zola's attire and wasn't too thrilled.

"Lovely dress, Zola."

"Thank you."

"Where did you get it, from a Black Lives Matter convention?"

Zola looked down at her black dress. It was plain but cute. That was how she liked it.

"No, I didn't. Maybe it's something you should attend someday, though."

Darshan cleared his throat. He didn't expect to see Anushka. Suddenly, he felt hot.

"Try this, Zola. I made it," said Anushka, passing her a bowl of a deep red sauce. Zola spooned it over yellow rice. She tasted it, and her mouth was on fire. She tossed back a mouthful of champagne, the gold bubbles blistering down her throat, gold flakes clung to her teeth. Rapid French and Hindi was flung across the table. Zola heard her name in the mix and felt embarrassed.

"What did you give her, Anushka?" Darshan quickly spooned *crème fraiche* onto Zola's plate which looked like yogurt with diced cucumbers and mint. Zola scooped a spoonful into her mouth. The mint and thick cream soothed her quickly. She glared at Anushka, who wore a slippery grin.

"I thought you could handle spice. It was vindaloo."

Zola had never had it before and would never touch it again. Anushka spooned the lethal hot red curry onto her plate and took in a hefty bite.

Darshan handed Zola a mild curry.

Anushka challenged her to pronounce the curry's name. Zola wasn't in the mood to make a complete ass of herself. So, she ignored the challenge. Zola couldn't help noticing Anushka eating with her hand. She did it with ease and grace.

"Wait, wait, wait," said the cousin, putting up his curry-soaked fingers. "You're telling me Darshan hasn't showed you the right way to eat Indian food?" Zola shook her head. "Here, let me show you." He took his long fingers and mixed a few grains of rice with the curry and tossed it in his mouth. He made it look effortless. If Zola attempted it, she knew it would end horribly. She couldn't afford to ruin her new black dress from Paris, a dress she was planning to wear more than once on this trip.

"Why do Indians eat with their hands?" asked Zola, wondering why Darshan hadn't told her about this etiquette before meeting his family.

"It makes the food taste better." Anushka chimed in.

Mrs. Singh posed a question to Zola "What do your parents do for a living?"

Zola swallowed hard; she thought the question was a little intrusive. "My father is deceased, but he was a cook, and he owned a small market in the neighborhood where I grew up in Atlanta."

"Your mother. What does she do?"

"She works in retail."

Mrs. Singh shifted uncomfortably in her seat. "And your siblings, what do they do?"

Zola looked over at Darshan for help. She felt like she was sinking like a ship. She couldn't take this interrogation anymore.

"I'm the only child."

"What school did you attend?" asked Anushka.

Zola wanted to tell her to mind her own damn business. But thought she should be nice. "I didn't attend college." She suddenly wanted to run outside and head back to America, where social distancing was still in practice.

"Oh! I thought owning a cafe, you would have gone to some prestigious culinary school," said Anushka, enjoying every minute of this humiliation.

"A cafe! What kind of cafe?" the cousin asked, sucking the rich sauce from his fingers.

"It's called the Spice Café. I specialize in Southern cuisine. I serve candied yams, macaroni and cheese, corn bread, smothered pork chops, fried chicken, peach cobbler, collard greens, you name it." Everyone stared at each other in silence, not sure if they had tried any of these dishes. Mac and cheese, yes. But not the way Zola made it, with eggs, cream, and butter.

"Wow! That sounds delicious. Maybe you and Darshan should have a cook off…Indo-French Bistro vs. Spice Café," said the cousin, grinning.

Zola looked confused. "Indo-French Bistro?"

"Yeah, our family owns restaurants all over the world. We're opening another one in Paris. That's why Darshan was there this past month. How's the business going anyway, Darshan?"

Darshan rubbed his hand over his face. Zola was totally stunned, lost for words. He was her competitor. Her enemy. Why didn't he tell her? Why did he make her look like a fool?

She excused herself from the table, and her heavy footsteps hit the floor frantically. Everyone's eyebrows tugged together in confusion, looking around the table as if to find some answers to what just happened. However, Mrs. Singh wore a happy expression.

Zola ran out of the house, footsteps pounding down the white porch. Crying. Wailing for mercy to save her from this nightmare.

⸋

The château and the full moon lit the night. The river flowed deceptively dark and slow. Zola stood on a terrace, sucking in the cool air. She was having second thoughts about marrying Darshan. His culture was too different from her own. His family would never accept her into their stock. Why did Darshan have to lie to her? Why couldn't he tell her about the restaurants? The money.

Darshan appeared behind her. "Hey, Zo, what was that all about back there?"

"Are you kidding me? When were you planning on telling me you were the CEO at Indo-French bistro?"

"The reason why I didn't tell you because I didn't want you to look at me differently. I hear the things you say about the bistro. How you despise the place. The place I'm trying hard to keep afloat. An empire I'm trying to maintain that my great-grandparents started. I see the look of disdain in your eyes when the name is brought up."

"Because you guys put me through hell. All the lies, all the torments."

"I don't know what you are talking about."

"Telling the world I was exploiting illegal immigrants, the break-ins…stealing our customers. It has all been too much. Now this! How could you let your family ask me all those personal questions? Interrogating me like a criminal."

"Look, Zola, I didn't find anything wrong with them asking you questions. Indians do that. It's a part of our culture to find out what friends and family do for a living, especially if they know you are the love of my life."

A boat sailed by filled with tourists. They flashed pictures of the château. It caught Darshan's attention. He thought this part of the river was restricted after a certain hour.

"But what about me? What about my Black heritage? What about my feelings? Do I discard everything I am just to assimilate to yours? Huh? Do I?" she said with tears streaming, stabbing a finger into his chest, once, twice, three times. He took a step back, giving her space. She wanted him to hurt the way she was hurting. Cry the way she was crying. Make him feel her humiliation.

She looked off into the night. A thin layer of clouds crossed the moon, creating shadows over the water and over their faces. Darshan's eyebrows were set demonically heavy and glossy. His lashes whispered seduction. His eyes resembling espresso-chocolate-drops.

"To ask what my family does for a living? Really? It's none of their damn business, especially Anushka's. Why is she here anyway?" She gave him a searching glance. For someone who was photogenic, he was so hard to read. They were trying to figure each other out, like two people on a boat lost at sea in the dark.

"I don't know. But look, don't make this about Anushka. She doesn't matter."

"And your mother! Sitting there with that smirk on her face, enjoying every second of the massacre. I'm surprised she didn't join in for the kill."

"Do you think you're overreacting just a bit?"

Zola locked her arms. "Just leave me be."

He looked at Zola for a long while and felt a pang of guilt. He realized he was being a jerk. He also realized he was insensitive to her feelings. He should've informed her about the Indian customs; it hadn't entered his mind that it would affect her. He grew up with them. It was second nature. He was stuck between two worlds.

"Zola. I'm sorry. I do realize that I fucked up. Can you forgive me?" Zola's face softened. He pulled her into a hug, her hair ever shifting to a maze of smells: avocado, coconut cream, shea butter, and toasted almonds. Zola thought he smelled like strawberries growing out of a burning log. She felt small in his arms. It felt good to hear his heartbeat against her ear.

She needed time to be alone. She wanted to go back to the hotel and soak in a hot bath. He didn't fight her; instead, he called for the driver, who came within minutes. Zola told Darshan to stay and enjoy the party. She would be okay. He didn't argue. She wanted him to spend time with his family. She climbed into the back seat of the black car and pulled off into the night.

Darshan stood there in the dark until the car melted behind trees. He ran his fingers through his hair and punched the air. He kicked a rock into the river, messing up his expensive black shoes. French music was playing from the house. He would make sure to call Zola to see she made it back safely.

It was midnight. His eyes were midnight. Everything about him was midnight. That was the thing Zola loved about him. He reminded her of midnight, her favorite time of the day, but he didn't know this. He wondered if she loved him the way he loved her.

He sure hoped that was still the case.

# CHAPTER 32

**L**etters were littered across the coffee table.

Pizza was ordered. Two slices were already eaten. Italian sausage perfumed Pierre's apartment.

Pierre decided to do some investigation. In Marquis's letters, the Indo-French bistro used to be called India 65. Mrs. Singh renamed it after losing her husband. Some of their restaurants around the world still had the original name. The menu was still Indian. It was Darshan's idea to turn the Toronto bistro into a fusion place in memory of his father. Mrs. Singh just helped execute it.

The computer swirled to life. He wondered if Marquis had ever reached out to his biological mother. Did Marquis need answers? Closure? Was he still upset with her? Did he desire her back into his life? Had she ever reached out to him?

In his letters, he said Mrs. Singh raised him. However, never treated him like her own. Never showed him love and affection like she did Darshan, her true son.

Facebook opened. Pierre clicked on Marquis's profile. Immediately a picture of him and Darshan as young boys popped up at the CN Tower with their father. Another picture showed Darshan in Paris with his mother. Marquis was tagged in the photo, but he was nowhere to be found. Darshan was eating a stuffed crêpe, ham and cheese, perhaps with Nutella. He was eating it joyfully underneath the Eiffel Tower, wind blowing into his carrot-top-hair. There were so many answers Pierre needed to know, especially if he was going to be in a serious relationship with Marquis.

He clicked on Marquis's Facebook gallery. He looked so good in his chef coat. Pierre foraged through his galleries, shifting through old memories. More pictures popped up of him wearing his chef's whites. Anushka appeared in a few snapshots, some in Marquis's embrace. Jealousy simmered through Pierre. He had to admit they made a cute couple. He clicked off their picture.

Pierre's cell buzzed next to him. It was a text from Zola. She might be ending her vacation early and coming home. Good! Pierre thought. He couldn't help but feel like he was doing everything at the cafe. Cooking. Cleaning. Blogging. Ordering. Taking customers' bullshit. Firing. Hiring. You name it, he did it.

Pierre continued to forage through the photos. Some with Marquis with short puffy hair. Knees knocking. Eyes bright. Lashes wide. Skin lighter than cocoa butter. Pierre couldn't believe Marquis looked so innocent. How could anyone leave that face? Darshan was taller than Marquis by a few inches, arms wrapped around his little brother's shoulders. Darshan's hair falling into his eyes. Straight and black. Eyes deep and rich. Pierre tried to imagine their childhood together but couldn't.

There was an open bottle of red wine on the coffee table. Pierre topped up his glass and plopped the bottle partially onto Marquis's letters. *Oops!* He didn't mean to be so reckless; the wine was beginning to talk to him. He took a lingering sip. Blackberries sloshed down his throat giving him the flavor of black figs. He also tasted his favorite notes: bramble bush and boysenberry which gave the wine its devilish look.

He continued foraging. More happy moments. More celebrations. More family gatherings. More missed school plays. More missed singing rehearsals. Then Pierre froze. He leaned close to examine the next picture. There was a woman dressed in jeans that looked like it was carried over from the eighties and a tucked in white shirt that looked burrowed from a dear friend. Hair puffy and curly. Marquis in her embrace. Maybe their last embrace.

The wine had started to make Pierre feel numb. The room became quiet, exhausted even, from all the memories attached to it. He started to hear the faint sounds of people coming home from work, slamming their apartment doors, the hum of the night's traffic.

Pierre squinted. Marquis's and his mother's hair was identical. Smooth. Glossy. Wavy. Curly. He read the comments section. Nothing. No caption. He checked the likes. Five. Pierre debated if he should like it. The alcohol was making him bold. The dark fruits hummed in his throat like a sloppy French kiss. The glass of wine sat on the coffee table, being his cheerleader. If he liked it, Marquis would know he was snooping around, digging through his past, a past he was trying to leave behind.

Pierre imagined how many people looked at the photo and refused to like it. Ignoring Marquis's past. Ignoring his pain, ignoring the mother-and-son bond. Ignoring all the missed years between them. Ignoring all the missed birthdays. Ignoring all the missed celebrations. Missed Christmases. Missed graduations.

Pierre heart the photo. *Shit! What have I done?* Too late to reverse it. Marquis probably already saw it. He was always glued to his phone. Pierre stared at his name under the photo: Pierre Jackson. He almost had second thoughts to unlike it. Maybe Marquis didn't see it yet. But Pierre left it. Somehow it felt like a symbolic acceptance, an acceptance of Marquis's past, the acceptance of their growing relationship. He checked the list of names of people who liked it too. All South Asian names. Pierre assumed some were estranged relatives, people who were merely important in Marquis's memories.

Pierre saw three women's names. He clicked on one. She wore a sari. She had pale skin and straight hair. He clicked on another. Hair curly. Retro clothes. It was her. She had filled out a bit around the face, but it was her, maintaining the same icy expression. He noticed Marquis had liked her profile picture; there was some hope there after all. Pierre foraged through her gallery. She was remarried and had more children.

The night air blew generously through the window. Pierre had forgotten to close it. Buttercup stretched out on his foot. He didn't want to disturb her, so he stayed put. He had an urge to rub her head but refrained. This was too good to lose focus. He looked at her location: Ottawa. A four-hour drive. Pierre picked up his glass of wine and took a long sip.

❧

A few days later, Pierre arrived at Marquis's mother's cottage. It was snugged around pine trees and open land. It overlooked the Ottawa River, and the sky was the color of milk. The clouds seemed thicker out here. The air seemed fresher. A cool breeze whistled. A small dollar-store Canadian flag stabbed the ground, flapping weakly. The white paint on the cottage was chipping by years of heavy rain and snow. A clutter of flowers led up to a cracked porch. The heavy front door was open but the screen door was shut. A dark figure moved around inside.

The pastries in Pierre's hand shifted around in a pink box. Freshly baked from his cafe. The dark figure emerged.

"You Pierre?"

Her voice was smooth like butter cream. She looked like Marquis, skin sweet as ginger and eyes the color of whisky. Black hair thick and curly like an angry storm of clouds. The wind picked up, and her hair barely fought against it. She stood with arms locked on the porch. She seemed alone.

"Yes. I'm Pierre Jackson. A friend of Marquis."

She looked over Pierre's shoulder, perhaps expecting to see her son. A chance to smell his scent once again. A chance to embrace him. But he wasn't there.

"Please come in."

She held the screen door open, and Pierre stepped inside. It seemed like the house had lost its smell of cooking. No mess to clean up after. No more lunches needed to be made. No more trying out new recipes. Food was no longer a topic or priority.

A faded image of Jesus hung on the wall, surrounded by figurines and pictures. Pierre wondered if she was Catholic. It looked like a life different from Marquis's apartment. No restaurant books or Hindu pictures. No chef's awards. No images of fast cars and hot girls.

They sat across from each other in short silence. Dark circles marked her face. She stared at Pierre's red plaid jeans for a moment before offering something to drink.

"Would you like some tea?"

"Yes, please."

She moved with a tiredness in her walk. She touched her lower back as if the pain been keeping her company throughout these lonely years. Flowered wallpaper in the kitchen could be seen from the hallway. The kitchen looked as if it was big enough for two people, maybe three; four would cause chaos. Clinking cups were heard. She nuked the tea in the microwave. She couldn't be bothered watching it boil on the stove.

She handed Pierre a cup decorated with flowers. He took a small sip and thought it tasted like metal. Pierre was hoping for something little more flare; like dirty chai made with heavy cream and brown sugar, or saffron tea made with condense milk.

"Thanks for responding to my Facebook message and agreeing to meet with me. Sorry that Marquis couldn't come. I didn't tell him I was coming."

The sound of her son's name caused her to lower her head. Pierre didn't know if it was out of shame, guilt, or disappointment. Maybe all three.

"You're his friend, right?"

Pierre cleared his throat. "You can say that. I'm a close friend."

"What brings you here, Pierre?"

"I'm here to talk about your son. I know it bothers him that you are no longer in his life. Excuse my directness, but why did you two stop talking? I would have asked you this over the phone, but I thought meeting in person would be better."

"It wasn't my choice. It was his father's."

"Excuse me?"

"His father didn't want me to come back into Marquis's life after abandoning him on their doorstep. He thought it would be best. I was young and foolish. What did I know what was best for my son?" She looked away out the window, then back at Pierre. "But he was right, I guess. Me coming back into the picture would've complicated things."

"But you're his mother."

"There are things I regret. Things I wish I could take back. Things I wish I could undo. But it's already done. I only can live in the moment. During those times it was hard. I'm not proud of what I've done."

"Were you two ever in a relationship? You know… You and Mr. Singh."

"No, darling. We weren't." She looked off again to a distant place and turned back. "He was already married. I was his mistress and housemaid. I know I shouldn't have, but I did. He was a lonely man. It happened so quickly. The look on Mrs. Sigh's face when she caught us in the kitchen. The trouble I caused. I had to leave, of course. Later on, I got pregnant. I couldn't make ends meet. I was living on the streets for a while. After Marquis was born, I stayed at a women's shelter; he was a precious baby. Never caused a fuss. The most beautiful thing I have ever seen. Look…" She suddenly rose, disappeared into a dark hall.

Pierre looked about the space. He smelt a dog, but there were no animals around. She came back with a baby photo of her cradling Marquis wrapped in a pink blanket. Pierre's eyes glistened; he pinched the corner, studying it as if he had magic to bring it to life. The photo was worn and cracked like the bottom of her foot. The picture looked as if it was touched many times. "It was hard for me to leave him, you know. It wasn't easy. He was the cutest thing. But I wanted him to have the best in life. A life I couldn't offer him. But I know now that me being there was enough. Rumor has it I ran off with another man. All lies. There was no man. Just Mr. Singh."

"Did you love each other… You know…you and Mr. Singh."

"He offered to run away with me once. But I told him to stay. I didn't want him to leave Darshan. It would've broken his little heart. What a beautiful boy he was and still is. I loved cooking for him. He enjoyed my Indian dishes, more than his mother's." She paused and taking a birdlike sip of her tea. "I knew he would be a great big brother to Marquis, and I was right. I've heard he made him head chef at that fancy French Bistro."

"Yes, he is."

"Those boys loved their father, especially Marquis. I would see pictures of them on Facebook, fishing, hunting, hiking, and cooking." Her voice sounded like sun on flourishing grass. "His father even taught him how to cook French food. His father was so proud of him."

"How did he die?"

"In a plane crash."

Pierre's eyebrows shot up.

"It was very unexpected. He was coming back from his yearly trip from Paris. He loved France. If you asked me, I think he wanted to retire there. Maybe because his parents were from there. Who knows?" She shrugged. She looked down at her tea that was now cold. Pierre saw a fly land on the rim. She waved it away like she was used to it.

"Marquis never told me that."

"I can imagine he wouldn't."

"Are you married? I see family pictures."

"I never married. Just short-lived relationships."

"You should come to Toronto to eat at my cafe and perhaps see Marquis."

She took a moment to respond. "I'm pretty sure he wouldn't want to see me." She paused again, voice starting to sound like cold tea left too long on a switched-off stove. "I probably would conjure up too many bad memories for him. I still remember him pulling on my leg to stay. I had to pry his little fingers off. Tears were rolling down his cheeks. I cried so much on the bus that day. It felt like someone had ripped out my heart. I don't deserve to be forgiven. I was a horrible mother. I thought I was doing the right thing. Perhaps I didn't want the responsibility of raising a child. I don't know why I did the things I've done." There was a small tear begging to fall.

"Well, just think about it. I'm sure he'll be happy to see you."

"I sent him messages before on Facebook, but they went ignored."

"Just give it some thought." With that said, Pierre rose from the dingy sofa marked by years of spilled juice and coffee. He gave her a warm hung. She smelled like cherry blossoms and sweet vanilla. She watched as he took leave, arms back in a tight fold, the house a yawn of darkness behind her.

Pierre did all he could do; he hoped he didn't make matters worse. The phone buzzed in his pocket once he got inside the rental car; he grabbed it from the folds of his jeans. He looked down at his phone and read: *What have you done!*

⁀

Mina thought there was no point in getting up in the morning. There was no job to go to. No floors to scrub. No meals to cook. No clothes to wash. No sheets to fold. She was tossed out like a broken coconut.

She deserved it. She had no right sleeping with someone's husband. She knew this time would come; she just didn't know when. Now she was pregnant. How in the hell she was going to take care of a baby? She was barely a baby herself. Nineteen years old and uneducated. How would she send him to college? How would she give him the things he needed? How would she make him suitable for an Indian marriage? Make him the man he needed to be. This baby would hate her. Hate her for not providing. Hate her for not giving him a better life. Hate her for not giving him privileges. She was unprepared, too irresponsible to have a child.

Just like her mother who grew up in the slums of Mumbai, born on a mud floor. Her mother watched women outside her shack carry buckets of filthy water after washing dirty clothes and dirty dishes, spilling some as they balanced it on their heads. Men squatting, some chewing and spitting pan, others brushing their rotten teeth with the same water they used to bath themselves. Mina's mother knew she wanted more. She travelled farther in the inner city for better work. She was tired of seeing her parents barely making any money.

She got a job as a maid. However, she didn't keep the job long. She fooled around with the delivery boy who came daily. They flirted every chance they got. He asked her to run away with him, and she did. He loved her, and she loved him. She became pregnant months later in a rundown apartment. When her boyfriend found out about her pregnancy, he started acting out, no longer wanting to be held down by a relationship, and certainly not a baby. He left her for another, much prettier woman. A woman she considered a friend. Her heart was broken. Blinking back tears that burned her eyes, she looked down at her black skin, black as a truffle. How could she compete with the other woman?

She was scared as hell bringing a baby into this cruel world. If she went back home pregnant without a husband, she'd be looked at as a failure, a fast girl, a *chutiya*. A woman no smarter than her own mother selling vegetables at the corner on a dirty mat. When Mina was born, she gave her daughter away to an orphanage, leaving her on their doorstep. She thought the baby would have a better life, a better future.

Mina now was grown and moved to Canada with little to her name. Some would think it was courageous of her. It wasn't hard for her to leave. She didn't have any parents to miss, any relatives or friends to mourn her disappearance. She was merely a ghost moving through this crazy world.

When Mina arrived in Toronto, she saw an ad for housekeeping. She went to the job opening and got the job on the spot. She thought Mrs. Singh was a formidable woman, very sure of herself, something Mina wasn't. Mrs. Singh had a nice home, the biggest Mina had ever seen. In her eyes it was a mansion, but to Mrs. Singh it was a modest home. For Mina, it was a place she could never imagine for herself; it didn't matter how many floors she scrubbed, she could never afford something this spacious and beautiful. She was accustomed to being poor. Poverty clung to her like a good friend.

Mrs. Singh was nice to Mina. They became close, almost sister-like. Mrs. Singh was only a few years older than her. When Mrs. Singh and her husband got into a heated argument, it was Mina that Mrs. Singh would run to for consolation and reasoning.

"How could he not care for my restaurant, Mina? He said I was selfish. How am I selfish? I'm doing it for our family." Mina nodded. "It isn't true, is it, Mina? You will tell me the truth if I was being selfish, would you?"

Mina stayed quiet, watching the tears flow down her boss's face. If one was watching, they would've thought Mina was being callous towards Mrs. Singh's feelings, but Mina handled the situation the best way she knew how. She would sit still and rub Mrs. Singh's back, occasionally giving her a tissue for her tears. "Why was he so mean to me? Tell me, *na*? Does he see what I'm doing is providing for our children? It isn't my fault he hates his job being a bus driver. Who told him to take that stupid job?" She cried more into the tissue; she talked more, but it was muddled. Mina looked at her cautiously, lost for words.

The following day, Mina cooked butter chicken, Darshan's favorite. He would beg her to make it every Tuesday and Wednesday. He loved it so much that Mrs. Singh wrote down the recipe; she couldn't help feeling a little jealous. Mina would go even further to make flatbread from scratch smothered with garlic and butter.

One day, Darshan noticed her baby bump. His little hands touched it lovingly. He didn't say anything. Mina thought he must think it was extra fat. Mrs. Singh didn't notice the small bump; she thought it was extra weight too.

When Mr. Singh waited for his wife to go to work and children left for school, he snuck into the kitchen and grabbed Mina's by the waist. Today, he hadn't noticed anything different about her. Not even the baby bump. She fisted and twisted his dark hair. His hand went up her dress, squeezing her heavy breasts. They were round, like melons. He pressed harder against her. She arched her neck like a beautiful swan. She loved it. He loved it. The moans increased. The touching increased. The temperature in the kitchen increased. He remembered the first night he wanted to touch her. The night he sucked greedily at her breast. A night when he got into a heated fight with his wife, and she left in anger and went to that stupid restaurant. He hated that place. He loved French food. He didn't grow up eating Indian food. The flavors were foreign to him. The bistro always got in the way of their romance. He confided in Mina, hoping she could understand his troubles. His loneliness. His frustrations. She nodded but didn't rub his back like she did Mrs. Singh's. She didn't know why. But the way he looked made her want to cradle him in her arms.

She loved these feelings he gave her. It made her feel wanted and needed, even desirable. She'd never been looked at this way before by another man. His eyes were pressing. Dark and savory. One would think he had on eyeliner. Mina got lost in them. His skin was black. Black like roasted cinnamon left in a smoker. He looked as if he only breathed in sweet air.

The butter chicken was burning. He pulled down her undergarments. Her hand tried to turn off the stove while the other clutched her breast. Before he could dive inside her, there was a scream. They froze.

It was Mrs. Singh.

# CHAPTER 33

**P**aris **woke up** to clapping thunder.

It rained hard and fierce. Staring Zola in the face like a bad omen. She rose from the bed and closed the French windows to prevent water from coming in.

When the rain stopped, a fog settled over the city, crushing everything into a romantic French gray. It encouraged some people to pull out their old manuscripts, others to go for a long stroll along the river while sipping on hot chocolate while dodging murky puddles.

Zola felt like a souffle taken out of the oven too soon. All the life in her seemed sucked out. She made a complete ass of herself at Darshan's family château. How could she face them again?

Darshan left early to check on the new bistro. They barely spoke about what happened that night. Maybe it was a good thing. Zola needed to sort out her thoughts. She didn't want to say anything she didn't mean.

She picked up her bowl of mango mousse. It was coated with an edible gold leaf. A gourmet chef had delivered it minutes ago, ordered by Darshan to make his fiancée feel better. He was not going to let the woman of his life starve, even when he was far away.

A chef carried the mousse carefully to Zola's suite, as if his life depended on it. He was almost tempted to asked Zola for identification before handing it off. She showed up to the door looking a hot mess, thick hair shooting out in all directions, wrapped up in old clothes.

She hit the golden leaf with a spoon, it shattered like beautiful glass. With each bite, her emotions were rebooted. The embarrassment, the shame, the impulsiveness, the anger.

Zola decided to call Courtney. She needed to talk to someone.

"Get the fuck out! You're engaged to Darshan Singh?"

"Yes, why is that so hard to believe?"

"Hello to Zola! He owns restaurants all over the freak'n world. He's practically a business tycoon."

"Darshan?"

"No, Mother Teresa. Of course, Darshan."

"You're getting him confused with someone else."

"Fuck, no. It's him. I'm sure of it. He owns the bistro in Toronto, also a few in India and Dubai, and maybe a few more in Singapore and Bali. Didn't you know?"

"No, I didn't know…well…yes. I knew about the Toronto one, and the new one in Paris."

"Come again? You're telling me you about to marry someone you don't even know. Damn! Is the sex that good?"

Zola sat quietly. Courtney must be mistaken. She must be talking about someone else. If this was true, she felt ridiculous. How could she not known all of this about the man she was going to marry? Should she also tell Courtney he lived in a castle too?

"Listen, Courtney. If this was true, I would've known about it. He only have two bistros."

Zola's phone buzzed a few times with incoming pictures. Zola checked the pictures that Courtney sent. *Fuck!* It was him. Pictures of Darshan cooking at various bistros.

'Tell me that isn't him."

"Yes…it is."

"I knew it! So, tell me how did it happened? How did he propose?"

"He proposed in Paris."

"Freakin' PARIS! Fuck, Zo! Talk about a big spender. I can't get a man to take me to Red Lobster. What else did y'all do?"

"He rented a helicopter, and we flew over the city. The Louvre was so beautiful from the sky. He took me to a Michelin star restaurant, and all we did was talk about food, food, food, food, and more FOOD! It was crazy. I never dated someone who enjoys food as much as me. Most guys I date just glaze over the subject. Not Darshan. We talked about all different types of food, from escargot to oysters to sea urchin…you name it…we even talked about—"

"Yeah, yeah, yeah…did y'all have hot sex?"

"*Courtney!*"

"Get to the freak'n point, geez." Courtney was popping buttery popcorn in the microwave. Zola heard the timer peep. She imagined Courtney wearing her pajamas in the late afternoon.

"Yes, and it was fantastic. He had me walking bowleg throughout the whole trip."

This made Courtney squeal like a banshee. "Damn, Zola. He's rich, ambitious, good-looking, and knows how to put it down in the bedroom. You're one lucky bitch. Darshan sounds like he's really into you. Guys like him are predatorial. When they see something they like, they go after it. Pounce on it like there's no tomorrow. Sounds like he's been hunting you for a while."

Zola rose and sat on the edge of the bed. "I don't know. Maybe we're rushing things."

"There you go. Now don't you go sabotaging yourself. You're always trying to find an excuse to fall back single."

"I've been burned before, and I just don't want to delude myself. This could be nothing but a fling."

"The man flew you first-class to Paris, took you on an all-exclusive shopping spree, screwed you like a ravenous beast. What more do you want? Him to declare a national holiday after you?"

Courtney's tone was dismissive now. Her patience was wearing thin. "Listen, Zo, he sounds like an amazing guy. He really does. I think he's the one, and you're the one for him. Yes, he was bit of a jerk for not being hundred percent honest with you about the restaurants, but he probably had a good reason. Maybe he wanted you to see him, just for him, and not for his money or status, or maybe he was trying to protect you, and y'all relationship. But I don't know, I'm just guessing."

Zola felt better after speaking with Courtney. Zola sat on her bed trying to make sense of the jumbled puzzle that had become her life this past month. Maybe Courtney was right. Maybe she should stop focusing on the past. She needed to live in the present.

But she still couldn't jeopardize her cafe. Couldn't her dear friend understand that? Courtney didn't know how it feels to have all your coins in a restaurant. It felt like the world was weighing on Zola's shoulders. She couldn't give up what she worked so hard for over a man she met within a month. Or could she? Zola knew very little about Indian marriages. She also knew very little about French men and how marriages worked in France.

She didn't know if she could live with someone that was always so neat. Melting her messy life with Darshan's would be challenging. He had so many nice things. She loved her little apartment. A place where she can be loud, crazy, and spill things without suffering any repercussions.

There was more she needed to know about Darshan. First, she needed to find out about all the restaurants he owned. Zola refused to believe he was as rich as Courtney claimed him to be. Courtney was known to be extra and melodramatic. Darshan had been in many kitchens. That was his job being a food writer. The pictures Courtney sent could have meant anything. Yes, he had a nice car and place, but maybe he was just good with his finances. Numbers got on Zola's nerves. If she could afford an accountant, she would have nice things too.

Zola reached for her phone. She googled the Singh family and their restaurants. Immediately, loads of photos and articles popped up of the culinary family's dynasty. Darshan was in a few shots. Zola assumed he didn't like being in the limelight. But the ones he was in, he looked devilishly handsome. Courtney was right. He certainly was an acclaimed chef who owned restaurants all over the world. Zola felt silly that she was engaged to a man with a secret identity.

Zola saw a photo of herself in one of the articles. She clicked on it, and it took her directly to a French blogger's page. The photo was incriminating, showing her crying profusely into Darshan's chest on the château's terrace. The article read:

*Darshan flies off to South of France to rip apart another restaurant. Is he giving bad reviews out of anger due to relationship troubles? Or should he be worried about his own Paris bistro falling underneath the wire of a Michelin star? And who is this new lady friend, Zola Washington? Or should we be focused on his new hot chef, Anushka Black?*

*Will bad boy Darshan ever settle for one woman? Ladies pucker up, you might be next on his simmering list of hookups.* Underneath the picture it said: *Zola Washington is later spotted fighting with Darshan Singh in front of the family's château before storming off into the night, drunk and alone. A drunken Zola makes a scene at the premiere party of Paris 65, embarrassing herself and the duke of culinary arts.*

Zola was mortified. She plunged her face into her hands. *How can this be happening?* She needed a drink. She ordered French wine to be brought up to her suite. She poured it and sauntered to the balcony to watch the Seine River. Only a few weeks in Paris, and Zola was already in the headlines. Media was speculating who she was. Would she live up to the family's royal status? Would she be the head chef at Paris 65? There were more pictures of herself online than on her phone. She was so wrapped up having a good time in Paris, she forgot to check social media. She was never a social media whore. Foodists were already dubbing her the new princess of culinary cuisine. Her Instagram followers went up by the thousands. This was crazy. She touched her head and couldn't believe she was suddenly famous.

∽

Paris 65 bistro was empty when Darshan arrived that morning. Zola was fast asleep when he left the hotel. His heavy footsteps echoed throughout the restaurant. There was a strong scent of jasmine and peach colored roses that peppered space. The crew wasn't expected to be in for another hour. He would have to go over the new menu and show them how to cook the new dishes.

He wore black shoes, a black button-up shirt, black slacks, and his favorite black watch; even the intensity of his face screamed black. His glossy eyebrows sat heavy on his face as he studied *the book.*

The current menu looked like a wedding invitation. He scratched out the lamb chutney burgers. He thought it must have been Marquis's idea. He added tandoori fish and fennel garnished with pomegranate seeds and grilled pine nuts. He crossed off more items and added masala omelet stuffed with camembert and grilled broccolini. For dessert he canceled crème brulée and wrote in poached pears in a spiced red wine reduction, served with *paan* ice cream.

His eyebrows were gleaming from the morning light starting to come through the window. The muscles in his neck and back were beginning to ache from hunching over the counter. He stretched a little and went back to revamping the menu. Adding, cancelling, adding and cancelling. He thought about Zola's philosophy on creating the perfect dish at her cafe... *Food should be playful... Food should look like food... Food should be made with love... Food should transport the eater into memories... Food should be satisfying.* But to Darshan, food should look like art. His dishes had to look like a complicated painting worth a thousand words. Coming in second and third was never an option. Mrs. Singh instilled in her children that they must come in first place in anything they do. It was all about being the best.

He checked his phone and listened to his voicemail. He had several news outlets wanting him to do an interview about the bistro. Another message was a celebrity TV show asking him to do a competition cook-off. He deleted it. It wasn't his thing. There were a few Parisian girls hitting him out the blue after he gave them his number years ago. He remembered a few of them being supermodels and yoga instructors. He deleted them all.

He looked out the window and saw Zola across the street. She wore more lip gloss than usual to compete with the fabulous Parisian women. She was holding a bag of artisanal chocolates. She was looking at a for-sale sign on a cookie shop. He leaned forward onto the marble counter and watched her. He lowered his lashes, veiling his midnight eyes. She didn't look toward him. He started to get offended. Didn't she like his restaurant? Didn't she find it interesting? He continued to observe her with hawk-like vision. Lashes on fleek once again. She pulled out her cellphone and snapped pictures, not once looking at the Paris 65 bistro before walking away.

Why was Zola taking a picture of that empty shop? Why didn't she text him when she woke up? Didn't she recognize his black Porsche parked outside? The one they drove back to Paris in from the chateau. Questions raced through his mind. He thought about what Anushka said when he overheard her conversation at the party: *Zola just wants to use the family's name for the success of her café and then destroy the bistro.* He suddenly had an urge to flag Zola down.

But something prevented him. Was Anushka telling the truth? Was Zola planning on using their name to open a restaurant of her own, in Paris? Was she trying to destroy them, wipe them clean off the map? He shook free from the nefarious thoughts. He went back to revamping the menu. Then his eyes flung back to the for-sale sign.

⁓

Later that evening, Zola found a little cafe. The sign over the door was too cute to ignore. She entered and it made a satisfying ring. She settled at a table near the window and looked around the room. Clean sunlight reflected off every surface. A chandelier hung in the center painted metallic gold. The walls were the shade of French vanilla, and the floors were the darkest shade of coffee. The sweet aroma made Zola feel better already.

A skinny waitress set a plate of complimentary macarons in front of her. They came out as if they were apart of the décor, dusted with gold powder and filled with champagne buttercream. They were giving French couture attitude all the way. Some dark as jewels and some light as autumn leaves. She tries to think if she ever tried macarons before, the tiny desserts foreign to her American eyes. She takes a bite. The weight and balance seem perfect in her mouth.

She looks behind the counter and watch a short man sweet-talk a customer into paying some madeleines, some dipped in melting milk chocolate that fell from a fountain that looked like healing magic. The short man looked as if he was curing problems every day. Zola ordered a few too but plain. She wanted to taste them in their original state.

The waitress brought some to her table. Zola thought the madeleines looked like beautiful seashells. The crunch and buttery taste reminded her of sweet cornbread, or pound cake. She imagined eating it with collard greens. It would be a smash hit at the Spice Café. She jots down the idea on her phone. Fingers moving fast. She over-heard a book club chatting about a particular book set in Paris.

Their British accents light and fluffy. The ladies were gossipy and full of smiles and laughs. Zola started to crave some company of her own. She text Darshan to join her. He showed up within minutes, holding a dozen of black roses, the color contrasting beautifully with his dark olive skin and espresso eyes.

"What are these for?"

"For being a jerk."

"I told you all is forgiven."

He flagged down a waitress and ordered coffee.

"We need to talk."

"About what?" Her eyes became concerned. Was he calling off the engagement? Before he could answer, the waitress came back with his coffee, he added brown sugar and stirred the black liquid around and around as if he was forming his thoughts; fumbling with the facts, moving and rearranging them into the proper order.

The smell of the strong French coffee intensified his presence. The five o'clock shadow on his jawline made him appear darker. The dusting of black chest hair peeking out of his midnight shirt warranted double glances.

Zola took a bite of a macaron and moan out of goodness. Butterscotch was her favorite flavor, maybe because of the word butter. The use of rock salt made it tastier. It was so good that she forgot Darshan had something important to say.

A woman sitting across from them wearing leopard pants and smoking a cigarette, gave Darshan a flirtatious look. He paid her no mind. He leaned onto the table taking in Zola's sweet perfume. She was still smelling her black roses. She didn't question the color. Anything coming from Darshan was beautiful.

"So, what did you want to talk about?"

"About the new restaurant I opened in Paris."

"The restaurant you failed to tell me about?" Her voice became crossed.

"I told you, I didn't know how you would've taken the news. I wanted everything to go smoothly during your stay here. I thought I was doing the right thing. I eventually would've told you. I was waiting for the right time."

"I'm over it..really."

"There's more."

Zola stopped sniffing her roses and set them aside. She didn't like the sound of his voice.

"I will be staying in Paris to run the new bistro."

"Let me get this straight…you want me to shut down the Spice Café to live in Paris?"

Darshan closed his eyes as if he were meditating. "Why don't you become a head chef, you know, at the new bistro."

"At your restaurant?"

"*Our* restaurant. We can make something beautiful with your creativity and my experience."

"And you just want me to abandon my cafe and work for you? Is that what you're saying?"

"Zola, it's just an idea."

"You want me to give up on my dream to cater to yours?"

Darshan snaked his hand in his dark hair. It was growing out a bit, licking his ears. Almost looking like a mop of curls. He was having so much fun with Zola, and running the new bistro, that he missed his weekly hair appointments.

"You have a lot of nerve asking me to shut down my cafe."

"Look, I don't mean to upset you."

"Well, you did." The black roses laid limp on the table, hanging precariously on the edge like their engagement. Their beauty and presence became more like an afterthought to Zola. He placed a tatted hand on hers, and she snatched it away as if it was a hot stove.

"Can we talk about this later, Zola? I have a plane to catch. I have to review a restaurant in London."

"You've always got a plane to catch these days."

"This is my life, you know that."

"Why can't they send somebody else?"

"The *Gourmet* needs this review as soon as possible. I'm the only journalist closer to the story."

Zola locked her arms. "Darshan, I'm not leaving the Spice Café to be some French chef at one of your luxurious bistros in Paris; it's not who I am. I don't even know how to cook French food, let alone Indian."

"I can teach you."

"You don't have to teach me anything. I'm not doing it. You can forget it. I'm not in the mood to talk about this anymore." Zola's put up her hands and snapped her gaze towards the river in the distance, cheeks burning.

Darshan sighed, his eyes becoming darker with the burning truth. "Look, Zola, I'm going to be straight with you; if you can't take the position as head chef at the new bistro, I would have to ask Anushka."

"Anushka?!"

"Yes."

Zola's mouth suddenly was filled with a horrible taste, like burnt fish and motel coffee soaked in a stale coconut cake left out too long. "Are you giving me an ultimatum? Because if you are…this engagement is—"

"Zola, she's the only person that knows our recipes, and right now she has proven to be our best employee and my mother trusts her. Marquis turned down the position of executive chef which threw me for a loop. He likes his life in Toronto. Besides, it's not totally my decision. My partner is my mother. It was her idea; she owns majority of the company."

"So, you're telling me you and Anushka will be working together?"

"I have no choice, my hands are tied."

"Darsha—"

"All I'm saying is think about it. I'm not pressing you to do anything that you don't want to do. If you want to keep running the Spice Café…so be it. We will somehow work around it. I just thought since you are having so much fun in Paris, you would like to spend the rest of our lives here."

Darshan kissed her on the lips and left. Zola didn't know what to do or how to react to what just happened. Should she live in Paris? Should she shut down the cafe? What would Pierre think if she abandoned him? The thought of Anushka near her man set her blood simmering. Anushka had a thing for Darshan. She knew it.

Zola never dreamed about living in Paris and working as a master chef at a French bistro. She flirted with the idea. It sounded beautiful. Living in Paris with a gorgeous man, cooking gourmet French food. That life didn't sound too shabby.

# CHAPTER 34

**C**hampagne and a private jet were waiting.

Zola's phone buzzed on the white marble dresser. It danced a few minutes before dropping onto the plush carpet. It was Darshan's sisters. They wanted to meet up with Zola to take her to an exclusive spa in South of France.

Zola's hair was wild and puffy like a mass of black clouds. Mouth feeling like cotton candy. Eyes heavy like rocks. It was Sunday morning. The day yawned emptily before her, as if everyone was at home with their loved ones sipping coffee.

Darshan had left to do a review somewhere in France. She missed him already. She wished he could come along whatever his sisters had planned. He told her to have fun and enjoy herself. However, all she wanted to do was binge on Netflix, watching romantic movies set in foreign countries while sabotaging her waistline eating French chocolates and pastries. She had a horrible time over Mrs. Singh's dinner party. Zola made a complete fool of herself. How could she face his family again? She should've stayed and sucked it up. She still couldn't believe her fiancé was rich and famous.

The sisters opened the door to the château. Sunlight hit the marble floor, detailing gold and blue against white. French doors were opened on balconies to let in fresh country air. Flowers were in bloom all around the compound. An ideal place to have summer gatherings.

Zola had on a fitted *I love Paris* T-shirt and black yoga pants. While she was walking up to the door, she heard a dog bark out in the forest. The sound echoed around the estate. She felt her anxiety blossom into full nerves. She couldn't believe she was putting herself back in front of embarrassment. The sisters wore matching cream cashmere thin sweaters with scalloped edges. Their faces were vibrant, as if they just had a chemical peel and a detox juice cleanse.

They greeted Zola with a bottle of vanilla vodka and shot glasses, wearing their biggest, darkest shades. They attacked her with hugs and smooches. Zola protested it was too early to drink. They waved her off and poured her a glass anyway. They downed their shots. It actually went down smoothly. Zola couldn't believe they had their own private plane. These girls were living it up. She wondered once she married Darshan, would this be her life? Jet-setting to places like Paris, London and India.

"We're going to get beautified."

"Beautified?

"Facials. Pedicures. The works!"

"Is Darshan coming?"

"No, silly. Just us girls."

The plane landed at a lush green resort. They were surrounded by beautiful trees and exotic flowers somewhere on a hill station.

The doorman helped the ladies with their bags and showed them to their suite. This one-night getaway was probably what Zola needed to take her mind off things. A place to clear her mind. She needed to still herself. She was indecisive about whether she should marry Darshan or leave Paris and cut her loses.

Zola's master suite overlooked the French Riviera. Big umbrellas littered the beaches stretching for miles and miles. Wild exotic flowers the color of purple, yellow and deep pink stretched down to the blue water where boats bobbed like mini castles. She sauntered onto the balcony. White clouds blew slowly across the blue sky. Seagulls circled overhead. She took a deep breath, sucking in the country air.

A few minutes later, the sisters knocked on the door wearing white robes holding glasses of expensive champagne.

"Come. We're going to get a massage."

"A massage?"

"The best one you will ever experience." They handed her a flute of pink champagne. "We come here every month to get one."

"Every month?"

"Yes, silly. Now come. They are waiting."

⤝

Indian men stood outside the spa doors, shirtless, looking like a reincarnation of Shiva. Chestnut skin oiled up and strong. Refreshments were laid out on long tables. Prosciutto, stuffed olives, and creamy milk cheeses were artfully arranged. Zola looked at the sisters in confusion. She thought there was a no-men policy. The sisters giggled at her naïveté. Zola went into the massage room with the sisters pinned to her hips, leaving a trail of perfume behind for the men to savor.

The décor was bamboo wood and Moroccan title. Imported ceramic Buddhas hung out in corners, cracked with age from India's old palaces. Jewel-colored satin pillows littered the ground in one section for mediation. Incense burned and whispered out into the air.

They shed out of their robes, naked. They lay across the massage tables, face down. The air was misty and warm. Hot rocks were placed gently on their spines. Zola immediately felt the tension leave her body. All the drama surrounding the Spice Café and Darshan's family evaporated.

One of the sisters moaned in pleasure. Zola wondered was it from the hot rocks, or from the hot man massaging her feet?

The other sister opted out of a massage and decided to lounge on a marshmallow sofa studded with quarter-sized-gold buttons. She popped open a frosty bottle of champagne and poured herself a glass. It tasted so good that it suddenly became best friends with the vodka shots she had earlier. Her belly felt warm and cozy.

"Zola, you looked upset at our party. What happened?"

"I just needed some air."

"Was it our cousin? He can be very nosy. But you can't blame him. He's a lawyer and restaurateur. He interrogates and feeds people for a living."

"Oh. I see."

"Mother was thrilled to meet you, though. She couldn't stop talking about you at brunch."

"Really?"

"Yes. She thought you were charming and would love the wedding to be in India."

"India?"

"Yes, it's our mother's dying wish to have the wedding in her homeland."

"What did Darshan say?"

The sisters exchanged looks and giggled. "Darshan? He will do whatever she tells him to do. He's such a momma's boy. Don't let the tough exterior fool you. Everything is going to be amazing. After the wedding, we're going on a culinary tour to Singapore and Japan. It's a tradition in our family. We got to show you all the chef's tables. You're practically a Singh now. You have to live like one."

Everything was moving so fast that Zola couldn't catch up. Why didn't Darshan tell her about this?

"What about the viewing?"

"The viewing? What about it?"

"I read in the French blogs that your mother wanted Darshan to marry Anushka."

"Anushka!" The sisters giggled.

"What's so funny?"

"It's just that we never got along with her."

"How come?"

"She dated our half-brother Marquis. Mother doesn't know. Their relationship lasted for a brief moment. Word has it she got with him to be closer to Darshan."

"No way."

"Yes way."

Zola wondered if Pierre knew about Marquis being with Anushka. She also wondered did he know Marquis was related to the Singhs. She couldn't remember the last time she gossiped with Pierre. Whenever she called him, he was either at the cafe or with Marquis. She wondered if the sisters know about Marquis being bisexual.

"But what about me? You guys don't know me."

"We like you, Zola. If Darshan likes you, that's good enough."

This made Zola smile.

"How do you feel about having the wedding in India?"

Zola sat up, towel wrapped around her breast, essential oils running down her back. She never gave a thought to getting married in India. Everything was happening so fast. She always imagined getting married in a white dress with all her friends and family there. How could she have her dream wedding if she got married in India? She suddenly felt lightheaded.

∽

*"Food poisoning!"*

Darshan's voice boomed through the phone. The sisters tried to explain that Zola would be okay, and everything would be fine, and they would stay in South of France until she recovers.

Zola laid in bed, moaning in pain. Why her? Why this day? Why her at all? This was the worst pain she had ever felt. If giving birth felt this way, she didn't want kids. EVER! She twisted and turned.

The sisters sent the private jet for Darshan. He wanted to be by Zola's side and observe the situation himself. One of the sisters held a warm towel on Zola's forehead. Zola wondered if this was a ploy, some mean joke so she wouldn't marry Darshan.

The doctor arrived an hour later. He looked down at Zola, who looked like a wounded animal.

Darshan arrived a few hours later. He drags a tired hand over his face. He was upset with his sisters. How could they have let this happen?

"You of all people are supposed to be looking out for her. She is my fiancée for crying out loud. The woman I want to marry."

"We wanted to venture outside of the city, Lyon could be so dreadfully boring at times, so we did the countryside. Who knew she would fall sick eating street food?"

"You two took her out to eat street food, where was this place? In a back alley?"

"We eaten street food here all the time and never gotten sick; it isn't our fault your American girlfriend can't handle a little spice. How is she ever going to survive in India?" .

"Listen, if she gets worse, it's going to be on you two heads."

Darshan strode into the bedroom. He was carrying a cup of rose tea made with too much sugar and cream. She was still fast asleep. She smelled tangy and sweet, like she been throwing up all day. He lay beside her and she shifted closer to him. He held her tight. He vowed he wouldn't let anything else bad happen to her. He cursed himself for not being there. How could he be so stupid? His hawkish features darkened as he stared down at Zola. He loved her brown eyes, her cute nose, and gentle smile. He knew she was the woman he wanted to spend the rest of his life with.

He fell asleep, and his snoring woke Zola. She sat up and looked at the clock. It was midnight. The room was pitch black. She felt better. She loved his embrace. It made her feel safe. She played with the idea of living in Paris. Would she like it? Or would she hate it?

Then she played with the idea having a wedding in India. How would she learn Hindi in time to greet all of Darshan's relatives and how would she fly out all her friends and family?

She felt like nothing was really going to plan. She thought she would get married to Darshan in Canada. Why wouldn't she think he would want a wedding in India for all his friends and family to see? How could she be so selfish? Maybe he should marry Anushka. Maybe an arranged marriage was the way to go.

Zola thought about maxing out her credit card to fly back to Toronto. She could look up the next flight out of France and be done with it all. She could write a note saying: *family emergency to attend to. Sorry to cut the trip short. Didn't want to alarm you guys while sleep. Talk soon.* She thought that would do the trick.

She had everything invested in her café, she wasn't going to shut it down. Darshan had another thing coming. That was where she needed to be. Not denying her Blackness and her culture and dreams.

She could go back home and live a regular life. She was so blessed to have her own business, so why push her luck with love too? What made her think she could have it all in one year? A husband. A successful business and a baby. *Two out of three isn't bad,* she thought. She rubs a gentle hand on her stomach. *Fuck! I'm pregnant.*

# CHAPTER 35

Mrs. Singh sat on the bed in her son's Paris suite.
Trying to make sense of it all. She didn't understand what
she had done in her past life to deserve this travesty. Darshan was
happy that Zola was out shopping. He didn't want her to hear his
mother's antics.

"Mother, I believe she's the one."

"The one what? The Pointer Sisters?"

Darshan thought it was funny that his mother knew who the
singing group were. There was hope after all.

"I'm pretty sure you know what I meant."

"But I found a beautiful Indian girl for you who cooks, cleans,
travels, and comes from a decent family. Now what should I tell her
poor parents, each of whom were equally excited for the match. Huh?
You tell me, *na*?" she shouted, pushing up her glasses against the
bridge of her nose.

Darshan rolled his dark eyes in the back of his head. He looked
at his mother with hooded lashes. "What would you like me to do?

Call it off with the woman I love and have an arranged marriage like nothing ever happened?"

Mrs. Singh let the heavy silence speak for her. She actually liked that idea. Darshan continued, "I know what I should do. Call the Chopras and tell them things have changed. That I'm no longer marrying their daughter."

"What about the dowry? Who will all our family belongings go to? The jewelry is worth more than our château."

"Mother, I think you know the answer, and for the record I'm not concerned about the money and jewelry."

Mrs. Singh clenched her expensive necklace, a family heirloom. "I didn't know I had given birth to such a selfish child." she cries into a napkin. Darshan left the room as if he was fighting a losing battle.

When Mrs. Singh got into her BMW, she touched the Hindu gods on her dashboard; head bent. She couldn't believe her only son had turned down the arranged marriage she lovingly set up. How could he be so ungrateful? All she wanted was the best for him. What would she do now? What would she do next to salvage this union between Anushka and him? What would she tell her friends? Her family? She tried to conjure up a scheme. Nothing came to mind.

After she was finished praying, she took a deep breath and was startled when she saw Zola staring into her car, meters away.

⌒

Anushka's father came to see his daughter in action at the new bistro. She was running the front of house. She was all legs and wearing a cocktail smile. She was flushed with new confidence. She looked as if she was in her element, bustling around, checking orders and tables with a bright energy that didn't match her love life.

Anushka was surprised to see him and beelined in his direction. A hostess showed him to a table near a window viewing the busy streets of Paris. He sat and looked up at his daughter approaching in haste.

"Dad, what are you doing here?"

"To see how my beautiful daughter was doing at her new job." He looked around, and his eyes landed on the sparkling chandeliers and then back to his daughter. Mr. Chopra was dressed old-school in brown pants and a light blue button-up shirt. His hair was as creamy as white chocolate, and his skin was as rich as roasted tobacco.

Anushka fixed the Hermès scarf around her neck and took a seat across from him.

"You could have called, you know. I'm working."

"I was in the area and thought I'd drop in."

"In Paris?"

"Can't a father check up on his baby girl?"

Anushka rolled her eyes, which was caked with high-quality mascara. She sunk back in the chair, arms locked. Hunger was already putting her in a bad mood. She had a few almonds and a slice of burnt toast this morning. She got to work late, and now her father decided to pay her an unexpected visit.

"I'm fine, Dad. Everything is fine."

"Sorry to hear about you and Darshan. It seems to be all over the French blogs."

"There was never anything going on between us."

He sipped a glass of water that a waitress brought to the table.

"Are you still upset with us about not supporting you in your last marriage?"

"That could be it."

"I'm sorry about that. We should've supported you and your decisions. And you don't have to do this kind of work to make up for your mistakes to please me."

"Who said I'm doing this to please you, Dad?"

"Look, I know my restaurant failed. I wanted a Michelin star. I wanted to be the best chef in the world. But life didn't turn out the way I thought it would." He tapped his two fingers on the marble table. "I just want you to live your dream."

"I *am* living my dream. "

He screwed up his lips. "So, you really want to become a chef and have your own restaurant like your old man, eh?"

Anushka smiled. "Yes."

"And working here will help you achieve that?" He looked around again, taking in all the expensive fixtures and the handsome staff.

"Working for Mrs. Singh will give me the opportunity to make a name for myself."

"You know I can give you the money and you can open your own restaurant."

Anushka let out a breath, not quite sure her father understood at all.

"Anyway, whatever happened to that fellow?"

"My ex?"

"Yeah. One minute you two were together, then the next yall not."

"I left him."

Her father's eyebrows rose. "How come?"

Anushka took a breath, she wasn't for sure this was the time or place to get into it. She had a bistro to run. "We had a disagreement. We wanted different things in life. We always argued. Things just didn't work out. He never saw my side of the story in any situation. It was time to leave."

"Have you ever tried counseling?"

"It was past that point."

Anushka crossed her arms tighter.

"Maybe you two should give it another chance. He still calls me, you know."

"My ex calls you?"

"Yes."

"And you're just telling me this?"

"Well, your mother and I thought you had something going on with the Singh boy, and we didn't want to mess that up for you. But since there's nothing going on between you two, maybe you should give your marriage with Mark another shot."

"I don't know about that, Dad. We've tried. I don't want to go back to that dark place. We had nasty fights." She remembered smashing her favorite vase on the living room floor out of burning anger. Rage so intense, she almost blacked out.

"Every relationship has its share of problems. Marriage takes a lot of work. That's why me and your mother are still together."

"But you two never needed counseling."

"We're from a different generation. I sought counsel from my older brother."

"I'll think about it, Dad."

"I know you still love him."

"And how you know that?"

"Because you still have his last name and not mine." He smirked.

"Are you here to harass me or you going to order something?"

"Both."

She side-eyed him.

"Listen, just know I am here for you. Whatever decision you make."

She rose and gave her father the biggest hug, the ones she used to give as a little girl. She pulled apart from him and wiped a tear from his wrinkled cheek.

She went to the kitchen to pour him some coffee. The customers were just starting to trickle in for brunch. Her father liked his coffee strong and extra hot. He liked to see the steam from it. She threw in some macarons for good measure, one saffron, one rose, and two pistachios. All sitting on a small white plate like precious stones, made with rock salt to give a savory edge.

She thought about what her father said. Maybe she should give her ex-husband another chance. But she didn't know. Everything was such a fog.

She set the macarons and coffee on the table. The smell was rich and intoxicating. He took a bite of the rose-flavored macaron. It crumbles under his teeth. The cream melting on the roof of his mouth and tongue. It was baked to perfection. Her father ate it in three bites and washed it down with French coffee, which left a thin layer of froth on his lip. It took him a moment to lick it off and start on another macaron. This time saffron. He gobbled it up. His favorite so far. He wondered would they ever do *paan* flavored.

There was a situation in the dining room, and Anushka rushed to attend to it. A hostess had sat a group of five at the bar. They argued to have reservations. The hostess tried defusing the situation by giving them complimentary cocktails. They refused the offer. They didn't drink alcohol. Their tone acidic and sour. Anushka cut in and apologizes and escorted them to a private room that viewed the Eiffel Tower. She poured them a free bottle of sparkling cider. The good stuff. Nice and dry. This gesture seemed to please them.

Another incident occurred in the dining room where a customer didn't receive white truffle shavings on their roasted duck korma. He was leaning his large, unhealthy, gut against the table while a tie hung from his meaty neck. Anushka grated a generous amount until the customer looked satisfied. Tables were filling up. Rapid French was thrown around. She was speed-walking all over the place. She was functioning on coffee. She wished Godiva was here, she could use the help. The buzz of the new bistro swallowed all her time and thoughts.

Her father looked at his daughter as if he was watching a tennis match. He rose from the table getting ready to leave. Anushka jogs over towards him before he reached the door.

"Leaving so soon?"

"Yeah, I'll leave you to your new job. Take care of yourself, sweetheart. I love you."

She hugs him tight and pulls away.

"I love you too, Dad."

# CHAPTER 36

"**I have wonderful news!**"

The sisters gathered around their mother like a flock of hens at the chateau. Mrs. Singh let the girls know that Darshan has went to visit with Anushka's parents; they were in Paris for a few days.

"Oh, I hope everything goes well," said Mrs. Singh.

The sisters looked at each other in confusion. They had no clue that their brother was still interested in Anushka. They wondered how Zola would take the news. This would crush her heart into a million pieces.

They heard footsteps behind them. Zola was wearing a cream-colored sari. She wanted to show the sisters she had chosen a dress for the reception. But what she overheard made her eyes moist. Anger rose. Her chest became heavy with emotion.

Mrs. Singh looked up at Zola. She had no idea her daughters had flown Zola out to the chateau to try on garments. Zola heard enough. She stormed out of the chateau, leaving all the beautiful saris and dresses behind. Why should she take them? She had no use for them anyway. Why didn't Darshan tell her he was going to see Anushka's parents? Was that the reason why he was so pushy for her to spend time at the beautiful chateau? She couldn't believe he was doing this behind her back. Why did she keep leaving her heart open for it to get trampled over? Yesterday she knew Darshan was behaving strangely. Very quiet. She would ask him what was wrong, and he would brush it off by saying *nothing*. But now she knew there was something. He was having doubts about her. Maybe he chose the wrong one, the wrong woman. He was too afraid to say it. How could she be so stupid? When Zola got outside, hot tears streamed down her face.

∽

Zola confronted Darshan the moment he stepped in the door.

She needed answers. Why would he led her to think he wanted them to be together? Hakeem suddenly popped in her mind. She should have chosen him. Maybe they were meant to be together. However, he would never take her back after choosing Darshan over him. She fucked up big-time. She sucked when it came to love and men. She might as well be single for the rest of her life. Zola looked out the window to prevent from crying. She wouldn't allow him to see her so weak, so broken. Maybe she judged everything too soon.

"Why did you go to see Anushka?"

"To talk to her…to…"

"Have sex?"

"No, of course not."

"Be honest with me."

"I love you, Zola."

"Well, you have a fine way of showing it."

Darshan ran his fingers through his hair. "Are you going to let me explain?"

"Explain that you can't keep your dick in your pants. Yes, please do explain."

"Geez, Zola, you're taking this out of context. It even didn't go down like that. If you only knew the…"

"I know everything I needed to know. You prefer her over me… and your child. You'd rather please your mother than marry me. I was foolish to think we could have…."

Darshan's eyes widened. "What do you mean child?

"I'm pregnant."

# CHAPTER 37

"Send out the wedding invitations!"

When Mrs. Singh found out her son wasn't interested in marrying Anushka, she had to think fast. She wasn't letting her son go another day unmarried. Not on her watch. Not if she could help it. Hell no. She was going to see to it her son got hitched right away, even if it was with someone that has a different custom than her own. She didn't know when this time was going to present itself again.

"Invitations?"

Darshan looked confused when he visited his mother at the chateau.

"Yes, dear. You and Zola are engaged, correct?"

"Yes, but…"

"Well, it's settled. The wedding will be arranged this month. No ands or buts. Your mother isn't getting any younger, you know. And Zola, you don't mind, do you?"

Zola stood next to Darshan; their hands locked. They were a united front. Mrs. Singh's sudden change of heart surprised her.

"What about my mother?"

"Don't you worry, darling; we can fly her out here with our private plane. Anyone you would like to come just let me know. I will add them to the V.I.P list. Nothing to fear. I will handle everything." The smile on Mrs. Singh's face hit her cheekbone. Zola couldn't believe this was the same woman who treated her like dirt on the bottom of her shoe.

Mrs. Singh's daughter spoke while looking up from her phone. "Perhaps we shouldn't rush the two love birds"

"You hush up! What do you know? I say they should have a wedding before the year is out."

Darshan turned to Zola and said:

"You decide."

She swallowed hard. She didn't want to piss off Mrs. Singh and was appreciative she was paying and planning for everything.

"Sure."

Mrs. Singh beamed from ear to ear.

Darshan was shocked. "Really?"

"Yeah, I mean, it would be cool to have a French wedding."

"Great!" exclaimed Mrs. Singh. "Well, it's settled." She almost knocked over the maids as she rushed to fetch her phone to inform everyone.

"Maybe we should have told her we were expecting."

Darshan chuckled. "Too much excitement for one day."

They both looked down at her stomach while Darshan rubbed circles around it. He couldn't believe she was having his child. The hollowness in his eyes disappeared, replaced by joy.

⌒

The sisters took Zola around Paris to sample wedding cakes.

They went to high-end bridal shops and markets. Brainstorming centerpieces that represented both Zola's African American culture and Darshan's Indian heritage. They shopped around to Indian stores to buy elaborate saris that hung like expensive jewels. They strode down a village-like block in Paris, stealing glances into shop windows. Cafes. Coffee shops. Bookstores. Yoga studios. Vegan restaurants were all in reach.

The sisters went to their favorite Indian clothing store, a place where they got the most unique saris specially tailored to their liking. Every time the sisters walked into the store, the thin young salesmen would go nuts, running up and down the stairs for saris that were placed especially on hold for them.

Colorful saris were laid out on the glass counter like beautiful Persian rugs. The sisters looked at each garment with discontent, as if they had seen them all before. However, Zola's eyes were dazzled.

A man measured her waist and height. The sisters coached her to suck it in. More saris were spread out onto the counters and floor. A melon sari and apricot-colored sari were a strong no. The men catered to the ladies as if they were Bollywood stars. The owner even locked the door to prevent interruptions.

Zola couldn't believe how well they were being treated. It was something out of the movies. One minute she was slaving over a hot stove, and now she was being treated like royalty holding a glass of champagne for fittings. She thought she could get used to this.

She still hasn't decided what she was going to do with the café. It was something she was trying to avoid but couldn't. She wondered if she could handle a long-distance relationship with Darshan. They could travel back and forth in the meantime, at least until they figured things out. Maybe she could bring the Spice Café to Paris. That's an idea. She knew Pierre would love that. He always wanted to live in Paris. Or does she want to be head chef at Darshan's new bistro? She couldn't bear the thought Anushka rubbing elbows with her man, attending grand openings and premieres on his arm.

Zola knew she had to think of something…fast.

⚬❧

Zola was in Mrs. Singh's master bedroom at the château, picking out henna designs from a scrap book. Yesterday, Zola decided on her wedding dress. She loved her choice. It was a cream and gold sari with exquisite beading that shimmered beneath the perfect lighting.

The wedding date was set. The closer it got, the more nervous Zola became. What if Darshan's aunties didn't like her? What if she did or say something stupid or insulting at the wedding out of ignorance? She couldn't survive another embarrassing moment like the one at Mrs. Singh's dinner party.

The sisters wanted to give Zola an Indian traditional bath in turmeric. Zola only used the spice in her cooking, not on her body. But she was open-minded and wanted everything to go smoothly. She was going to put all her American ways aside and emerge herself in the Indian culture and traditions. How was she going to marry an Indian man and not love every aspect of him? Darshan told her she did not have to go through with it. But she wanted to. She wanted to please his mother and make her happy.

She looked down at the yellow water before she got into the tub. The sisters and Mrs. Singh rubbed her arms and legs with the yellow spice. The water felt warm and soothing against her brown skin.

She came out of the bath with a yellow tinge, looking like a golden goddess.

# CHAPTER 38

Zola squeezed into her wedding dress.

Her baby bump was getting bigger. Still, nobody knew. The sisters thought it was from eating too many pastries. Trying on dresses was starting to make Zola's head spin.

Zola tried on a garment for a dinner party tonight. Darshan was going to announce their engagement to the world. The sisters iron-pressed Zola's hair and beat her face into submission with the finest makeup products that Paris had to offer. Once satisfied, the sisters spread out a few beautiful arrays of garments across the bed. Zola chose a buttercream-yellow kameez that she picked up at the market, a knee-length, tummy-hugging sleeveless shirt with splits running along the sides. She wore white leggings.

She stood in a full-length mirror. The sisters gave each other approving looks. Her make-up was soft and simple with nothing more than a little lip gloss and dark eyeliner that made her lashes look fuller and beautiful. Her black hair was parted down the center with a thin gold chain, a charm dangling at her hairline.

A cool breeze gently blew through the window, lightly fluttering the ends of her white scarf draped down her back. Her eyebrows plucked and tweaked into angles like soaring birds. Expensive encrusted earrings hung from her ears like chandeliers. Her hands were lavishly henna. Silver bangles cascaded down her arm. She was ready to marry the man she loved. It was going to be a joyous celebration. She just hoped his mother doesn't wear...you know... black.

# CHAPTER 39

**P**ierre arrived at his hotel suite in Paris.

He had a powerful view of the Eiffel Tower. The flashing lights danced on his face like some divine sign. It felt unreal. It also felt unreal that Zola will be married in a couple of days. The Spice Café was closed until his returned. He thought about leaving one of the staff in charge until he got back, but he didn't want to take the risk of something happening. Zola told him about her plan bringing the Spice Café to Paris and Pierre didn't like the idea initially. He didn't' want her to move her business because of some man. But once he saw Zola and Darshan together at the dinner party last night at the chateau, he knew they were in love and wanted nothing but the best for them. He loved Paris. But him leaving Toronto would be challenging. That meant leaving Marquis behind; he already been abandoned once. However, Marquis wasn't talking to him anyway. Pierre hadn't heard from him ever since Pierre went to see his mother at her cottage.

Pierre's phone buzzed in his pocket. It was Marquis. They were staying at the same hotel. Pierre wondered why he wasn't staying at the chateau with the rest of his family. He texted Pierre to come to his suite.

"Bruh! Are you serious! You went to see my mother?"

"I'm happy to see you too."

"This isn't some game Pierre."

"Do you think you're being a bit selfish? There are two sides to every story. Besides, it wasn't like I didn't ask you to come."

"Dude, there's a reason I said no. That didn't mean you had to go."

"You don't have any control over me, Marquis."

"Obviously."

"I feel you need to speak to your mother, let some things out."

"And how do you know I hadn't already?"

Pierre fell silent for a moment. He was right. He didn't know. "I'm sorry, maybe I shouldn't have gone."

"Yeah, maybe you shouldn't."

"I'm not perfect, you know."

"I didn't say you were."

"Why can't you meet with her?"

"It's complicated."

"To talk to your biological mother?"

"She has her own life."

"Maybe she wants to talk to you."

"Bullshit."

"How do you know it's bullshit?"

"If she wanted to talk to me, she would've come to my graduations, birthdays, and school plays. You don't know, Pierre, just keep living in your fantasy world. At least you have a mother and father who cares."

He was right again. Pierre didn't know how it felt to be abandoned by a parent. His parents were always supportive, even coming out as gay.

"You're right, I had no right to visit your mother behind your back."

"You damn straight."

"How did you know I went to see her anyway?"

"Anushka."

"Of course."

"Yeah man, she knows my mother."

"She does?"

"We dated, remember?"

"Y'all only dated briefly."

"Yeah, but she became nosy, like you. Snooping around my place like the FBI."

Pierre couldn't blame her; Marquis was like a closed book.

"Anushka found those handwritten letters in my room." Pierre's mouth formed an O. "She added my mother on social media and stayed in touch ever since. My mother must have contacted her before your visit. Perhaps to find out more info on you.

"So, that must mean your mother knows we are…"

Marquis nodded.

"I'm sorry Marquis, I didn't mean for her to know you were… you know…"

"That's okay, Pierre. It's out now." He sighs, taking a deep breath.

"Your mother wants to see you."

"She does?"

"Yes."

"Well, I don't want to see her."

"How come?"

"You know why, and don't ask again."

"But that was in the past."

Marquis took a minute to think.

"I don't know, Pierre. I'm good."

"But maybe she's feeling guilty for what she's done."

"Nah, man, she loves her life. Trust me."

Pierre didn't know what else to say. He had exhausted all his tactics. He wished he had taken up psychology instead of journalism in college.

"You don't know if that's true, Marquis, unless you talk to her face to face. Maybe she's dying of some horrible disease."

Marquis waved a dismissive hand at Pierre's theories and grabbed a beer out the mini fridge tucked in the corner of the room. He popped it open with a quick snap and tossed it back.

"She isn't"

Pierre let it go. No more persuading. No more convincing. He rose and rubbed Marquis's shoulder for comfort. He didn't flinch. He actually closed his eyes to the touch. His long eyelashes fluttered in the breeze from the open French window.

"Pierre, I have something to tell you." He rose and propped himself against the wall, Pierre remained seated on the sofa, he wondered if Marquis was going to pop the big question. Perhaps the Eiffel Tower sparkling in the background was working its magic. "Do you remember the break-in at your cafe?"

Pierre nodded slowly. Afraid Marquis would confess something that he didn't want to hear.

"Well, I know who done it."

Pierre sat up straight.

"Who?"

"It was Anushka. She was looking for your recipes."

"But why?"

Marquis shrugs.

"Maybe to get ahead at the bistro by recreating your food. I don't know exactly. I never asked."

"How do you know she was the one?"

"The night when me and you were fooling around in the alley, I stayed behind and had a smoke. She didn't see me behind a bush while she was sneaking out the Spice Café. Look, don't make it a big deal. She got want she wanted which is the new bistro."

Pierre thought he was right. Zola got Darshan, Anushka got the new bistro and the fame attached to it, and he had Marquis. Besides it's not like he had any concrete evidence against Anushka that would hold up in court.

"I have to use the bathroom," said Pierre.

"It's to your left. I'll be here when you get back." Marquis took another quick swig of his beer and flipped on some music.

Pierre flushed the toilet. The handle was gold, and the sink was gold too. Talk about luxury. He dried his hands on a fluffy white towel. When he strode back out, Marquis was no longer on the sofa or chill'n against the wall. Pierre looked around the spacious suite and he wasn't anywhere. He wondered did he step out for food. *Nah.* Pierre realized there was an empty box of Chinese takeout on the coffee table when he got there.

Smoke was coming from the balcony. Marquis was lighting a joint, staring at the Eiffel Tower sparkling down on the sleepy city. Pierre sauntered outside and leaned on the railing and took in the scenery. Marquis got closer and whispered in his ear: "I'm glad you're here."

The suite became quiet when Pierre left the next morning. Marquis rose from bed and sauntered into the living room and poured himself a cup of orange. His body golden from the hot sun shining in from the open French windows.

He looks over at the coffee table and saw a folded letter with his name written across the front. Tears started to burn the back of his eyes. He blinks them back. He hadn't read the letter since he wrote it. He picks it up and holds the page loosely in his hand.

Dear Mama,

Where did you go? I woke up the next morning and you weren't there. I spent the entire night crying in a strange bed. Why did you leave? Wondering will you come back. I think about you every night since you left. I keep having recurring dreams of me chasing after you. My tiny feet falling heavy on the pavement, heart racing in my chest feeling like birds trapped, beating their wings to get free. Hot fear and blood pumping through my veins. My hands fall to my knees to swallow air. Fighting back tears. Men didn't cry. I can't show weakness. I have to be strong. I couldn't catch you. You kept running and I keep screaming mama mama come back, please! Don't go! My voice is loud and desperate, like I'm falling off a fucking cliff. But you faded into the dark night, so dark it looked like death.

The first night without you was black and cold. It felt like I couldn't breathe. I thought you would come back for me and say everything was just a joke. This feels like a nightmare, knowing you are out there somewhere without me. A part of me hates you. I feel like screaming from the top of my lungs every night.

In my occurring dream, I found you in a dark café. People were staring at me through a fog of heavy smoke. You were placing a plate of food in front of a fat woman, her hair bright like gold. A man behind me places a hand on my shoulder. I jumped. He was tall, skinny and black. He said things in French which I didn't understand. He smells like coffee and old clothes. I wanted to run away, but my feet stuck to the dirty floor. He tried to pull me away from the café, I tried to shake loose. I called out to you, mama mama! Thinking for sure you would see me… but you didn't.

∽

Marquis's mother would take him for ice cream every Saturday.

He loved this as a young boy, especially their trips to the park to catch butterflies.

So, he thought today was any normal day. He hadn't notice anything out of the ordinary. He even woke up to his mother making his favorite breakfast; Chocolate chip pancakes, their edges crispy and golden. He would smear a lot of butter and maple syrup.

"You're the best, Mom."

She smiled and tussled his wild curls. He forked the triangular pieces into mouth, his tiny feet swinging, barely reaching the floor.

There was heavy knocks at the door. Marquis jumped, knocking over his orange juice across the hand-me-down table. He looked toward the door, confused. He wasn't used to anyone coming over at this hour, especially on the day of their outing. His mother answered it, wondering who it could be this early in the morning. She wiped butter on her faded jeans. The house was slightly cold; Thank goodness summer was just around the corner.

There were two men at the door. They were the biggest men Marquis had ever seen. His mother was confused. What was going on? Who were these men? And why were they showing up at her door unannounced? There were soft whispers between Marquis's mother and the men.

Before she closed the door, the men give the boy a stern look. They had on gloves and heavy boots. Marquis saw a U-Haul truck out the window.

Later that day, his mother took him out for a walk. She let him carry the jar of butterflies they caught at the park. He was happy she didn't make him release them. He marveled at them as he licked his ice cream which melted over his knuckles and droplets fell onto his shoe.

She stared at him, looking down occasionally. They passed a charity shop, a post office, and specialty store. The farther they walked, the more up-scale the neighborhood appeared. She took him up to a big house, hugged by beautiful flowers.

"Where are we, Mommy?"

She looks down at him as if she forgot he was attached to her hip. She kneeled to his level, aligning her coffee brown eyes with his, their faces alert and tight.

"At your new home."

"But I love the old one."

There was a tear in her eye.

"This has to be your home now."

"I don't like it here."

"You're going to love it. They even have a swing set." She pointed to the white swings on the side of the house. For a moment, the boy was dazzled, staring at it far too long than he wanted to. Her rapid knocking on the heavy wooden door tossed him out of the spell. He looked up at her and dropped his ice cream. He grabbed her leg preventing her from leaving.

"Don't leave me here, Mommy." She pried his little fingers off her jeans. The grip was like claws. He stumbled, sending his jar cashing to the ground. The butterflies fluttered around them. She kissed his forehead and took off running. He cried. His hair was a mess, thick curls looking like flames. Face distorted like a bad phone connection.

When Mr. Singh opened the door, she was gone.

༄

Marquis didn't know Mr. Singh was his father. He was in his teens when he found out. Mr. Singh told him the truth. The whole truth. The affair and all. He waited till Marquis had gotten to an age where he could handle it. Marquis wasn't surprised. People always thought they looked alike. The only thing that separates them was their complexion. Marquis loved his father, nonetheless.

Mrs. Singh didn't care too much for the boy. She looked at him like a bad omen that she couldn't get rid of, accusing him of things he didn't commit. He wasn't anything but collateral damage. At least that was how he felt.

He hated being alive sometimes, especially when Mrs. Singh would take Darshan to Paris, London and India. He didn't want to go anyway. He would spend most of time in his room listening to music. Mrs. Singh didn't explain why Marquis couldn't come along on her trips. She felt she didn't need to. She thought her husband better be grateful she even allowed the boy to live with them, which always felt a slap in her face.

She was always complaining that Marquis was always doing poorly in school and hanging out all sorts of hours, and that he never listens to her. She blames it all on Mr. Singh for spoiling him.

Marquis missed his real mother. It was never said, though. He wondered where she could be. What she might be doing. Who she might be with. Was she thinking about him? He went to their old house a few years ago when he learned how to catch the bus. He remembered the streets like the back of his hand.

Once he arrived, he was shocked. The house was gone. He placed his hands on his head, his eyelashes fluttering in the wind. He looked at the house that was once there. It was flat land now. Nothing but grass. Butterflies danced upon it. He tries blinking tears away but failed. A tear dropped on his black Jordans.

He suddenly remembered his mother tucking him into bed. Wrapping her arms around him. Lightly tinkling his arms, which made him fall asleep. One day they tried to learn some dance moves from an old Bollywood film, Marquis's body loose like a worm. The way he wiggled made his mother laughed. He could always make her laugh. He remembered running around the yard barefoot, feeling the grass and dirt underneath his tiny feet. His mother would clean them with a warm towel before he entered the house.

He was hoping he would find her here. Maybe things could go back the way they were. But he found nothing, as if his life never existed. A chunk of his childhood, gone. Thrown away. Tossed out like trash. *Does anybody care? Do I matter?* More tears fell on his shoe.

Cars drove by, whipping up wind in his hair. The neighborhood was a ghost town. The kids he played with were gone, their parents moved out. Nobody knew his mother's whereabouts. His father told him she ran off with some man, probably got married and went back to India.

One day, he watched his father paint. He loved his father's paintings. He even had one of his drawings hung up in his bedroom; a mother holding a baby with a dark figure lurking in the background. It was his father's least favorite piece. He never sold his work; he wasn't interested. He would just give them away to friends and family. Darshan tried to pressure him to open up an art gallery, but he would just reply, "I don't have the energy."

Marquis looked at his father's newest painting. He tilted his head this way and that way. He thought he sees spices and fruits. Plums and dates and apricots. These were his dad's favorite fruits. He saw spiced cashew nuts in a small bowl on the blanket. A woman standing. Her shadow casted on the ground, stretching out into the dark forest. Was she having a picnic? Was she by herself? Marquis tried to remember if Mrs. Singh liked cashews. He couldn't recall. He barely paid attention to what she liked.

The woman in the painting was slim and wearing a white dress. There was a bleak feeling of isolation. Chestnut horses were in the background with white streaks on their foreheads. Their hair was as black as the forest floor itself. The woman was staring into a hole on the ground. She was clutching herself tight. It looked like she wanted to crawl inside, or maybe bury some secrets. Or was she unearthing the truth? Marquis loved studying his father's drawings. It made him feel closer to his father. He could usually figure them out. But this one takes the cake. *What is this about? There's a black river. Chestnut horses. A dark forest. A woman. In white.*

Marquis scratched his head, his curls glossy with coconut oil. The dirt underneath his nails made him feel gross. He would have to clean and cut them after he deciphers the new painting. The room was silent. His father began to chuckle with a cigarette hanging from his mouth. He didn't smoke. He quit years ago. Having it in his mouth helped him think. His moustache was the color of chewed tobacco. His ears stuck out underneath thick hair.

Marquis heard the faint hum of the TV he left on in his bedroom. He wished he had switched it off so he could concentrate. He studied the painting closely; nothing came to mind. He wondered what it unlocked. He might never know.

# CHAPTER 40

The wedding was at the château. White lace cloths hung from trees. Kids chased one another screaming and laughing, women stood around dressed in their best saris and jewelry, some gossiping about the splendor of the event, others whispering about the travesty of it all. Some saying Mrs. Singh must be a bad mother for her son to go against her wishes.

Food was being catered by the finest French restaurants in Paris. Some servants' faces were shiny from the summer heat. Mrs. Singh helped by picking at the silver platters as they floated by. She saw Anushka and her mother chatting with a couple of Bengali ladies in gold saris with their hair immaculately pulled back. She thought Mrs. Chopra looked rather gaudy in a metallic blue sari. Mrs. Singh made her way over.

"Mrs. Chopra, I'm so glad you and your daughter could make it. Sorry to meet again under such circumstances. What a lovely sari you both have on." The Bengali women were eating up the conversation with their eyes. They couldn't wait to get home and gossip about this with the other aunties.

"Would you mine walking with me, Mrs. Chopra?" They excused themselves from the ladies, leaving Anushka behind.

"Is everything all right? I hope your daughter isn't too upset about Darshan not selecting her as his bride."

"No, she is fine. She probably looking a little blue because she is feeling under the weather, but she couldn't be happier for him... and the bride." Mrs. Chopra grabbed a samosa from a tray as a server strode past. She stuffed the samosa greedily into her mouth.

"She should be at home getting well. Not here. Let me know if you need me to fetch a private plane if she appears worst. I don't want the poor thing getting sicker over this. Besides I need her in top shape working at my new bistro."

Mrs. Chopra suddenly felt like a horrible mother leaving her daughter behind with those gossipy hens. They probably was asking Anushka why she wasn't the chosen one? Did she feel any shame for letting such a good man get away? They were probably making up stories about her daughter not being able to bear children. Mrs. Chopra thought about finding a suitable boy at the wedding. She wasn't going to let this opportunity slip through her chubby fingers. Most of the men there were rich, young, and available. Mrs. Chopra excused herself and shuffled back to the crowd.

∽

Marquis was in a black suit. His long curls were gone. He wanted to look nice for his brother's big day. Mrs. Singh almost didn't recognize him. She stared at him for a long while to the point that it freaked him out. He went outside to get away.

The guests had flown in from all over the world. It was a warm day with a blue sky. Heavy white clouds floated beautifully, birds soaring in the air. Champagne was flowing like the Seine River. The guests gawked at a Parisian wedding cake resembling the Eiffel Tower. The color was butterscotch and mocha, strings of caramelized sugars and chocolate flaring around and on top. Candied rose petals winked between its folds. It was a sight to behold. The inside oozed a butter-cream filling. Two doves sandwiched the creation made from white chocolate. Some guests snapped pictures, some posted immediately to their social media.

Marquis saw a woman staring at him. She looked familiar. He took a hard drag from his cigarette; white smoke feathered up his face, clouding his image. The sun hit his eyes occasionally, making them a gorgeous amber. The woman kept glancing his way. He was posted against the château. He looked at Pierre amongst the crowd and winked at him. He winked back. Before he could make his way toward Pierre, the woman approached him.

"*Bonjour, mademoiselle*, if you're looking for the drinks, they're being served inside."

"I'm your mother." She took off her shades. He double blinked with the cigarette hanging between his knuckles. Suddenly there was a strong breeze coming off the river.

"What are you doing here?"

"Mrs. Singh invited me."

"She what?"

"I know it's strange seeing me here, but…" She paused "You know what, I'll just leave…" Before she could say anything else, Marquis scoffed.

"Yes, do what you do best. Leave." He took a hard drag on his cigarette. She didn't know what to say. She wanted to say sorry, but she felt that wouldn't undo all the years of not hugging and wiping the tears from his eyes. The pain she caused him. The amount of damage that caused him to smoke and drink at such a young age.

Mrs. Singh stood in the house, staring at them, wondering if it was such a good idea inviting her deceased husband's mistress. If it weren't for Darshan, she wouldn't have. Darshan was always fond of her, and he wanted her at the wedding. Mrs. Singh was over the infidelity. Her husband was dead, and she was alive. There wasn't any need to be spiteful. The past was the past.

"I'm sorry, son. I didn't mean to leave you."

"But you did."

"Your father loved you. I knew he could take better care of you; I wasn't in the right space to take care of a child. "

"You should've tried harder."

"I did."

She looked down at the white concrete where a butterfly landed on a piece of cheese. Marquis kicked it. She watched the cheese fly into a fountain. "Is there anything I can say to make it better?"

Marquis shrugged while taking another puff, flicking ashes.

"I just wish you were a better mother."

The words stunned her. If she could do it all over again, she would. But she was young. She made poor choices. She knew very little about being a mother. She knew so little about being a single parent. She touched his face. He didn't flinch. The sun hid behind a thick cloud. His eyes were no longer amber but rather a smooth whiskey. He stomped out his cigarette. A maid witnessed the act and rushed over to sweep it up. Marquis had an urge to cuss and storm into the house and leave his mother hurt and abandoned. Make her feel the way he felt. It was hard to forgive. The pain hurts so bad. But Marquis also knew tomorrow wasn't promised.

He tried to behave like he didn't care. A mother he shared a lineage with didn't matter. The woman who made him pancakes and waffles in the morning. The woman who kissed his wounds after she bandaged it. The woman who read him stories before going to bed. The good he remembered.

He stepped forward and hugged her. She rubbed the back of his shaved head. A smile ghosted his face. She smelled like butter pecans and jasmine, floral and sweet. He assumed she was wearing perfume and some flavored lotion on top. Marquis smelled like smoke and pain. A bruised boy. She held him tight, not wanting to let him go, not ever.

The sun came back from behind the clouds. It was shining more confidently. Marquis pulled away from his mother. His eyes were now amber again. She wiped the tears from his cheeks. He spotted Pierre with Zola, and grabbed his mother's hand.

"It's about to start."

⌣◯⌢

Rose petals landed on Zola's dress.

She sparkled on Pierre's arm. Zola sauntered down the aisle in a beautiful gold and cream sari floating down to her feet. Some felt tears in their eyes, and others felt mesmerized. Zola wished her father was alive to share this magical moment with her. The summer air blew gently, harmonizing with everything around. Darshan's dark eyes were zeroed in on his wife-to-be. The woman of his life. Two cultures coming together.

After the priest was done, rice was thrown. Zola turned around and rubbed her stomach toward the crowd. Mrs. Singh's eyes popped out of her head and fainted. Her daughters caught her and revived her back to life.

Zola turned to Darshan and said:

"I love you."

He gave her a hard kiss.

"You stole the words right out of my mouth."

# CHAPTER 41

**M**rs. Singh walked into the Spice Café.

There was a soft haze. It dawned on her this was her first visit. She eyeballed the place as if she was walking into the NAACP headquarters. The wooden floor beneath her feet was the color of mahogany and smooth like cream. Pictures of spices hung along the walls, emphasizing their raw nature.

Golden desserts filled the pastry case. Red berries submerged in yellow custard were hugged by a buttery crust. A few desserts winked with almonds and nibs of chocolate, some with elusive designs. All baked minutes ago.

Zola emerged from the kitchen. She was carrying a tray of salted coconut curry chocolate truffles that Pierre made last night. The ladies froze. The sight of her new mother in-law in her cafe brought a strange feeling.

She slowly set the tray on the counter but then thought to offer one. Mrs. Singh placed the chocolate into her mouth, her teeth meeting the resistance of the exterior. Zola watched her perfect teeth sink into the chocolate and knew exactly how it melted on her tongue. The rich silkiness drugged her thoughts, inducing her to crawl into the corners of memories. Mrs. Singh thought of traveling. She thought of Paris. The elusive flavors behaved like a striptease, seducing her deeper and deeper into the earth where everything grows so rich. The fudginess French kissing the back of her throat. She thought of India next, spices flooding her senses.

"Exquisite."

It was evening, and a few customers lingered. Mrs. Singh took a table. She rubbed her hands on the smooth reclaimed wood. Zola poured them both black coffees. There was a moment of silence between them. Nina Simone floated from the speakers. The melody reminded Mrs. Singh of her first trip to Paris. She couldn't remember the name of the song, though, but it sounded beautiful.

"You have...a...charming cafe here."

"Thanks."

"I'll bet you're wondering why I've come."

"I just married your son,"

"Yes. But there's more."

Mrs. Singh's bangles rattled on her arm, making her seem older and wise. She smelled like lavender and a soft breeze. She didn't know how to say what she came to say.

"My husband."

"Yes, I know he passed. I'm so sorry…"

"He had an affair."

Zola fell silent.

"It happened when Darshan was a young boy. It happened in our home."

Zola raised a hand to her mouth.

"She was our cook. Worked for us for many years." A tear formed in her eye. She grabs a napkin from the disperser on the table. "They were lovers."

"Mrs. Singh, you don't have to tell me anymo—"

"I was coming home from the bistro, I had forgot my purse. When I heard noises coming from kitchen, I knew it was them." She paused "After my husband passed away, Darshan wanted to turn the restaurant into a French fusion bistro. I was against it. I didn't want to honor that man. It was my business. A business I opened and placed blood and sweat into. A place I operated before meeting him."

The smoke detector went off in the kitchen. Zola forgot she left pumpkin muffins in the oven. They had solidified into doorknobs. She heard Pierre tossing them out.

"I met my husband in Montreal. He taught me French." She giggled at the memory. "Oh, I was so horrible speaking the language. But he was patient, teaching me at night. Oh, he was so handsome. Tall and dark." She raised a brow and smirked. "But somewhere, things went wrong between us. He said I was never home. I was always at the bistro. I had to be there. It was my bistro. How could I abandon it? My parents were proud of me for moving to Toronto and continuing the family's business. It was my baby. My own bistro. My own space. My own independence away from home." She looked down at the rubies and diamonds on her fingers and toyed with them.

Pierre strode out the kitchen with a tray of butter cookies studded with almonds and cashews. Mrs. Singh's eyes grew big. Pierre places some on a plate and set it on their table. Before heading back into the kitchen, he refilled their coffee. Mrs. Singh tasted the cookie and almost fell out her chair. The butter was prominent. The cookie crumbed, melting fast between teeth and tongue. It was so good, she forgot the reason why she was there.

"Marquis's mother left him on our doorstep. Young thing was wailing like a banshee. It scared me right out of my sleep. Marquis's mother left town. No one knew where she disappeared to. Not even my husband, so he says."

She paused and took another nibble at her cookie "The poor boy was frightened. Not knowing who the hell we were. A note was attached to his shirt, saying he belonged to my husband. There was a DNA test done, and it was true. Another moment in my life shattered. But I tried to raise him like he was my own. But he was so rebellious. Always getting into trouble, always running the streets in Brampton and Scarborough with those thugs. But Darshan pulled him out. Mentored him. Gave him a position at the bistro. That's when I saw a change in Marquis. However, I can't say that about his love life. I hear things, you know." She stopped and looked over at Pierre behind the counter. He pretended not to hear. He changes the R&B station back to French music. Maybe it would take the attention off him. The song was familiar to Mrs. Singh, one that her and her husband danced to on their wedding day.

Zola sat back in her chair and looked out the window. Mrs. Singh was finished with her story and was probably hungry for a proper meal. How many times could she eat at her own bistro? Zola thought. She had a plan to cook for Mrs. Singh. She grabbed Pierre by the arm, and they went to work. Mrs. Singh looked confused. Zola just told her to sit tight.

They got to cooking, moving around the kitchen like seasoned dancers. Collard greens were sautéing in bacon fat. A thick steak searing in butter. It was later smothered in a creamy brown sauce with onions.

Eggs were cracked in a bowl with sharp cheddar, butter, paprika, pepper, and evaporated milk. Noodles were added then baked until bubbly brown. Mrs. Singh watched at the door, amused. She even laughed. They placed the dishes in front of her and said Bon Appetit.

Mrs. Singh looked at them suspiciously. She dug into her purse and broke out a bottle of truffle spice. Before she could add a sprinkle, Zola stopped her:

"Not necessary Mrs. Singh. Please try it without."

She forked the tender meat and mixed it with the greens. She slowly chewed. The savory fried steak balanced the earthiness of the greens. The mac and cheese was cheesy and had a nice string pull. With each bite, her expressions changed like a sun moving over open water. She was surprised she had never eaten Southern food.

When Mrs. Singh left the Spice Café, she sat quietly in the car with her thoughts. A memory of her late husband washed up onto shore that she had long forgotten. One day, she was watching him paint in their tiny hotel room in Paris. She never dreamed of being engaged to someone who spoke French. She always dreamed of marrying a Bollywood star.

She gripped the large white cup in her hand. It was filled with cream and coffee. She secretly watched her fiancé paint shirtless near an open French window. He was unaware of her presence. Her parents were furious she wasn't having an arranged marriage. She didn't care. Durian's parents had an arrangement, but they didn't impose one on their son.

She picked up a French audio tape laying on a wooden coffee table. Durian promised to teach her his language. She was horrible at it. He laughed at her pronunciations. He didn't know Hindi. She wanted to teach him, but he wasn't interested. When she spoke to her parents on the phone, it was only in Hindi. When they spoke to Durian, their voices slipped between Hindi and broken English. Durian barely understood them. A few words were exchanged, and the phone was passed back to her. She tried to get him to use Indian terms like uncle and auntie whenever talking to her relatives; he did it to please her. She wanted her parents to love him, but there was a disconnect. A disconnect she wanted to fix. Even though he was Indian, it didn't matter to her parents. He didn't follow their customs and speak their language.

She nibbled on a piece of semi-dark chocolate. It reminded her the color of his skin. His nipples were even darker against it. She snuck up behind him and planted a kiss on his cheek. He swung her around and she fell into his lap.

"What are you painting?"

"Can you guess?"

She took a minute to think. She studied the colors of white, pinks, yellows and blues.

"Me?"

"You guessed it."

She smiled. "You are too sweet."

"Sweet like this chocolate?"

"Even sweeter."

She popped one into his mouth. He chewed seductively.

"What you want to do today?"

"Take a stroll to the open markets."

"We did that yesterday and the day before."

"I know, but I never get tired of it."

"Why don't we move here?"

"What about my bistro?"

"Move it here."

She thought for a second. She was so attached to her little bistro in Toronto, leaving it would make her feel horrible. She designed and decorated everything herself. She was going to miss her regular customers.

"But I love Toronto."

"You can love this place too."

"But Toronto is our home."

"I'm your home."

They visited an open market down the street. She squeezed a tomato. It gave way to her touch, and she placed it in her basket.

"What you plan on cooking?"

"Chicken tikka."

He screwed up his face.

"What's wrong, do you not like it?"

"You know how I feel about spice."

"I'll make it less spicy."

He pointed at a stall selling prawns and fish. "Why don't you make something using mussels and white wine?"

She frowned a little, but all she wanted to do was make him happy. Tomatoes and garlic were diced the moment she got home. White wine was open, ready for use. Noodles were boiling away. He wanted her to use shallots instead of onions, and truffle oil instead of ghee.

At this stage, she was itching to add some spice. She snuck in a little smoked paprika. She wanted to add chili powder but that would be going overboard. She didn't want to push her luck. She tossed in the mussels after cleaning them. She poured in the wine, and white smoke cloud her face.

She covered it and let it simmer. She started to smell the earthiness of the thyme she added. She sliced bread in thick chunks, smothered them in creamy French butter, and toasted it off in the oven. Durian was in the middle of a new painting again, looking like a glossy black espresso bean in the moonlight. He was whistling to himself. The night breeze feathered through his shiny hair. She imagined his dark lashes fluttering too.

She served him the food at the table. He loved every mouthful, eating it like it was going out of fashion. A vase of white roses sat between them; their edges touched with black. They cost as much as the bottle of white wine that she used to cook the mussels. Durian always bought her white roses on their Sunday walks.

She added a dash of chili powder to her bowl; it was too bland for her liking. But she was happy Durian was enjoying the food. Every greedy slurp made her smile. She got satisfaction watching him eat. It was so satisfying in a way that she couldn't explain. The way his beautiful face was so close to the bowl. The way his dark eyebrows glistened in the moonlight, like ravens in flight. He felt her watching him. After he finished his last bite, he looked up at her.

"You ready to learn French?"

# EPILOGUE

**B**lack Truffle & Spice *was* now open.

The cooking session was held at Black Truffle & Spice Café. The newest fusion restaurant in Toronto, earning multiple Michelin stars. The first restaurant in Canada to achieve such high culinary honor.

The kitchen was medium-sized. The cabinets were black and open-faced, housing white plates and cups. Black and cream filigree tiles detailing ebony flowers with gold centers. Sparkling chandeliers hung like Chanel jewelry. Black slab tables. Open front windows.

Darshan decided to move back to Toronto. This where he needed to be. It was Zola's idea to revamp the Spice Café and start something new after her trip to Paris.

Her and Darshan were hosting a cooking class at their new café. Today they were teaching the students how to cook Southern fry chicken.

The inspired cooks gathered around in their whites. Zola's father's picture hung on the kitchen wall besides Darshan's father.

The CN Tower could be seen from the French windows. One

cook was trying to fry chicken in a sea of butter. It took time for the cubes of butter to melt; it was slow, like a wave sinking into thick sand. She told the cooks that frying chicken is a technique. It must come from the heart and soul.

Pierre stood next to one student, helping her season chicken.

"Girl, add more seasoning than that, and don't forget the flour. There you go. You got it. Now add some pepper. Put a little bit of that Moroccan spice too. Don't be afraid, add more. I love Moroccan men. A little more. There you go. Now you got it."

"What about garlic powder?" she asked meekly.

"That works too."

"Onion powder, smoked paprika, cayenne?"

"Yes, yes and yes. Don't be afraid of spices. They are your friends. The chicken is so bland it's begging to be bitch-slapped with some spice. Grab that curry powder too!"

Pierre melted a block of lard into a Dutch pot.

"If I don't want to use lard, can I use vegetable oil?"

"That's actually the best. But I am frying this chicken ol' school. Now look closely and always make sure you have a good amount of grease in the pot. That's the trick to frying some good chicken. When the chicken wing or drumstick is done, it will float to the top. Watch and learn, people, watch and learn." Some men in the class eyed Pierre. Some wanted to be as great as him, others wanted to secretly screw him.

The oil sizzled then bubbled when the first piece of chicken dropped in. The kitchen smelled heavenly. The chicken turned a light brown with specks of spices showing throughout and slowly drifted to the surface. "Ta-da! It's done." Pierre let the chicken cool on paper towel and let the cooks have a taste. They moaned. The skin was flavorful and crispy, the meat white and juicy.

Zola coached one cook to follow his instinct. To go with his heart. Let the soul guide you. Don't think. Feel. Dance. Twirl. Feel the heart. Silence yourself to know what it needs. What it is telling you to add. Throw dashes of this and dashes of that. Rectify it later.

One student marinated his chicken with truffle salt, lavender and sage and a squeeze of lemon juice. He patted them good in white flour and gently fried them in coconut oil.

The chicken was sampled with a creamy truffle white sauce that looked like *Velouté*. The combination was exquisite, all thanks to Darshan teaching the students how to make the sauce the day before. Some cooks loved it. Others hated it. Zola thought the sauce needed some spice, like smoked paprika. She also thought it would be better using chicken broth instead of vegetable. She told the class, "Not everyone is going to love your cooking, but those who does matter. Take that and strive."

Darshan came back into the kitchen after greeting and seating some customers. The place was buzzing with food critics and food bloggers. *Gourmet* magazine and other gastronomical outlets deemed it the best upcoming fusion restaurant in Toronto.

Darshan and Zola embraced each other. They stood as a united front. Nothing was going to tear them apart—or maybe something would. A little boy ran into the kitchen, snuggling between his parents, licking French buttercream off his chubby fingers. His hair smelled like strawberries and sunshine.

Zola rested her head on Darshan's chest. She took a deep breath and looked around the kitchen buzzing with activity.

She was ready for a new beginning.

# ABOUT THE AUTHOR

**Mathis Bailey is** a LGBTQ author and a foodie at heart. He was born and raised in Detroit, Michigan. He graduated in Journalism from York University Seneca and was a production assistant at a glamorous South Asian magazine. When he's not writing, you can find him exploring trending new restaurants, cooking, reading, traveling, and visiting farmer's markets. He currently resides in Toronto, Ontario.

You can follow him at www.MathisBailey.com

# ACKNOWLEDGEMENTS

A million-chocolate sweet thanks to all the fantastic chefs and cooks out there. I salute you for feeding our hungry hearts and souls. You're awesome! Also sweet thanks to all the readers who picked up this book. I appreciate you for coming along for the ride. *Merci!* I hope you enjoyed *Black Truffle & Spice*, the third book in the *Confused Spice* series. This book was inspired by my travels to France. The moment I stepped foot on the cobblestone streets of Paris, I was in love. All I did was eat and eat and marveled at the historical buildings and eat some more.

A short backstory on how the book got its title. This book took on three titles. The rough draft was called *Finding Zola,* which started off as a boy-meets-girl romance. Then, when I gave the manuscript a rest and looked at it again a few years later, I thought it should be called *The Spice Café…* due to the added food elements. Then bam! The pandemic hits. Nowhere to go. The world stopped. This put me in a heavy mood, physically and mentally. I can't say I was in a great space of mind during the revision of this book. I thought about death, loss and family and other things, which the story picked up a darker tone. As I foraged deeper and deeper into the characters, *Black Truffle & Spice* emerged.

Thank you to my loving parents, Deborah and Charles, for their undying guidance, love, and support. I love you dearly. Also, thank you to all my friends and family for encouraging me.

Thank you to my sister-in-law, Rachel Abraham, for reading my first draft when it was called *Finding Zola*. Sorry for making you suffer through that horrible ordeal. I really needed that critical feedback, which was a hard pill to swallow. But I needed to hear it. You're awesome!

Thank you to my beautiful siblings Akinya Bailey, Latara Bailey and Charles Jr. Bailey for always being in my corner when the chips are down.

Thank you to all the bookstores for promoting my books and having me in for book signings to meet all the wonderful readers and staff.

Much love to all the book bloggers and book lovers for spreading the word every time I release a new book into the world.

Thank you to my editor, Allister Thompson, for your wonderful insight and making *Black Truffle & Spice* the best it can be. And sweet kisses to Katie Anderson for creating a scrumptious cover, and chocolate sweet thanks to Sagar Pusalkar for tweaking my book covers whenever I run into a crisis. You're the BEST!

A million thanks to Keith Fernandez for planting the seed to start my writing journey. Who would've thought writing a food review would lead to three novels. Thank you for the opportunity.

Thanks to Estefania Bernardo and Kailee Singh for your undying support. You ladies are awesome. Whenever I need help figuring things out with my books, you guys are always there with wonderful suggestions.

Last but not least, thank you to my sweet husband, Sharon Abraham, for an awesome ride and inspiring me to write *Confused Spice*. My first published novel. Thanks for giving me alone time to write and introducing me to tasty Indian and French cuisines. A true foodist. I'm looking forward to more adventures with you. I love you.

You can find me at mathisbailey.com for updates and appearances, or you can follow me on social media.

Instagram: Mathis Bailey

Facebook: Mathis Bailey

#Blacktruffleandspice

Please leave a review on Amazon or Goodreads. I would love to know your thoughts.

# PLAYLIST

Need You Tonight – INXS/Marquis

Slum Cake – Gangi Khan/Marquis

Ride It – Regard/Marquis

Dream a little Dream – Pink Martini/Marquis

My Oh My – Camila Cabello/Pierre

Dance Monkey – Tones and I/Pierre

Boyfriend – Selena Gomez/Anushka

Paparazzi – Lady Gaga/Anushka

Flight Attendant – Josh Rouse/Darshan

Back to Black – Amy Winehouse/Darshan

Bittersweet – 05/Zola

Addictive – Truth Hurts/Zola

How deep is your Love – Calvin & Disciples/Zola

I put a Spell on You – Nina Simone/Mrs. Singh

La Vie En Rose – Edith Paif/Mrs. Singh

"Bailey's novel is smart, captivating, and hilarious, seasoned with spicy moments of intimacy..."
- KIRKUS REVIEWS

Confused
Spice

MATHIS BAILEY

A Novel

Available Now on Amazon

BROWN SUGAR & SPICE

*a novel*

MATHIS BAILEY

Available Now on Amazon

# BLACK TRUFFLES

Black Truffles are balls of hidden gems grown underground on roots
of trees. They belong to the mushroom family and thrives in darkness. They have showboated their way into the culinary world and are
famously used in French and Italian cuisine. These beauties are considered the most expensive food and much respected ingredient. The
taste is meaty and pungent that packs a bold punch. These divas have
couture attitude and are found in specialty shops, gourmet stores and
farmer markets. They are best enjoyed as a garnish over pasta dishes,
eggs or creamy rice. A little goes a long way, and it complements
white and red wines.

# RECIPES

# CHOCOLATE CHIA PUDDING

This is a decadent dessert that is friendly to the waistline, and easy to make.

Servings: 1 person
1 8oz Mason jar
Half cup of chia seeds
1 cup of almond milk
Half cup of sliced strawberries (cooked and smashed)
Half cup of water
3 tbsps. of honey (or any sweetener)
1 tsp of cinnamon (optional)
1 tbsp of cocoa powder (unsweetened)
Garnish with fresh raspberries and dark chocolate chips.

On medium high heat, add sliced strawberries, water, and honey. Bring to boil. Roughly smash the strawberries, cook until it looks slightly pulpy. Take it off heat and let cool.

In a bowl, add chia seeds, almond milk, cinnamon and cocoa powder. Mix well until cocoa lumps are gone. Let it sit in freezer for 10 minutes until it thickens.

Take strawberry mixture and spoon some into Mason jar, then add chocolate chia pudding and repeat. Refrigerate for 10 minutes or overnight.

Garnish with fresh raspberries and dark chocolate chips. Enjoy!

# COCONUT SALMON

This delicate dish is light and summery.

4 square pieces of salmon
2 tbsp truffle oil or vegetable oil
2 garlic cloves, chopped
1 tbsp capers
1 tsp of Dijon mustard
1 can thick coconut milk
½ cup of dill herbs, chopped

On med. high heat, season salmon with salt and pepper (optional). Heat frying pan with truffle oil. Sear the salmon on both sides for 3 minutes. Take out and rest on plate.

In the same pan, throw in garlic and capers. Cook for 1 minute. Add coconut milk, Dijon mustard, and stir.

Add back salmon and chopped dill. Cover and simmer for 3 minutes.

Serve over grilled asparagus or rice. *Bon appétit!*

# MIXED BERRY GALETTE

This is an extremely easy French dessert. When I became interested in French cuisine, this was one of the first recipes I tried and loved. You could make your dough from scratch and use butter! Yum! But this one is just as nice and quick.

> 1 box of Pillsbury Pie crust
> 1 cup of strawberries (diced)
> 1 cup of blueberries
> 1 cup of blackberries
> 1 cup white sugar
> 1 tsp of cornstarch
> 1 tsp of cinnamon
> 1 knob of melted butter
> 1 tbsp of lemon juice or lemon zest (optional)
> Garnish with vanilla ice cream

Mixed the fresh berries in a bowl with cinnamon, cornstarch, melted butter, sugar, and lemon juice.

Take a baking sheet and spread out one pie dough onto it. Pour mixed berries onto of the dough and smooth it out with your hands. Deeply fold the edges of the pie over the mixed fruit, creating an encased bowl shape to hold in the juices.

Bake at 350 F for 45 minutes. Let cool for 5 minutes and serve with vanilla ice cream. *Bon appétit!*

# PUMPKIN BUTTER GOOEY CAKE

This is a decadent dessert that is perfect for gatherings and holidays. My favorite recipe for a dessert quick and easy. My favorite recipe.

1 Box of vanilla cake mix
2 sticks of butter
4 eggs
15 oz can pumpkin puree (no sugar added)
Cup of powder sugar (Slowly add, adjust sweetness to taste)
1 pack of cream cheese
1 teaspoon of cinnamon
1 teaspoon of vanilla extract
1 teaspoon of nutmeg
Preheat oven 350. Bake for 40 mins.

With a hand mixer, combine cake mix, 1 stick of melted butter, and 1 egg. Pat the dough into a rectangle 13 x 9 baking pan. This is your crust.

In a separate bowl, combine cream cheese, pumpkin puree, 3 eggs, powder sugar, vanilla extract, cinnamon, nutmeg and mix well until silky smooth.

Pour pumpkin mixture onto dough and bake for 40 minutes.

Serve with a scoop of vanilla Ice cream. Bon Appetit!

# THE BEST JALAPEÑO CORNBREAD

A good friend made this for me years ago, and it was so good that I hijacked the recipe. It is spicy, moist, and delicious. If you try this recipe, your family and friends will not stop eating it.

1 cup of cornmeal
1 cup of flour
1 tsp baking soda
1 tsp baking powder
1 tsp of jalapeño powder (optional)
1/4 cup of sugar
2 eggs
1 stick of salted butter
1/2 cup of sour cream
1 cup of butter milk
1 4.5 oz can of Old El Paso chopped green chilies
1 cup of corn
1 cup of Monterey Jack cheese

Preheat oven 350 F and bake for 20 minutes.

In a big bowl, combine wet ingredients: eggs, melted butter, buttermilk, and sour cream. Then add flour, cornmeal, baking soda, baking powder, jalapeño powder, suga, and mix. Then add corn, cheese, and green chilies. Mix well. Place in a rectangular baking pan and bake on 350 F for 20 minutes until lightly golden.

# ZOLA'S MAC & CHEESE

1 bag of spiral pasta
1 bag (2 cups) of shredded aged sharp cheddar cheese
1 bag (2 cups) of shredded Colby & Monterey jack cheese
1/2 cup of cubed Gruyère cheese
1 stick of melted butter
4 eggs
2 cans of evaporated milk
1 cup sour cream
1 tsp smoked paprika
2 tsp coarse black pepper

Preheat the oven at 350 F

Reserve one cup of shredded cheese for topping.

Boil noodles in salted water for 15 minutes then drain and set aside.

Mix eggs, evaporated milk, butter, and sour cream. Then add noodles, cheeses, and coarse pepper. Pour mixture into a rectangular baking glass dish. Place reserved shredded cheese on top, then sprinkle smoked paprika. The smoked paprika will give the dish a nice color. Bake for 25 minutes on 350 F degrees covered with aluminum foil. Last 5 minutes back uncovered.

Enjoy this yummy, cheesy goodness.

# CREAMY CHICKEN AND MUSHROOMS

4 chicken thighs
3 knobs of butter
1 small onion diced.
3 gloves of garlic, diced
1 cup of chicken stock or white wine
½ cup of mushrooms, roughly chopped.
Truffle salt (or salt)
Pepper
A splash of heavy cream
Fresh thyme
Season chicken thighs with salt and pepper.

Add twos knob of butter to frying pan on med. high heat. Add chopped onions, garlic, truffle salt, black pepper, and sauté until soften and transparent. Then add mushrooms and thyme. Cooked for 10 minutes covered. Once cooked, pour mixture in bowl and set aside.

Add another butter knob and sauté chicken on both sides 8 to 10 minutes until lightly brown. Add back mushroom mixture. Add chicken broth and a splash of heavy cream (add more if needed). Simmer for 5 minutes on low heat.

Serve over rice or pasta. *Bon appétit*!

# ZOLA'S COLLARD GREENS

1 medium size bunch of collard greens
2 strips of bacon
1 small onion (chopped)
1 teaspoon of garlic
1 teaspoon of Cajun seasoning
1 teaspoon of black pepper
1 teaspoon of tabasco sauce
4 cups of vegetable broth (or any broth of your choice)

Cut and discard stems from the collard greens. Roughly chop the greens, rinse in colander and set aside.

Fry two strip of bacon in a skillet on moderate high heat. Cook until all the fat has rendered. Reserve the grease, and roughly chop the bacon and place it aside.

In a Dutch pot on moderate high heat, add the reserved bacon grease and chopped onions. Cook until translucent. Add garlic and spices. Give a good stir. Toss in collard greens and vegetable broth and bacon. Simmer for 15 to 20 minutes until greens are tender.

Add more salt and pepper if needed.

Ladle the greens in a bowl and garnish with dashes of tabasco sauce.

Best served with jalapeno cornbread or samosas. Enjoy!

Made in the USA
Middletown, DE
31 January 2022

59287733R00158